30 Days to Empathy

By

Taylor Berghoff, Sydney Burdin,
Joli Chandler, Mateusz Chorazy,
Zachary Deitz, Marc Deming,
Adeyanira Escuadra, Justin Galowich,
Jasmine Grayson, Jacob Haase,
Susan Jiang, Alyssa Komish,
Victoria Lei, Marlene Lenthang,
Patryk Lipski, Ashanti Marshall,
Logan McClure, Somyiah Nance,
Kevin Ngo, Aidan O'Carroll,
Sarah Quinn, Jay C. Rehak,
Antonio Romo, Brian Scheff,
Matthew Scott, Veronica Skital,
Da'Manise Smith,
Jonathan Villasenor, Rielle Walker,
Cory Wong, Hannah Wong

From a story idea by Jay C. Rehak

To every student who has ever had the courage to enter into the Wonderful World of Knowledge and become vulnerable to the joyful task of sharing who they are.

Acknowledgements

This book would not have been possible without the outstanding professional support of the entire Whitney Young administrative team. Principal Doctor Joyce Kenner and Assistant Principal Mr. Mark Grishaber have cultivated and nurtured an academic environment of excellence that has developed the creativity and community necessary for such an endeavor.

Additionally, good friend and technical genius Mr. Melvin Soto was instrumental in seeing us through this process. It was his encouragement and technological expertise that ensured that this project was actualized.

Of course, the entire faculty and staff at Whitney Young also had a hand in the creation of this book, as did all of the teachers in CPS and other districts who helped develop the writing and thinking skills of these talented authors. While we are not able to name all of those educators, we'd like to acknowledge the Whitney Young English Department for their direct and indirect efforts in the creation of this book. Specifically, Department Chair Mr. Jim English and Curriculum Coordinator Dagny Bloland were extremely supportive as were my colleagues: John Fanning, Melissa Fett, Charlene Floreani, Rosemarie Foy, Erin Freier, JaNean Gayles, Liz Graff, Porscha Henderson, Angela Iagaru, Michael Johnson, Natalie Leki-Albano, Josh Locks, Ian McCarthy, Brigid Pasulka, Donnie Smith, and Dan Winkler.

Special thanks to Joseph Scotese for providing insight and encouragement on a daily basis.

We're also appreciative of Somyiah Nance for her cover design and Brian Scheff for his additions and edits to the cover. Mr. Nick Gorisch, from the WY Art Department also played a pivotal role in the successful design, layout, and completion of the art work for the cover.

Thanks also to Veronica Skital for her work editing the authors' biographies, Adeyanira Escuadra for her early contributions to editing of the overall novel and Lisa Goldberg for her masterful editing of the second edition.

Special thanks to our pro bono legal team that helped us navigate the copyright issues of this class-sourced novel, especially Thad Chaloemtiarana and Andrew R.W. Hughesof Pattishall, McAuliffe, Newbury, Hilliard & Geraldson LLP.

Finally, thanks to Susan Salidor, Hannah Rehak, Hope Rehak, Ali Malik, Bruce Boyer, Julie Biehl and the core team for their contributions to the actualization of this work.

CHAPTER 1
The Countdown Begins

I woke up with the satisfying feeling that I was one day closer to getting out of high school. I rolled over and tore off the latest sheet of a handwritten calendar I had made to survive. That morning I tore off the sheet that read, "31 days left of meaningless drivel."

Slowly, I rubbed my face and headed to the shower. My parents were just getting up, and although I wasn't hungry, I knew my mother would insist her only child eat something before I made my way out into the cold Chicago winter. I grabbed a yogurt, a banana, and the lunch my mother had made for me, and headed out to the family's 2007 Honda Civic. I was bored beyond belief, but I had to go to school.

Although Sojourner Truth High School didn't post class rankings, I was at the top of my class, and I really hadn't tried all that hard. You might reasonably ask, if everything was so easy, why wasn't I lined up to be valedictorian in June? Well, the answer is simple enough. It's because of the rigged playing field at my school. You see, I entered ST as a freshman; by then, there were students who had attended the school for two years, in a 7th and 8th grade program called "the academic center." Since the school's founding some thirty-five years earlier, the school included not only a four-year high school, but also a two-year intermediate school, which included the top 200 seventh and eighth graders in Chicago. Those kids were called "Ackies" and they had all earned high school credits before I ever got there, so although my overall GPA was impeccable. (I had never gotten less than an "A" in any course I took, although a gym teacher once threatened me with a "B," not because of my athletic abilities but because of my "attitude.") I had no chance of being valedictorian. That "honor" was annually reserved for an "Ackie." It bothered me my freshman year, for about a day, until I realized that while subjective truth might suggest that someone in the building was smarter than I was, objectively, that simply wasn't true. I'd have to endure.

And so I did. I went through the first three and one quarter years of high school doing what I had to do, taking the classes I needed to take, and preparing myself as best as I could for the day that couldn't come soon enough: liberation from high school and what I hoped would be a more challenging experience in college.

When I arrived at ST that morning, I immediately headed for the tech lab and printed my paper. It was an essay on Existentialism and why Jean Paul Sartre and Albert Camus were on to something, although, from my point of view, it wasn't so much as "Hell is other people" as Sartre had suggested, but more, as my thesis clearly articulated, "People create their own Hell."

I knew I had overwritten the assignment, but I was bored the night before, and spent more time on it than I might have otherwise. To be completely honest, I was also trying to impress my English teacher, Ms. Julie Glass, who was one of the few teachers I'd ever had who challenged me in any significant way. She had sort of a mystical hold on me. She was an older woman, probably about fifty-five, so it wasn't like I had some sort of puppy love teacher crush. She was old enough to be my grandmother, and I had my own grandmother, so it wasn't like I was looking for some parental figure that was absent in my life. No, I just wanted to impress her because I considered her some sort of intellectual mentor, someone that, if she liked my work, somehow validated me. Not that I needed the validation; I got that all the time. But if she liked what I wrote, I knew it was legit; she actually read what students wrote and she pulled few punches. If she thought you were a slacker, she told you, in her own cutting way.

My second period math AP Calc teacher, Mr. Maskus, droned on about differential equations until he got bogged down in a problem he couldn't answer. He looked around the room for someone to rescue him, and when no one did, I volunteered, went up, and solved the problem. When I returned to my seat I pulled out George Bernard Shaw's *Man and Superman* and waited for the bell to ring.

Third period AP French took forever, but since we'd met in the tech lab, no one bothered me as I put on a headset and listened to news from the BBC.

Fourth period lunch came and went quickly, as I went around the corner from school and picked up a Starbucks on Taylor Street to keep me awake through the rest of the day.

I got to fifth period, a minute after the bell rang, and Ms. Glass gave me a look of disappointment but did not write me a tardy. I think she thought she was doing me a favor by not writing me up, but the truth was, I didn't mind detention. At ST, it meant giving up your lunch and sitting quietly in the library. Not a tragedy for me. But Ms. Glass never wrote me up. She liked me too much, I suppose, and I think she wanted to be liked. So for her, to give me a detention was to risk her best student suddenly not liking her. If she only knew.

I took my seat behind Nia, a girl I had a crush on. She seemed to be happy all the time so I knew, as much as I liked her, we'd probably never get along. My discontentment ran too deep and she probably had a boyfriend anyway.

I handed my paper in with a hidden smugness that still oozed out of me. Students around me knew I considered my writing to be above theirs. I suppose I had a very standoffish attitude towards my fellow students, which I now regret, but at the time seemed appropriate. After most of us handed in our papers (3 students didn't) I waited patiently in the hopes that Ms. Glass might have something to teach that I didn't already know. She was my last best chance of the day, as I'd heard my 6th period AP Chem teacher was absent, and my 7th period AP Statistics class was essentially a blow off.

"Today we're going to review 'sympathy' versus 'empathy' and all that implies," Ms. Glass began. I sighed.

"Oh, please" I thought. "Do we really have to go over this?"

"Now some of you might be thinking, 'do we really have to go over this?'" she said, looking straight at me. I nodded in acknowledgement of her perspicacity. She continued, "We need to review this because a number of you still seem confused by the difference between "sympathy" and "empathy," and too many of you want to use the words interchangeably. So, can anyone give me a working definition of both?"

Not much of a response from the class, but I knew everyone knew the difference. I didn't want to get involved even though no one was answering. I'd bail Ms. Glass out if the silence kept up for more than a minute, but my hope was someone would jump in and answer the softball question so I could save my one class response of the day for later in the class. (For years I'd played an internal game called "Teacher Rescue" where I promised myself I'd only save the classroom discussion from the sound of crickets once per class. After that, the teacher was on her own.)

Finally, an answer came from the front of the room, and I was chagrinned when the speaker clumsily misidentified both. "Empathy's when you feel bad for someone and sympathy's when you've felt their pain."

"You're on the right track, but not quite." Ms.

Glass responded patiently. How did she do it? How did she put up with people not knowing the obvious?

More students answered and muttered, none quite on point until finally, from a classmate I didn't know existed, "I think it's the other way around. Sympathy is when we feel badly for others but we haven't experienced their pain. Empathy is when we have experienced someone's pain and consider ourselves very much in touch with that individual's pain. In other words, sympathy has some distance between the person feeling the pain and experiencing the pain, while empathy narrows that distance and makes us understand someone else's pain almost as he or she must experience it. It's the difference between feeling an arm's length sadness for someone and feeling a deep sense of oneness with another person's pain."

"Wow," I thought. "Where did that come from?" A bit late to be learning kids' names but I suddenly wanted class to end so I could go over and introduce myself. But I never got the chance. Just before the bell rang, Ms. Glass asked me to stop by her desk after class. I forgot about my classmate and readied myself for what I assumed would be some pleasant chat with an intellectual equal. When the bell rang I took my time leaving my desk, watching a little sadly as Nia left the room. I wouldn't see her again until tomorrow. I waited for everyone to leave and then headed to the front of the room.

"Jake?"

"Yes, Ms. Glass."

"I understand you're leaving Sojourner Truth a semester early."

"Yes, I think it's time."

"What about your AP tests?"

"I'll come back and take them in May. Doesn't really matter anyway, because most Ivy League schools don't accept them for credit anyway."

"Oh, then you're set for college."

"Well, not exactly. All my applications are in. I'm just waiting to see what colleges accept me, and which one is the best fit for me."

"I see. So you don't think another semester in high school might provide you some modicum of learning?"

"No, I'm good. No offense, Ms. Glass. I've enjoyed being in your class this semester. I'm just done. Done with tardy slips, asking to go to the bathroom, pointless fire drills, small talk at lunch. I'm just done."

"I noticed today in class you didn't speak at all. Especially during the discussion about sympathy and empathy."

"Yeah, well, I didn't think you needed me."

"I beg your pardon?"

"I thought the discussion went well enough. No need for my input when it's going well."

"Ah, I see. You only answer questions in class when no one else does. You sort of feel sorry for me?"

"Something like that."

"I appreciate the sympathy."

"Well, I don't mean to come across as arrogant."

"I know. You try your best to hide it. Still... You don't have a lot of respect for your classmates, do you?"

"Sure I do."

"Jake?"

"Okay, well, maybe I don't. I mean, I'm not into the same things they are. I'm not much of a partier, I like dating and all, but it's not the be all and end all of my existence. I don't really obsess about the Bears or who's running for prom queen. I'm just interested in other things, that's all."

"Really? What kind of things?"

"Well, things that are important."

"Like what?"

"Oh, I don't want to sound too philosophic, you might think I'm pretentious."

"It's always a risk," she said, gently nodding. "Still, I'd like to know what you think is important."

Somehow I believed she really was interested, and so I blurted out, almost involuntarily. "Elements of the human condition."

"Really? That sounds deep. What 'elements of the human condition' are you interested in?"

"Everything. That's what I hope to study when I get to Princeton or Harvard or wherever I decide to go."

"You sound pretty confident that you'll get into one of those places."

"If I don't get into either one of those, I'll go somewhere else, and it'll be their loss. But wherever I go, I hope to dig a little deeper into the nature of what it is that makes us human and why, as a species, we seem to be such morons."

"And you think leaving high school early will help you learn that?"

"Not sure. But I can tell you one thing. Staying here isn't going to get me anywhere. I've learned everything I can from this place."

"I'm not sure I agree, and I'm actually a bit disappointed in your certainty."

I wish she hadn't done that. Said she was disappointed in me. That's not why I stopped by her desk at the end of class. The word 'disappointed' bothered me. Especially coming from her.

"Well, I guess I'm not 100% certain about anything. Let's call it 99.9% certain that I'm done here."

"Okay, good to know. Can I get a chance at that one-tenth of a percent?"

"What do you mean? What are you talking about?"

11

"I'm wondering if you'll let me suggest to you the one-tenth of one percent learning that Sojourner Truth can still teach you. Can I suggest that to you?"

"Sure. What is it?"

"Empathy."

"Empathy? What do you mean? I mean, I know what it means."

"Yes, I know you know what it means, but do you feel it? Have you internalized it? It's one thing to know the book definition, but do you understand in your bones, the meaning of empathy?"

"Yeah, sure, I know."

"You're sure?"

"Ninety-nine point nine percent."

"But you'll let me have a crack at the one-tenth of one percent?"

"Go for it."

"Thank you. I appreciate you giving me the chance to reach you on this. Look at me. Tonight I want you to go home and think about being empathetic. And every night, until you leave this school, I want you to think about it. Will you do that for me?"

"Sure, when I have the time. If it means that much to you. I mean, I can't promise you that I'll spend that much time on it, but when I get the chance, sure, I'll think about it."

"That's all I ask. Thanks, Jake. You'd better get to your next class."

I was going to tell her that I had a sub for my next class, but realized it would only prolong the conversation. I was spooked by the intensity of her stare when she was talking to me. It was as if she were hypnotizing me into thinking about a part of the human condition I hadn't fully considered. I got out of there as fast as I could and vowed I wouldn't dwell on it. But it was sort of like when people say "Don't think about elephants" and then all you can think about is elephants. I was annoyed all day, my brain gnawing on what seemed to me to be a bit of an insult and definitely a challenge. That night, just before I went to sleep, I couldn't stop thinking about it. What the hell was she talking about, I'm the most empathetic guy I know.

CHAPTER 2
Sex Change

There's my alarm clock. It's ringing and I slowly turn on my side to stop the annoyance. As I do my usual morning roll to the left side of my queen bed, I realize something. My bed has shrunk, and now I'm on the floor. "The hell?" Suddenly I'm no longer tired. Am I being dumb? I look around as the foggy layer on my eyes fades. It's as if I got too drunk last night, but I don't drink. What's going on? This is *not* my room, this is *not* my bed, and this is *definitely* not my wall color. How is it that just yesterday I was waking up to a wonderful breakfast cooked by my mom and now I'm in this foreign place? Where are my radio and my alarm clock? Puke green walls? A twin sized bed? Bubbly hanging lights? Did I sleepwalk? Is this a nightmare? I stand up slowly. This has to be a dream. And yet, they say if you're consciously telling yourself it's a dream, then it's not. The floor's messy, and there's clothes thrown over a small chair pushed into a desk. A guitar is hanging from the wall.

"That alarm clock...."

I look around for the buzzing that won't stop. At this point, I'm sure I'm not looking for the dull black alarm clock on my side table, but something else. There, under the bed is an iPhone. I grab it quickly and press "snooze." Now that my thoughts are left to communicate with the rest of my body, I stand up. From the looks of it, it's a girl's room. The boots and scarves are the giveaway, and the tacky sparkling pink earring tree just tops it off. It'd bother me too much to leave my room in such disarray, with no place to put my feet comfortably on the floor. I kick over some of the stacked books and papers lying next to the bed.

This could be fun; the Paranoid Android poster

14

would look much better hanging on my wall. What time is it anyway? Where'd that damn phone go? Am I alone in this place? The thought suddenly hits me -- what if I'm not supposed to be here? And what if there are people moving about the house that don't want me here? I have to be quiet. I check the phone for the time. It says 6:45. Wait, how far am I from school? Guess I'll be wearing my sleep attire to class this morning. I'm surprised by how awake my mind is at the moment; it's 6:45 and I have an endless array of voices in my head.

I begin to walk to a door that appears to lead to a bathroom. As I make my way, I realize the full-length mirror propped against the slit of wall on my left. Oh, that's amusing, that's really... funny.... That they would... I slowly move my arm up and down to make sure there is no image printed onto the mirror. No optical illusion deal. I fall silent and I feel light headed. The figure, in the mirror, that is not Jake Holomann. That isn't even a guy. From the looks of it, I stand about 5"8, with red/blonde hair, and skinny legs. I inch closer to take a better look at my face. Why is it that I look familiar, like I've seen this face before? I search my memory banks for some recollection. It's my 5th period writing class. What's her name? I swear I've seen her sitting in the front of the class a couple of times. I need to find a name. But something immediately stops my train of thought. I glance down, at my new chest.

"*Look at this! I have tits!*" I suddenly burst into a laughing fit, feeling like I've somehow accomplished my ultimate dream. Being able to glance at boobs whenever I feel fit. But wait, if I have tits...

I run into the bathroom and shut the door. I hear someone bustling outside and become cautious. A voice.

"Tess?" Tess? That should be my question. Is that a full name? It's probably Tessa. But wait, what if I'm not Tessa? I stay silent. The door handle jiggles from the outside.

15

"I'm in here." It stops. Okay good, I know my name is Tess. This will be fun trying to find small pieces of information about myself all day. I'm still wondering how I'll get to school, and now, how I'll get dressed. Where are the sweatpants and sweatshirts? I hope this chick doesn't brush her hair or put on makeup. HA! I could completely ruin her reputation when I get to school. Oh, now I really want to get there on time.

I go back into the room where I woke up and look through the black wardrobe in the corner. Girly underwear and bras; I feel like I'm on Room Raiders. I manage to find a bright orange t-shirt and red gray sweatpants. I skip the bra, not ever understanding those clips on the back. We'll save the ruining of her reputation for later; it's too much to deal with right now. Socks. I scan to the bottom drawer where I find an array of gray and black tights and one pair of mix match socks. It will do. I look around for some shoes when the voice that was calling before appears in the doorway. I watch her groggily look my way as she drags her feet down the wooden steps. Good thing it's the morning; no one talks then. I won't give myself away. Though I'm still not sure what would happen if I did… Could that even happen?

I go back into the bathroom to the four rectangular mirrors positioned with long salon-like light bulbs in between each. I search for some sort of deodorant or perfume simply because BO has always bothered me. I find PINK perfume. It's glittery.

Now that I'm confident I won't be annoyed with my smell the rest of the day, I exit the bathroom. To my left looks like another bedroom; the door is only slightly ajar. To the right is the rest of the hallway and another door to "Tess's" room. I turn to the right and stop at the top of the wooden stairs the other girl had gone down earlier. It'd probably be helpful to learn her name, since it appears she's a sibling. I take a quick glance into the door directly on my right and search for some clue to a name.

Okay, there's softball gear everywhere, she's sporty, and, trophies on the wall. There, an academic award hanging. "Certificate of Achievement: Sam Walsh."

Now this tells me two things. My full name is Tessa Walsh, and my sister's name is Sam Walsh. Am I the eldest? Because it appears Sam is definitely taller than me. And is she my only sibling? *Oh, the mysteries!* I decide to make the trip downstairs.

"Here goes nothing." I still couldn't get over the boob thing. I touch them again because they feel funny.

I walk down to the base of the stairs to a large wooden door in my view. This family really loves wood. I do a 180 turn to walk into a very modern looking kitchen where I see Sam, a younger red headed girl, and someone that appears to be a motherly figure.

"Hello." My "mom" glances up and gives me an odd look. Bad choice. Should've stayed quiet.

"I put your tea on the counter, you still have to add sugar, and your lunch is on the table." Oh, I like this woman, she reminds me of my mom. Motherly.

"Okay." I reply. Trying to keep my responses as short as possible.

"Halle, time to go!" Halle. That must be my other sister's name. She is obviously the youngest; she looks like she's in the range of nine to ten. I glance at the clock on the oven and it says 7:10. I guess that'd be a good time to leave, but I decide to follow Sam's lead.

"Do you know where your keys are?"

"Yes." I lie. I don't know where my keys are. I decide to go back upstairs to search for them and to my surprise I find a pair of keys sitting on the black desk in the corner. I quickly grab them and head back downstairs. I then take the tea and my lunch and head out the front door. My new sister follows me out and I assume I'm driving her as well.

I open the door and sit in the driver's seat. I notice the stickers on the dashboard and a slight stench of

17

some sort of smoke. I notice the key does not fit completely in the ignition, and soon figure out that the quarter of the key dangling from the chain is the one I should use. I notice an audio jack connected to an old cassette player and plug Tessa's iPod in. I choose shuffle to get a taste of who this girl is. Lastly, I pull out the iPhone in my pocket and get directions to school. We are off.

Though to say the least her array of techno and metal music was not to my highest regards, we did, by some miracle, make it to school. As I park my car in the lot, I realize Sam and I have maintained a steady silence throughout the ride, and the walk to the door required some sort of conversation. I wait for Sam to speak first so as not to blow my cover. She asks me where Julian is. I don't know who that is so I reply with a simple "I don't know." As the conversation comes to an abrupt halt, I enter the arts building; I check her ID and head to my first period class.

I make it through my second, third, and fourth period quite smoothly. By having my headphones in in the hallway I avoid any type of interaction. The teachers also seem to be looking at me quite normally, so I assume I'm acting "Tess-like." My fifth period class is when I notice something. I sit down in my normal seat in the back row of Ms. Glass's class. Within the first five minutes of class, Ms. Glass reminds me that my name is Tessa.

"Tessa, isn't your seat in the front row?" I realize that my face looks quite surprised and soon try to hide it.

"Oh, right." The other kids in the class seem to be staring at me. All I can think is *don't look at them, don't look at them, and don't look at them.* As I sit down in my seat I wonder, *why this girl?* I don't believe I have once interacted with her throughout the year and now I am suddenly living her life? I look down at my journal and scribble down random thoughts to fill the vacant space.

Just please get me through this day. The school day ends after 8th period and her iPhone is suddenly buzzing with texts. "Where are you?" "What are you doing?" I decide to respond to one of them and choose the text marked "Korbin." I tell her I'm in the Red House lunchroom (one of four cafeterias in the school, each creatively named for a color) and I suddenly see a smiling girl walking towards me, I'm guessing this is "Korbin."

"What's up friend?" Korbin says.

"You want to go to Starbucks?"

"Of course I do."

We walk back out to my car and I feel myself unzipping the side pocket of my book bag. As I open the door I pull out a pack of cigarettes. Korbin doesn't look surprised, so I'm guessing this is a habit of Tessa's. As much as I don't want to, I find myself being partially impacted by Tessa's thoughts and partially by my own. Korbin and I drive to Starbucks and I tell her I have to leave soon. Though it was nice talking to her, I have a feeling she knows that something is different. I drop Korbin off at the CTA Blue Line and I tell her I'll see her tomorrow. I haven't gotten any texts from Sam so I am assuming she doesn't need a ride home.

As I sit at the train waiting for Google maps to load so I can get back "home," I get a call from Julian.

"Hello?"

"You want to go finish that song we were working on earlier?" I guess I make music.

"Sure, where are you?" I think I've seen Julian around school before.

"By the Bridge."

"I'll be there in a second." I hang up the phone and drive. I see Julian waiting by the doors of the Arts Building and honk. He looks up and walks over to my car. I have seen this kid before. As we drive home, more techno bullshit is played, and more cigarettes are smoked. I'm not sure what I think of these kids yet.

We arrive back at the house, and go upstairs to "my room." The laptop sitting on the floor is pulled onto the bed. Julian opens the computer and asks me where the song is. To my surprise, the GarageBand file is still sitting on the screen. I guess I really had been working on it earlier. He takes the computer back as he adds kick drums and snares to the track. To be honest I find the whole process sort of interesting. He constantly searches my face for approval every time he adds a new instrument, or every time there's a slight change in tempo. I try my hand at the program and suddenly feel myself enjoying the genre much more than before. I like being in control of the beat and giving my own direction to the piece. I wonder if I can sing.

I start to hum softly over the beat, and soon it turns into words. They smoothly flow off my tongue unlike ever before. I like being able to have the talent of this girl, but still see through her eyes. There's a drive within Tessa I find quite admirable. If only I could harness a passion in the way she has. As hours pass we dabble on multiple projects and decide it's finally time for Julian to go home. As his mom picks him up, I decide to sleep. I ponder where such a passion could take a person. Where could that take me? My eyes slowly close from the weight of the long day.

CHAPTER 3
Paying the Rent

A shrill, mechanical beeping awakens me. I know I'm not Tessa anymore, but I also know that I am not at home. What's going on? The bed is spacious and comfortable like my own, but the noise, the location of the window, and the fact that two kittens are curled on top of my chest are very unfamiliar. I locate the source of the sound by feel and find that it is a cell phone plugged into the wall, resting on the bed beside me. I turn off the alarm, thankful there is no screen lock preventing me from doing so, and notice that it is five o'clock in the morning. This person must live far from school. I push off the covers to stretch and discover that I appear to be female...again. It was fun to be someone new yesterday, but I thought I might be dreaming. This being another person is just too weird. Two days in a row? What's going on?

The scant light coming through the window allows my eyes to make out the outline of a lamp, on what I'm guessing is a side table, but its surface is not flat. I manage to get the lamp on, but it is one of those dim-to-bright light bulbs, so it barely helps. I can, however, see that it is a side table; it's littered with bowls, water bottles, empty chip bags, and more food paraphernalia. Looking out at the rest of the room impresses me even less. The place is filthy. I can only see the smoothness of the hardwood floor in certain areas; the rest is completely covered with what are, at the moment, shapeless lumps.

I make my way to the door, in the hopes that the rest of the house might be tidier. It certainly is cleaner, but it also gives me the impression that this home is unbearably small. The room I step out to is divided into two separate areas: a living space with disgusting thrift store furniture, and what appears to be an art area with paint, brushes, pastels, paper, and other art supplies stuffed into the bottom of a bookshelf. The desk on the side and a couple large bookcases on the other create a sort of pseudo-hallway on this side of the room.

The only good things about this space are the windows that line the entire outside wall. I walk over to them and look out onto the tin roof of another building. What a great view. I guess the windows aren't such good things after all. I walk back to the artsy side, and decide to check out where the obviously DIY door leads. Aha! A bathroom. I figure I'll leave the rest of the tour for later and take a shower. I pause for a second before I remove these clothes. I wouldn't have such a similar dream one after another would I? Besides, I distinctly remember falling asleep last night, and you don't sleep in dreams; it just makes you wake up. This is definitely real; I am absolutely in somebody else's body.

I feel as though undressing will be some sort of serious violation into this girl's privacy, but then I realize that I am already violating her privacy by being inside her body. I don't, however, want to risk the odd possibility of being sexually attracted to myself, and decide not to look down. I test out the water since there are no labels on the handles and it feels warm enough. I hop in and wonder if girls shower differently than guys. There is only one option for shampoo and it smells sweet like flowers. I suck up my embarrassment and use it anyway, placating myself with the fact that nobody knows that I am the occupant of this body. Smelling sweet as a girl is perfectly acceptable. I wash my face, and to keep with avoiding arousal, I proceed to simply stand under the water for a few more minutes. This is cut short by a sudden drop in water pressure and the absence of hot water. I jump out of the shower and discover that there is not a single towel in the bathroom. What on earth do these people use to dry their hands?

Listening at the door for a minute lets me know that nobody else is awake yet. I open the door and start walking slowly and quietly to my room for today, so as not to wake anyone and avoid an awkward conversation. So much for that. I hear a throat clear, and look up from my feet to find another girl standing before me. I cry out in a raspy morning voice and rush to cover myself, forgetting momentarily that I have two spots to cover; I only go for the one down below and have to correct myself.

The thin, caramel skinned girl in front of me laughs and says "Nothing I haven't seen before." I ask her why, and she responds with "What?"

What kind of response is that? You can't answer a question with a question, and I am inclined to say so, but all I manage to get out is an equally elegant "What?" She laughs again at this, perhaps thinking that I am poking fun. I raise my hands in frustration with both this whole situation and myself, and am now standing fully nude in front of a stranger, which only adds to the absolute confusion that has become my life. I must have looked quite confused because she actually does answer my question.

"Sophie, do you not remember that this exact thing happened yesterday? You gotta remember to bring a towel to the bathroom, girl!"

"Oh. Right. Well, I'm going to get some clothes on." I get a "You do that" paired with yet another giggle in response. Girls laugh a lot. I make it back to the safety of my temporary room and shut the door tight. One good thing did come out of that interaction; I know my name for today. Sophie. It is a simple, boring, extremely common name. The lamp has become bright enough that I can see clearly, and I notice the towel hanging on the back of the door right away. I wrap myself in it and look at my face in the mirror. I look nothing like the thin girl I just met. We must not be related, unless one of us is

23

adopted. The girl staring back at me looks like she may not be as simple as her name suggests. She has piercing green eyes, a nose ring, and a partially shaved head.

Not exactly the kind of person whom I would fraternize with, but I suppose I can deal with it for a day. I dry off and locate undergarments in the dresser. After I finally figure out how to put a bra on myself, I start in on deciding what to wear. This should be simple; maybe just jeans and a t-shirt. The problem is, I can't find a single plain t-shirt, and the only pair of jeans I find are uncomfortable. They're tight in some places, loose in others. It all could be fixed with a belt, but they also scratch at a spot on my upper thigh. I take the jeans off in the hopes of finding a different, looser-fitting pair. I notice when I take them off they scrape over that same spot on my thigh. I look to see if something is caught in the seams, but all I find are healing wounds. They would explain the hair, the nose ring, and the messy room.

This girl is clearly depressed. That's probably why I've never seen her before. I bet she hangs out with her emo friends and they take turns cutting each other. That's not right though, because I realize I have seen her before. In fact, I've seen her with large groups of people, laughing. The hair was a recent change, or maybe not, I see now that if I part it differently, the shaven side is hidden. Her clothes aren't emo, that's for sure. Neither is her bedroom. It's messy but has a ton of color; what looks like an Indian theme. It's cozy. I wonder if the whole Indian thing has to do with the nose ring. There are clothes and books scattered everywhere. Her room tells me that she is a normal, girly bookworm. The cuts must be from these cats.

I study my new face more closely in the mirror. There are worry lines set in the forehead, wrinkles and darkness around the eyes, dry, cracked lips -- all signs of exhaustion. Once I see the extreme weariness etched onto this face, I begin to feel it in my muscles, the sag of my shoulders, the way my bones feel brittle like they could snap just from standing here. Behind it all though, is a strange surge of energy. I feel like a superhero, all my senses sharp and aware.

Another alarm goes off; it's already 6:15. I have been so involved in discovering things about my host, Sophie, that I have forgotten all about getting ready for school. I see a pair of black sweatpants peeking out of a corner and decide to wear those; they should be comfortable at least. I rarely wear such casual clothing outside, yet another "exciting" experience for today. The water-powered clock on the side table says 6:20 and I still don't know how I am getting to school, what my classes are, or where I am. Sophie's bag is lying next to the bed so I look through it. Of course, there are clothes and random papers just shoved inside, but surprisingly, I am able to find her schedule and a piece of mail. Using the laptop sitting at the end of the bed, I use the address on the letter to figure out how to get to school.

As the page loads, I examine her schedule. It looks easy; half honors and half regular's classes...I hope this girl isn't lazy. I'm not sure I know how she acts. It seems the quickest route would be to take the number 11 bus to the number 9, and walk the remaining block and a half to school. At 6:35 I am ready to leave. I throw on some furry boots and grab a coat. On my way through the kitchen, I stop at the fridge and see that there really isn't much food, so I decide to use the few dollars in Sophie's bag to buy a lunch at school. Reaching the end of the kitchen, I walk out the back door, down three flights of stairs, quickly get my bearings, and make my trek to the bus.

When I finally arrive at school, I have just enough time to sit in the library and collect my thoughts. I discover in this time that I severely miss my car rides to school, homemade lunches, and not having to deal with bras, the most uncomfortable article of clothing I have yet to wear.

The bell rings. First up: Honors Law. The class is quite basic, all things I learned in elementary school. The teacher makes it an enjoyable experience though, by being quick-witted and energetic first thing in the morning. The period goes by quickly and I make my way to Art.

Imagine that, a senior taking a freshman art class! It's ridiculous. Today, we are working on drawing hands, the only object I have ever had difficulty with, certainly not my forte. I quickly get frustrated and decide that I've done enough participating for the day. The girl to my right takes this as an invitation to talk my ear off. She mostly talks about boys and what she is going to do after school with boys, since today is Friday and she can be home late. I eventually put my head down, claiming I have a headache. She stops talking.

In Division a girl asks me how my old roommate, Tara, is. That must be the girl from this morning. So that's who she was, Tara, my roommate, not my adopted sister after all. After Division, "lunch" is written on Sophie's schedule. I am concerned about who Sophie's friends are after the annoying art girl, so I go to the library to "study." For some reason, I have this odd feeling in my head and body. It's like I am craving something with all of my being. I'm probably just hungry since I haven't eaten yet. I walk from the library to the vending machines for some snacks.

A couple minutes after the second bell rings, I get two text messages asking where I am. I respond to both, saying "in library, hw." Apparently, this is unusual for Sophie, because both recipients LOL me back. One of them texts again, telling me they have their car, but I don't see the significance of this and simply don't respond.

As I leave the library to make my way to fifth period, I spot myself standing outside the library doors.

Did I just comprehend that thought correctly? I see myself, Jake Holomann, standing in the hallway. I have to know if this other me knows what's going on. Maybe Sophie is in my body, like some weird *Freaky Friday* kind of thing.

As I approach him, he turns his body away as though to avoid me and pretend he's not there. That's odd. I already think of my physical body as a "him" and my host body as a "me." I grab his arm to restrain him from leaving. He looks at me like I've just stabbed him.

"What are you doing? Let go of my arm!" I realize that people don't usually just grab other people's arms in the middle of the hall and I lose my nerve. I was going to ask if he knew what was going on, but I'm not sure I can anymore. Even so, before I realize it, the words "What do you know? What are you hiding? Why am I a girl?" come flying out of my mouth. He now looks as though I belong in a psych ward and struggles to free his arm. I quickly let go, give him what I hope is a winning smile, and tell him I was kidding, that I just wanted to find an interesting way to break the ice; get to know him.

"You should have just said hello," he says, (I say?) as if he's some kind of royalty and I'm some sort of peasant. "You've never talked to me before. Saying hello would have been enough for me to notice you."

"Oh. Right. I guess that is what normal people do. Sorry if I freaked you out, you're just so cute that it made me nervous." Did I just hit on myself?

"Well, thanks, but I don't have time for this, I have to get to class." With that, he walks away. I shouldn't have tried to talk to Jake…I mean me…it was a complete disaster. Clearly Sophie isn't in my body; otherwise she would have said something. The strangest part of that was not even that I'm someone else while my body exists with nobody inside, but that myself just turned me down.

Am I ugly? No. I remember the face from this morning and I'm attractive enough. Why would I have such a negative response to a pretty girl? Am I always so arrogant? Maybe not, maybe I'm usually nicer, more approachable. I hope so anyway. None of this makes any sense. Why was I just able to talk to my body? What's happening inside of it? How come Jake is walking around like nothing is wrong? I try to clear my mind of this encounter that has left me with more questions and confusion than before. I move on to my next class.

Fifth period is the class I always have, Interdisciplinary Writing with Ms. Glass. As per usual, we mainly discuss things, although it's a different experience all the way in the back of the room. Apparently this is where Sophie always sits, though I hadn't noticed. It's much harder to focus back here. Next up is Discrete Math. I walk in a minute late, as I've learned to do, so that I know which seat is mine, but this class seems to have quite a few people missing. After having to change my seat three times, I finally choose the correct one.

Some people in the class laugh and ask me "what I'm on" but I ignore them all. I am actually intrigued by this subject so I listen to the lesson intently because this teacher has a hard time explaining the information. Mr. Sanders is my next teacher and we go way back. Today, as Sophie, I have him for World Literature. Two years ago, as Jake, I had him as a sophomore. He kind of hated me because I always pointed out the flaws in his logic or explanations, but we always had a good banter going.

I forget that I am not myself today, and as soon as I walk into the room, I say "Whaddup, Mista S, how is you today?" This is how I always greeted him, our inside joke. I immediately recognize the error of my ways, but surprisingly, he thinks nothing of it and responds as usual. Perhaps Sophie and he have a love-hate relationship, too; Mr. Sanders makes fun of me the entire class, so I know that this is correct.

28

My last class, regular Physics, is a breeze. I finish the class work early and nap the rest of the period. For some reason, in this body, I can't seem to get enough rest. I decide to skip my Seminar since it is also with Mr. Sanders, and I can tell that Sophie knows him well enough that he will not mark me absent. Even if he does, that craving from earlier is back and I just want to go to sleep so I can hopefully wake up as myself.

Just as I am walking up to the backstairs of today's dwelling, Sophie's MyTouch rings. The caller ID says "Potbelly Andersonville." I thought Potbelly was a sandwich shop, but maybe it is a nickname or something. Upon answering, I find out that it is, in fact, the sandwich shop. A woman on the other end exasperatingly reminds me that I have work right now and am already five minutes late. I apologize, telling her I will be right there. Using the map app on Sophie's phone, the Andersonville Potbelly turns out to be only 1.3 miles away. I walk to work and say hello to the guy working the register. He looks at me and tells me that I better have my uniform in my bag. I go straight back to the bathroom and open up Sophie's bag. Sure enough, the clothes I saw earlier are actually a uniform. I put the on the shirt and hat, and go back out into the store.

The man, whose nametag I now see says "Gary," laughs and inquires as to what I think I'm wearing. I ask, "What do you mean, Gary? This is the correct uniform, right?" Maybe Sophie has multiple jobs, but I remember seeing Potbelly written somewhere on this shirt. Gary then proceeds to look at me like I am insane, tells me that maybe I should go home because clearly I am not in my right mind to work if I think sweatpants are appropriate attire. He tells me that if I can't make my shift tomorrow he will understand. I apologize profusely, and then start walking home. I don't think I have ever walked this much in my whole life. It sucks not having a car.

I am finally home for the night, it's only six o'clock, but it feels like a lifetime. I walk in the kitchen door, and immediately hear Tara yell, "Sophie Bear, is it really you, are you home at last?" Following the direction of the voice takes me to a door in the hall to the right of the kitchen. I find it odd that someone would be that excited to see a person they just saw this morning, but I run with it. "Yes, Tara, it is I!" I speak into the door. "Well, come in, come in!" The smell of smoke with an undertone of minty citrus, hits me as soon as I open the door. A quick sweep of the room alerts me to the fact that there is a rat under a loft bed, a hookah burning on a low table, and Tara, sitting on her bed.

As I focus in, I notice that Tara is dragging a razor blade across the skin of her ankle, like it is usual occurrence, and I am not to say anything. I can't help myself, I hear the words come out of my mouth before I can stop them "Why are you cutting yourself, are you crazy?" Sophie's roommate smiles a knowing smile; it communicates that I should know why, that I hurt myself too. She verbally tells me to sit down, finish off the hookah, and she shall tell me about her day. I pick up the tubular thing coming out of the device as I sit, and she proceeds to tell me a horror story about a boy who doesn't love her back. I can't imagine treating a girl the way this Michael guy does. As much as I don't understand them, I do respect women. My hands and my lungs seem to know what they are doing, because as she tells me about Michael, I smoke. I hadn't smoked anything before yesterday, so I find it odd that I do not cough or have to be told what to do.

Every breath out, the smoke is cool, which doesn't make sense, since I am breathing fire, a citrus mint fire. I find that I do relax. I am at peace, my craving is gone, I almost feel my brain melting into oblivion, and yet, the world around me is so clear. I am in a body other than my own, a gender other than my own, a home other than my own, sitting in a room with a girl who makes blood flow from her ankles, smoking a thick, sweet substance, listening to a tale of betrayal, and yet, I am okay. She tells me to stay strong, not to let her relapse make me relapse, tells me that she will be fine, promises me that she won't cut again after today. Her story is over. I give her words of support and understanding. I try to leave, but find my balance is off. I move more slowly, and manage to exit the room. As I go, I hear her crying. My brain is abuzz. I slink back to Sophie's bed and I cannot sleep, although I try. I need to get out of this haze I am in. I don't like it.

I want to be back in my own bed, with my usual thoughts, my understanding of the world as a place to do trivial things. Instead I am here in a filthy room, with a bed in which I cannot sleep, with struggles I don't want. At last, the haze wears off. I find that I am just lying on her bed, a book on my lap, but I am not reading. It is 9:00 at night. Three hours doing nothing. I walk to the kitchen to find a note from Tara asking me to go get groceries tonight, along with a list of things to get, and some money. I search the Internet for the nearest grocery store, figuring that I am going to have to walk there. It is close though, only a few blocks away. There is a black cart, that I assume is for just this occasion, resting against the wall. It is dark out, and there are more shady characters outside here than in my neighborhood. I am not frightened, but I wouldn't want to be out much later than this. My trip to the store takes only half an hour.

When I get back, I put the perishables away, but I leave the rest out because I'm not sure where everything goes. The phone rings, I answer. It is another girl, asking if I am off of work. Rather than explain that I may have gotten my host body fired, I answer with a simple "Yes." The voice on the other end seems pleased, "I'll pick you up in ten minutes, and I'll help you figure out what to wear."

31

I can't imagine having company with a room that looks this disastrous. I decide to clean up a bit, to save Sophie some embarrassment. All I can really do is throw clothes into a laundry basket, but really, she needs about five. I am not at all satisfied with the result, but my ten minutes are up. I hear the back door open and close, and another girl I have seen before at school is standing in the doorway to the bedroom. She has been here recently, because she notices the room is cleaner than before. She starts pulling clothes out from the basket, and ends up handing me some tights, tiny shorts, and a chunky sweater, telling me to change fast. She starts messing around on the computer, so I take it that as I am supposed to change with her in the room. When I am done, she does my makeup. I didn't even want to try putting anything on this morning because it looked like there was a specific way to do things that I am not privy to. I was right.

The girl knows though; she makes sense of all the brushes and creams, and when I look in the mirror, I do not look bad. A bit too much makeup than I would normally like on a girl, but it suits my host, Sophie. We go downstairs, and enter a beat up old car. The drive to where we are going takes about 45 minutes. Once there, I realize that we are only a couple blocks away from school. The girl takes my hand and leads me to one of the loft buildings down the street. It feels nice holding someone's hand. The fourth floor is our destination; I can hear music blaring from where we stand in the hall, even though the loft we go to is six doors down. When we open the door, the music gets louder, some sort of electronic noise. The girl lets go of my hand and walks away.

Everywhere I look, there is some sort of illicit activity. Broken bottles litter the floor, people are doing lines of something off of cracked pieces of mirror, the bathroom door is open and there is someone on the toilet

32

with a belt wrapped tightly around his arm. This is overwhelming. I go through a door, hoping for some space alone, but walk in on two people having sex. They ask me to join so I walk out the door as a response. I bump into somebody with a bottle of pills, a couple fall to the floor and I'm handed the prescription. I'm not sure what to do with it, so I set it on a table a few feet away. I see sliding closet doors straight ahead, and make a beeline for them. I just want to get out of this situation, but it is too late for me to go home on public transportation alone. Something worse could happen than staying at this party.

Inside the closet, it is dark and comforting. I am finally alone. I check the phone, and discover that it is 12:00. There are two unread text messages. One from someone named Rachel; it reads "r we still on for writing tomorrow 8 am, at the coffee shop?" The other is from Sophie's dad, saying "staying in Michigan for a few more days, be back Thursday. I expect the rent by Friday."

So the apartment belongs to her dad. She pays her parent rent to stay in his home? My parents don't even make me pay for gas. I think about everything I just saw, and can't imagine how these people live. The girl whose body I inhabit seems so normal at school, how does she put on that front? She wakes up at five in the morning, goes to school, goes to work, and goes to parties late at night, then gets up early to write with a friend. Goes to work again and still has time to recover and do homework? She basically lives on her own, takes care of her pets and pays her dad...how? No wonder she has self-harm issues. This is a stressful, hectic lifestyle. I could never live this way. I don't know why anyone would want to. She is an adult trapped in an irresponsible teenager's body. She even emotionally supports her roommate, but who takes care of her? I can't keep thinking about all of this, because I can't wrap my head around it.

It makes me feel depressed just thinking about Sophie's life. She could just drop out of school; it would make her life easier for now, but she doesn't. I respect her for that. I do think she is making it harder on herself with all the drugs. I can feel in my bones that I want some of what the people out there, in the loft, are having. I can sense the longing for anything to numb her life. I won't let her do these things to her body tonight. I am in control right now, and I will give her the respite she needs, at least tonight. Maybe tomorrow or for however long I'm living her life. I step out of the closet and into a room that was once full of movement. Now, the music plays but everyone is slumped over the sparse furniture, on the floor, on each other. I walk out into the hall, close the door and sit against the wall. I check the phone for the time. It is now two, I have one last coherent thought of helping this poor girl, before I close my eyes and drift into the dreamless sleep that brings me to another day.

CHAPTER 4
My First Splash

An alarm goes off next to me and I wake in a daze, not in my body or my home but in another female's body somewhere in what I find out later is Rogers Park. I think about Sophie and about how much she goes through in one day and hope that I don't have another day like hers. I remember the alarm and begin to move to turn it off when someone above me shushes me. I turn off the alarm and notice that the time is 4:35. Why would I need to get up this early? There is no place in the City that is that far away from the school. The only other reason would be to finish homework that she didn't do the night before.

"Augie, you need to get up." Am I Augie? And why do I need to get up? "I know you're tired, but Elizabeth, your ride, is going to be here in forty minutes and you have to get dressed and make your lunch."

While getting up, I hit my head on the bed above mine, trip over clothes and shoes scattered around the room. I find my way through the dark and into the bathroom and assess the situation logically. The first thing I notice is the mess of hair that I don't know how to deal with; then I see the hair products on the table. The make-up comes next, and finally the tools.

I leave the bathroom flustered and still astonished at the amount of products females have for beautification. I wander into the kitchen and open to a fridge with some leftovers, yogurt, lunchmeat and salad. The pantry has cereal, applesauce, fruit cups, bread, and peanut butter. Sitting on the counter are a couple of apples. I go back for a bowl of cereal and realize that I have to leave in fifteen minutes. I throw an apple into what I assume is my lunch bag, pack a bag of cereal, make a peanut butter sandwich, and grab a yogurt for breakfast.

35

I throw on a sweater, find Augie's phone, and gather her backpack and a bag with clothes, and her lunch.

At around 5:15 I get a text saying my ride is here. I leave the house and enter a silent car. The car ride goes by fast because I fall asleep. We get to school and the other girls start heading toward the athletic building and the girls' locker room, a part of the school I am unfamiliar with. I follow not knowing what sport gets to school this early for practice.

Swimming. An easy sport without much physical exertion.

I manage to find my locker and a note on her phone with the combination so I have access to her suit and anything else she might have in her locker. After changing into the suit I grab the goggles and swimming cap inside, leave the locker room and enter the pool area, where I notice about six girls pulling lane dividers into the pool. I walk to where some people are gathered at the end of the pool and notice they each have a bag with equipment. I find one and walk back towards the pool. I put my cap on with everyone else and look at the sheet of paper they are all reading.

When I see what's on the paper, I begin to worry. There are numbers with abbreviations following; some parts are in brackets and multiplied by two or three, and others have asterisks next to them. Before I can ask one of my teammates to explain the paper and what everything means, everyone gets in the water and starts swimming. I go to ask someone who I assume is the coach what everything means, and he yells at me. Saying: "August, you are one of the captains of this team, and you have been swimming for four years, what are you doing? Get in the pool!" I don't know how to respond, so I blurt out an apology and jump into one of the lanes and follow what the other girls doing.

Just as I hit the water, I realize whose body I'm in. August in my 5th period class with Ms. Glass. A quiet girl

36

who sits in the back. So this is what she does when the rest of humanity is asleep or at some ridiculous party.

The beginning of the workout is nice because it feels as though I am stretching my body out while gliding through the water. After that, everything is much harder because I have to finish a certain amount of laps in a very short amount of time. The laps and times were numbers, of course, and how we are supposed to swim the laps were the abbreviations that followed. Some parts are kicking and other parts are drill or medley, meaning we swim a certain distance of every stroke, butterfly, backstroke, breaststroke, and freestyle.

When we finally get to the part of the workout in brackets, the coach explains each part inside the bracket and says we do everything three times. When I look over everything inside the bracket and imagine doing it three times, I think my arms are going to fall off. We begin swimming and I keep up the entire first time through. When we start swimming for the second round, my shoulders and legs start to burn, but I keep swimming and fall off a little towards the end. The third time around, I begin to have a harder time breathing and my goggles are fogged, so I can't see, and my shoulders and legs feel worse and are screaming for the end. After the third round the coach makes us continue swimming, but not timed, so we can stretch out our muscles so we aren't sore later. While swimming this, I realize that there is still a full day of school ahead of me. Then the coach reminds us we have practice after school, too. He's got to be kidding.

We leave the pool and return to the locker room where there is a radio set up blasting rap. We shower and change while gossiping and talking about anything from homework to the workout. The first bell rings and everyone scrambles to make themselves presentable, while I look at my schedule and see I have an extra twenty minutes to figure out how to deal with my hair and eat breakfast. I manage to put it in a ponytail, which is how she normally wears it, and while eating my yogurt I look over the homework she did the night before, correct anything I see is wrong, and finish anything she didn't.

She has scrap-booking for Seminar, which I get through easily. The teacher is very relaxed and plays music in the background while other students cut, mount and arrange pictures and journal entries. Her third period honors Calculus class teacher doesn't check the homework and rushes through every problem saying "Okay" at the end and not waiting for a reply to make sure everyone understands. No one pays the teacher any attention and he doesn't seem to mind. He just frequently reminds the students that he has no problem failing them.

Fourth Augie has lunch, which I was used to, but what's unfortunate is she doesn't have a car or any money to spend on Starbucks, so I sit at a table in Green House expecting to eat by myself when four people come and sit with me. Two of them I recognize from practice that morning but the rest of them I can't place. It turns out to not be that bad of a lunch, sitting and talking and even laughing with them. These people are the closest I've come to liking yet.

Fifth period is the class August and I share, English with Ms. Glass. We start class with the usual journal and Ms. Glass gathering her thoughts and informing us of anything new. Then she talks about our next book, *Like Water for Chocolate* by Laura Esquivel. I don't like Magic Realism, but it's not like I have a choice. I look over at myself and see I'm looking as arrogant as ever. The bell rings and the class disperses.

Discrete math, sixth period. Easy, all it is is logic. With almost no numbers involved anyone can do these problems without any trouble. That class ends quickly and it's off to Microbiology where I'm in a group learning how to plate bacteria and others are building lab equipment or writing grants for chemicals and supplies.

This class is too short as we rush through the steps hoping everything turns out in the end.

Eighth period is Fashion where I pick colors for an outfit Augie designed and drew. Hoping she likes what I pick, I decide to go with a soft green and yellow pastel. Finally, ninth period Spanish where we have a quiz that I finish quickly and take the rest of the period to nap.

When the bell rings for the end of the day, I'm momentarily overjoyed until I realize that I still have at least two and a half more hours to spend in practice. I take my time getting to the pool and when I do finally arrive most of the team is already starting to change. I follow along and when I finish I walk onto the pool area unsure of how my body will hold up to another grueling practice. I learn that practice will not start until four so we stretch as a team. When we get the workout I notice it's considerably shorter than the one from the morning and assume it will be easier.

As soon as we start swimming I know my assumption is wrong. We have fewer and shorter breaks and so I have no time to catch my breath. This, however, leaves me with lots of time to appreciate how much Augie has to deal with on a daily basis. She is maintaining decent grades and leading and participating on a swim team. The swim team takes up most of her time not only because she is in practice all the time but also because she is sore and in pain after practice, making it harder to sleep and concentrate on everything else. I am more surprised when I realize she never sleeps in class even though she has every right to and I know I would.

When practice is finally over at 6:00 I change into what I came to school in and am told that we have to take the CTA Red Line home because Elizabeth's mom came to school and picked the car up and no one's parents can take us home. Taking the train means I won't get back to her house until about 7:30. I try to work on her homework on the train but I need a book or the computer for all of my assignments. Once I get off the train I try to remember what her house looks like. I cannot remember a single detail about her house. I walk up and down a couple of blocks and none of the houses seem at all familiar so I go back to the train station and call my mom and ask her to meet me at the station because it is dark and I don't want to walk home by myself. She tells me my dad is coming and I wait about five minutes when a man walks up to me and asks me how my day and practice was. Her house is only a block and a half away from the train station but I still don't recognize it.

When I get inside I am greeted with the smells of a delicious dinner. I warm some up for myself and start to walk to the front of the house to watch TV when my mom clears her throat and looks at the table. I assume she is talking to me and sit down at the table and eat my dinner while working on some homework. I finish most of my homework by 9:00 when I begin to wilt with exhaustion. I look again at the clock to make sure it is not later and continue to push through my homework. When I finish it is 9:50 and I brush my teeth and fall into bed thinking: "How does she manage?"

CHAPTER 5
Mr. Popular

I wake up suddenly and again I don't know where I am. I realize it's happening again, but it can't have anything to do with drugs because I wasn't on anything yesterday. I spent all day swimming for God's sake. At least my arms don't ache right now. The comforter on the bed appears different and the room I'm in is still not my own. Posters of athletes line the walls, along with hand drawn art. "I don't care for any of this at all," I scoff almost silently before laying my head back down. I'm too afraid to go explore the house, out of fear that someone one of these days is going to recognize I'm not who they think I am.

I'm almost back into a dream state when I hear a voice calling "Zach, Zach." I stare up and see the outline of a woman whom I have obviously never seen before but who nonetheless has an inviting face.

"You're just going to stare at your own mother and not say good morning?" the woman says to me.

I stare at her and play along "Oh yeah, uh...hi there, mom" I say rather choppily. She leaves the room and I sit up with some alarm, although at the same time a bit relieved to be a guy this time around. Maybe it means I'm getting closer to getting back to being me.

I run to the bathroom and look in the mirror, and I can't believe what's staring back. I look in the mirror and recognize myself right away as one of my fellow 5th period classmates. I can't believe it. This is some kind of bizarre magic perpetrated by Ms. Glass, I'm sure of it. I get dressed, eat breakfast and walk out the door to the nearest train, hoping that I could pull off this charade again. I woke up hoping that this game the universe was playing with me might soon be coming to an end, but as I'd learn, this was only the start.

41

When I got to school everyone treated me differently. People came up to me in the halls and shook my hand and patted me on the back. I felt like I was at a party, not at school. It was almost as if people cared that I was present, that my aura made a difference. I went up to the group of friends I knew Zach hung out with and tried to act normal. I walked over and stood awkwardly and didn't say a word, as I did not want to blow my new cover. I was about to speak when the bell rang, thank God.

Saved by the bell, I quickly transitioned to my second period class, Creative Writing. This was only the start of what would be a heavy load of English courses. I sat in silence and tried to sleep, hoping I could somehow get back to being myself, but I couldn't keep my head down long enough before the teacher told me to pick it up.

I was like a bull in a china shop, the way I wanted to just bust out of this body. The bell rang again before I knew it and it was time for third. I scuffled to my next class and barged in the room.

Next was an AP class called AP Language. I took a deep breath and sat down. Ms. Biehl, the teacher, came over and asked me for the homework.

"What homework?" I replied.

My answer didn't fly with Ms. Biehl and she jotted down a zero. Wherever Zach was, he was not going to be pleased with me. I counted down the seconds until the bell rang and went to Division.

After that, my day breezed by. Fourth period was nothing short of a joke, a blow off math class called Honors Statistics. The teacher did not seem to have good control of the class and everyone talked out of turn and did whatever was on their own agenda. I saw three kids in the first five minutes ask to go to the bathroom so I tried my hand and asked. The teacher, Ms. Tintera, agreed and let me go. I spent the entire period in there and came back with two minutes left, grabbed my bag and left. I then went to fifth, which was the class I had with Zach. I didn't see myself present for the class and wondered where my real body was. I doodled in my journal looking for clues that Ms. Glass knew what was going on. I was convinced she did.

When the bell rang, I approached Ms. Glass with Zach's friendliness and my certainty.

"Ms. Glass."

"Yes, Zach."

Not wanting to repeat the fiasco I had when I was Sophie, I decided to proceed cautiously. "Do you notice anything different about me today?"

"No, you pretty much sat in the back of the class fooling around with your friends and doodling, pretty much like you always do." Same old Ms. Glass, trying to be funny at the same time trying to give me a gentle nudge towards participating more fully in class. If she knew something, she didn't let on, and I couldn't see through her.

"Nothing different at all?" I persisted.

"Nothing to speak of," sheshe said, in a way indicating the conversation had nowhere else to go. Having no other choice than coming off as insane, I left the room.

I went to sixth period happy that the day was half over. I walked in and a kind face greeted me. The teacher was one I recognized from around the school, Mr. Osinski. He had a reputation for being a very cool and lax teacher, and I saw that first hand. He made jokes with the class and tried to integrate the learning in a way to make it fun. I appreciated his effort and sweated my way through the class, counting down the seconds until it was over. The bell finally rang and I was relieved but I knew the biggest challenge was ahead of me. I had to stay stealthy during lunch, the social frenzy of the day.

I knew who Zach hung out with at lunch, but none

of these people were my friends. I knew what I had to do to remain safe. I went to the Arts Building and hid in the bathroom for the whole fifty minutes. Although I was bored to tears, it was a good alternative to being found out as a body-snatching imposter. When the bell finally rang, I was so relieved. The bell rang and I went to his last class of the day, Band. This was making me very nervous, as I didn't know how to play any instrument that would be in a band. I sat down in Zach's seat; it turned out he played saxophone, something I had no familiarity with. I was frozen in fear of being found out, but soon realized what I would do.

Every time the band played as a whole the teacher, Mr. Buttitta, couldn't distinguish my sound from the rest. I would puff out my cheeks, and look like I was putting forth a strenuous effort, when really I was not blowing any air. This charade worked and the bell finally rang after forty-five minutes of pretend playing. I was almost in the home stretch. Once the bell rang, I went to Seminar in Room 307 and sat down. No one said a word to me and the advisor, Mr. Sigelko, put on an episode of *Seinfeld*. I watched it, quiet as a church mouse. I was not going to be found out before I got to the bottom of what was going on and why I kept switching bodies.

I left last period and went straight to the Blue Line, trying to avoid all contact with anyone Zach knew which was proving to be almost impossible. This guy knew everybody. I got to the train and a kid ran up to me. He had shaggy blonde hair and a beard and I had seen him around school before with Zach. I think his name was Jake or Jack, something.

He said to me "ROC! What's up, baby bro!" and stuck out his hand with his pointer and ring finger out and other fingers tucked in, in gun form. He wanted to do a handshake with me, which I assumed was some form of secret bond.

"Uh...I can't shake up, I'm sick!" I said assuredly. I then bolted down the platform towards the back car as I heard the train coming. Jack screamed after me "What are you on!" But he didn't give chase.

"Jack may think Zach's insane now, but at least I'm out of that situation," I thought. I rode the train all the way to Zach's house in silence. When I arrived at his house his mother greeted me with a kiss.

"How was your day?" she asked.

"It was okay, nothing but the regular," I said, lying as big as I'd ever lied in my life.

She gave me a snack and told me to go do my homework in my room. I happily obliged. I had been worried that she was going to give me the longer clichéd parental "How was your day" dialogue, but was pleased to see that she was not interested. I couldn't stand being in Zach's body anymore. I needed to be in my own bed, even if Zach's was incredibly comfortable.

I went in his room and closed my eyes and counted to 100. Hopefully when I re-opened them and arose from my slumber, I'd be back home. I even considered clicking my heels and saying to myself "There's no place like home." Okay, I actually did do that. The fact was, I needed this body switching to stop; I had done nothing to deserve this. I hopped in his bed and closed my eyes, thinking of my amenities back home. I appreciated the lessons I have continued to learn through this empathic adventure, but man, I was tired. I started counting and things starting blurring. The room started spinning and then it all changed.

CHAPTER 6
Busted

I am flying over the earth at incredible speeds. I feel neither wind resistance nor a care in the world as I soar majestically across the sky. I'm not thinking about anything. All I am doing is flying weightlessly. Could this be real? Everything else seemed real... BUZZ! BUZZ! BUZZ! Am I still flying? The blazing, wretched sound of an alarm clock seeps into my dream and wakes me up. I groan because I am far too tired to be awake right now. Thinking back to 30 seconds ago, I conclude, yes, that was definitely a dream. This seems more real than it did a minute ago, but then again who am I to judge what's real and what isn't. I haven't seemed to have a grasp on that in quite a while.

I reach over for my alarm clock, not sure whether I am going to press the big snooze button or just turn off the alarm and start the day. I'm gonna hit snooze. I reach over, praying that the alarm clock has a snooze button. Every alarm clock has a snooze and it's always in the same place and it's always big and wide. Good. This one's no different. It's way too early. Most people at the school, I assume, wake up earlier than I just did, but it's still too early. My thoughts fade as I drift into a blank state. Before I'm well rested, that horrible noise pierces my eardrum and I'm forced to get up. How do I turn this damn thing off? I'm too tired for this; I unplug it. I zombie-walk over to the door and grab the big, blue towel hanging on the hook. I look around and start walking towards the bathroom. I run the water and start my shower. It's nice and hot. Breathing in the steam calms my nerves. God knows I need it. Do I use the soap? There are two bars of soap on two separate shelves and I have no way of knowing which one is mine. Even if I pick the right one, it's not really mine, is it? Whatever. I

46

get out of the shower, dry off, and go back to my room. I get dressed by picking the first items of clothing I see: jeans, a t-shirt, boxers and socks. While leaving the room, I catch my reflection in mirror. Why hadn't I looked at it until just now? Am I just too jaded by this whole ordeal to care? Maybe. So today I'm the white guy with a dirty blonde buzz cut who sits a few seats away from me. Never learned his name. I notice for some reason there's three dark spots in my hair. Is it like a medical condition? Should I be worried? Whatever, it's just a day. Unless it isn't...

There's a staircase to my left going only down, not up. I guess that's where I'm going. The entire floor is blocked by shut, white, double doors. I'll just keep going down. Ok, good, a kitchen. I assume the big cabinet doors are where the cereal is. First try! I'm getting good at this. But where are the bowls...? I search practically every one of the twenty something little cupboard doors before I find the bowls. Okay, so not that good. I find the spoons while looking for the bowls and I'm not too stupid as to have to look for the refrigerator. I eat a bowl of Chex and sit on a grayish brown couch. Am I getting a ride today, or what? I don't want to do the bus or the train; on the other hand, do I really want to talk to another group of strange family members? I know I want to be back as myself, but if I can't have that, I don't know what I want. I sit there for twenty or so minutes, contemplating how I'm going to get out of this situation. I have no idea. This whole thing makes no sense whatsoever. I'll just go to school. As I open the front door, I feel a cool breeze that's just too cool for me. I should get a coat; especially if I don't know where I'm going. I don't know where the coats are. Forget it. I'm too tired for this crap. I walk out into what looks like a courtyard. It looks as though a row of plants would line the walkway had the weather not been so horrid. All I see is dirt and a tiled ground. There's a staircase to my left going only down, not up. I guess that's where I'm going. Déjà vu. In the past that would have wowed me, but now I just don't care. I'm too tired to care. Tired from apparent lack of sleep and tired of going through this day after day in a seemingly endless cycle of constant foreign misery. I just want to go home, but right now I have no home, except for the one I just left.

I exit through a gate door after walking down the concrete stairs. I may be in an unfamiliar place, but it's still Chicago. I look up at the street signs and see that I'm somewhere north of downtown. There's a bus stop on both sides of this huge street. I need to go south to get on the Blue Line. Okay. Which one goes south? They obviously both go in opposing directions; I just need to choose the right one. I'm so cold. I should have gotten that coat. Crap. There's a bus coming right now. I'm too cold to just wait out here and if I don't go for it and it's the right bus, I'll just scream. I need to make a decision, fast. I sprint across the street to the bus stop. I get on the bus and realize that I don't have any money. I curse loudly, startling the bus driver, and then I get off. I just realized that I could have looked at the bus sign to see what direction it was going. Great... that was the right bus.

As I sit at the bus stop, I stare blankly into the street, ready to punch the next guy I see. So I have no money and no ride. And now I realize I have no keys. So I guess I'm not getting back into the house. Great. What do I do now? I can't do jack without money so I guess my only option is to go back to the house. But that's not even an option, is it? I could just hop the fence. It's not too high and there are plenty of ledges to climb on to get over. There's no barbed wire or anything. Yeah. I can do this. It's not illegal if it's my own house. I mean it's not my own house, but you know, it's this guy's house, and I'm this guy, so, I should be good. I reach up, grab the cement ledge, and pull myself up. I grab one of the

48

vertical bars of the gate next. I'm slipping. This looked easier from down there. I hang there for a few seconds, slowly slipping before I muster up my strength and do one big pull. I grab the top of the fence and hold onto it with both hands. WHEEE-OOOOO!!! WHEE-OOOOO!!!!

A cop car pulls up behind me, practically scaring me off of the fence. I didn't see it, but I heard it and that was enough. Should I just keep going? No, it's the police. Hiding behind the gate would just be futile. I give up and just drop to ground, defeated and scared. The 5-0's already out of the car, ready to get me. "Wait officer! I live here!" I exasperatedly exclaim. He looks about ready to just cuff me and throw me in the back of the car. I've never been arrested before. He pauses, just in case he's making a mistake. "So you live here, huh?" the officer asked skeptically. "What's your name?" I have no idea. I try to reach into my pocket to check for an ID that might help, when the cop yells the command. "Keep your hands on the ground!"

"Officer, I live here, I really do." I whine. The way I said it, I wouldn't believe it either.

"Which one's yours?" He sneers. My heart is racing. I have to think quickly. I remember the address in front of the door I exited from and tell it to the cop. "Who're your mom and dad?" … I pause, thinking of what to say. Apparently I pause for too long, because next thing I know, I'm being pushed onto the car. He aggressively tells me to put my hands behind my back, and before I know it, I'm sitting handcuffed in the back of a police car. This is the most surreal thing that's happened to me so far.

I sit there, waiting in the back seat. These handcuffs are way too tight and are hurting my wrists. There's no legroom in here and if I try to lean back I'll just sit on my twisted hands. I'm still waiting. What's probably about five minutes feels like forty-five. My brain speaks to me a mile a minute. "Is he, like, deciding whether or not to let me go? Please let me go. Please let me go. I hopped a fence. No big deal. He thinks I just tried to break into a residence; he's not going to let me go. I didn't actually break in. Maybe I was just playing around on the gate. No, I just told him I lived there. It's obvious that I tried to break in; and that's stupid anyway."

The officer opens the door and enters the car. I can't see anything except the top of the windshield through the mesh Boyer protecting the cop from me, the big criminal. I hear the sound of the engine starting and we start to move. This is really happening. He hasn't said a word to me during the entirety of the drive. This drive is taking forever, but I don't want it to end. I had completely forgotten that this wasn't me.

When we pull up to the station, I notice that we're a couple blocks away from my school. I noted the cruel irony. The car stopped and so did the engine. The officer exits the car and opens my door. "Get out," he says in a terse, gruff voice. I swing my legs over and do a sort of jump, pushing off of the seat with my cuffed hands. He puts his hand on my back and pushes me. He continuously pushes me up the stairs and opens the door for me. How nice of him. "Move!" he barks. My short-lived sense of humor about the matter dies with that command. "Sit down," he barks again, pointing at a metal chair. I sit down and wait; and wait. This is less comfortable than the back of the car. Don't I get to sit in a jail cell? These handcuffs hurt. Don't I get a phone call? Never mind, who would I call? Another cop points at me and says, "Come over here." I do as he says. He takes off my handcuffs and takes my fingerprints.

I'm then directed into a cell after being asked if I want to make a phone call. I decline. I'm feeling all alone, but I'm not. I sit in the cell, more sad now than scared. There's one other man in the cell and he's sleeping. God, I hope he doesn't wake up. I wonder about whether I will

50

be zapped out of this body or whatever, or if I had just screwed this guy into a jail cell that he didn't deserve to be in (not that I deserved to be in it either). I trace the day over and over in my head. There's one part that I just can't shake: when they took my prints. The experience was worse than I had expected. I felt like more of a criminal than I had before. When the guy grabbed my wrist and forced my hand into the ink and onto the paper, I could only notice two things. I noticed the deep creases on my wrists, left over from the handcuffs; and I noticed the date on the top of the page. It's Saturday. There was no school today.

CHAPTER 7
Down But Not Out

I woke up, staring at a random piece of blue tape on a white ceiling, trying to grasp the idea that once again I had woken up in someone else's body, grateful at least that I was no longer in jail. As I got up to see who I was, I fell out of the bed. I didn't think to look at how high the bed was before I tried to descend.

As I walked around searching for the light switch I questioned, "Why is this room so little?" Comparing my room and this one was like comparing a flashlight to a star; there was little comparison. When I reached the wall I felt a light switch and flicked it.

"Finally!"

I turned and viewed the room, which only included a bed that took up almost half of the room, a vanity set, and a television. I peered into the mirror to realize that I had taken the body of another female. She was an African American girl with curly hair. She had bags under her eyes as if she was sleep deprived. I glanced harder at her face trying to remember seeing her in class or even around campus for that matter, I couldn't. As I looked closely on the vanity set I noticed three prescription pill bottles. As I read the labels the names sounded familiar; they were usually prescribed for people who suffered from depression. Unaware of what might happen if I didn't take them, I decided to take them as a precaution.

As I looked over on the bed I noticed an iPhone and I realized that it was already going on 8 o'clock. I slowly walked down a long narrow hallway but I was stopped abruptly by a voice yelling.

"Lea, start getting ready for church."

"Church," I silently thought to myself. My family attended church, but I always just threw on slacks and a collared shirt; I have no idea how to dress a girl. I walked to a door, which I assumed was Lea's closet. There were clothes everywhere; luckily on one side she had hung only attire I thought was suitable for church. I grabbed a skirt and blouse. I'm not sure what it meant, but I was getting a little better at dressing like a girl.

I wandered down a narrow hallway, stopping to look at pictures along the way. I noticed there were a lot of pictures of two small children; I didn't hear any children running around so I figured they were baby pictures of Lea and a sibling. I walked into the bathroom and closed the door. Rushing so this lady, "my mother" wouldn't be late, I hopped in the shower. After fully undressing I realized I didn't know how to turn the shower on. I played with the showerhead and after mistakenly pressing a button the water began to trickle over my body. I tried to keep my head up and not look down so that I wouldn't invade this girl's privacy, something I seemed to be doing a lot lately.

I finished getting dressed and went back into the girl's room looking for something that would give me a sense of who she was. She didn't have any pictures of her with friends or family from the recent years; all the pictures said they were from age eight and younger. I dropped one of the pictures and noticed a pink notebook. I decided it must be important since she had attempted to hide it.

"Maybe I shouldn't read it, it's personal," I thought. Okay. But then I thought, "I'll only read some of it then I'll put it away." I walked to the door and locked it and began to read the notebook. As I flipped through the pages I began to become more and more intrigued. In the first couple pages she wrote about an abusive father, who she hated with a passion. Then she went on to describe the two hospitalizations she had gone through during her sophomore and junior year. That was it, that's why I thought she had recently transferred in;

53

she had missed so many days before due to the hospitalizations.

Page after page, I read about how she hated everyone and she thought everyone was insignificant. She rambled about how she looked forward to graduation and how she just knew life would be so much better afterwards. She reminded me of someone I knew all too well -- MYSELF.

I heard the lady yell that she was headed to the car and I rushed down the stairs, not because I didn't want to be late, but because I didn't know what or where the car was. When I stepped outside, I realized I was in the Lawndale community. I noted the amount of litter on the ground. From the looks of it, these people didn't know what a garbage can was created for. The second thing I noticed were the guys standing on the corner like in the movies, only this time it was real. I put my head down and walked briskly to avoid any trouble, but out the corner of my eye I noticed one of them smile at me as if we had some type of bond or friendship.

About twenty minutes later we pulled into the parking lot of this fancy church. There were stained glass windows, elevators, and cameras, even a sound room. I mean, of course, I had been inside nice churches, but I had never expected to see one like this. Unfortunately, instead of being able to enjoy the sight I was attacked by screaming children.

"Sister" a little girl said to me hugging my legs. Later I found out she was the daughter of a family friend. Unfortunately, she wasn't the only person that hugged me that day. More children, teens, and even adults made their way across the sanctuary to greet me with open arms, something I was not accustomed to.

After numerous hugs, a man began to sing and the service began. It began with an old man singing in an awful tone that I had no other option but to laugh at. Then I watched as more groups of people gathered to sing and finally a lady came to the podium and began lecturing about the Bible.

As soon as she began to lecture I pulled out Lea's phone and began to look through her messages to see what else I could learn about her. As I scrolled through her messages, I noticed a message from her brother. I questioned where he could be because I didn't see him when I left the house this morning. The only plausible assumption was that he was that he was older and in college.

"Boy, you acting like you do shit for me. Name the last time you did anything for me. Right, you can't. I don't have to do anything for you." As I read their messages I realized that their last conversation was almost two weeks ago and was an argument centered on her not allowing him to see her iPad. How could an iPad cause two siblings to not speak for weeks? I thought about it and I figured for Lea it wasn't about the iPad but that she wanted her brother to understand she didn't have to do anything for him and he should understand that. From the remainder of the messages I assumed that although Lea was younger, he had been the spoiled one. Tempted to text her brother, I decided it was best to put the phone away.

I began to think back over the past couple of days I had had. I thought about the first day I had woken up in Tessa's body. I reminisced on how I played with her chest and smoked cigarettes with that kid Julian. Then I thought about Sophie, the only girl I knew who worked and paid rent to her own father! Maybe Sophie and Lea should talk; I think they could help give each other some advice. My most horrendous day of them all was yesterday. I managed to go to school on a Saturday and then get arrested for trying to get into my own house. I'd much rather this calm boring life I had for the day. A light buzzing in my pocket brought me back to reality.

I checked the screen on the phone and the text read, "I need you to come in ASAP." Confused I simply showed it to my host-mother of the day to see what information and insight she could give me as to this new job I would have to work today. I watched as the lady tip-toed out the church so I did the same.

Once we reached the car she went on a rant about how my boss needed to give more notice. I tuned her out but caught some hints here and there in her lecture. By the time I had reached my job I knew that I was a waiter at a restaurant.

As I opened the car door, a man came to the door and began telling me how thankful he was that I could come on such short notice. He turned and told my mom the same thing and she responded by calling him by his first name. A guy I had seen in Lea's phone walked up and told me I should probably change before "Freeman," my manager, I assumed, saw me. Following him into the locker room I changed and clocked-in shortly after.

After eight straight hours of taking orders, listening to screaming babies and dealing with customers with terrible attitudes, it was time for me to clock out. Mr. Riley printed all my receipts and then told me the amount that I owed him. I had made $60 in tips; I assumed that was bad, but Eric, another waiter, came over and rectified my misconception. From his response to how much I had made, I realized that it was an impressive amount for their line of work.

As I headed for the door Mr. Riley called, "Lea, I need to have a word with you before you leave. I promise it won't take long." Unsure of what the conversation was about, I nervously walked towards his office.

"Eric told me about your acceptance letter."

"What acceptance letter?"

"The one everyone told me you were waving around all day yesterday. You must have left it in the locker room by mistake, because one of the busboys found it and gave it to me to give to you. Anyway, congratulations!"

"Thanks," I said, piecing it all together.

Not wanting to appear any more confused than I probably already had, I took the letter out from the opened envelope and read it as quickly as I could. I had earned a scholarship to a HBCU of my choice. I was momentarily proud. How did I, she, do it? This was amazing for the person I had lived as for the day, but then confusion swept over my mind. How was it possible for Lea, the girl I lived as for a day, to get this scholarship? She has depression; she takes medicine. She's from a single family home located in a drug infested neighborhood. Not to mention the fact that she associates herself with drug dealers. She works a full-time job where everyone's mean and rude to her because of their personal problems. Just how had this happened? These thoughts floated around in my head the entire ride home. Then it clicked: the situation doesn't make the person, the person has to make the best out of the situation and that's what Lea was doing.

As I walked up the stairs that led to the front door, I put my key into the lock and walked into the house. I turned to take one last glance at this horrendous neighborhood. I climbed the stairs that led to Lea's room and I picked up my book bag and pulled out my Pre Calc book and began to work on the only homework, according to her planner, she had for the weekend. I pulled out the envelope and stared at the letter. I decided to leave a note on Lea's mirror so that when she regained her body back in the morning she would once again feel the elation of great news. I took out some lipstick and scribbled on the mirror, "Congratulations, you did it, Lea."

I closed the bedroom door and the darkness of the room reminded me of the darkness in this girl's life. Her world revolved around dealing with people who weren't appreciative of her hard work and her depression. It wasn't until I lay down that I noticed that no one told me I seemed different, that I wasn't "myself" that day. Was Lea always this standoffish; or could it just be that no one really paid attention to her?

As I thought back to my writing class I tried to remember Lea. She always sat quietly on the other side of the room. It all made sense now; Lea struggled every day and due to my own selfish reasoning I didn't notice, maybe because I didn't care to see. I made myself oblivious to the people around me so that I wouldn't have to feel for them, but now I felt sorry for her. As I closed my eyes to go to sleep I heard Ms. Glass's voice repeat the word, "empathy."

CHAPTER 8
Beginning To Get It

"I don't want to get up yet!" I screamed, as I heard my alarm going off in the morning. As usual I reached to the left of my bed's headboard, but to my surprise my alarm clock wasn't there. Furiously I jumped out of bed and momentarily couldn't understand why my alarm clock was moved to the center of my headboard. "Oh, this again," I thought, irritated that I had yet to get back to being me. As I ran out of my bedroom to see who I am today, I ran into some woman who I assumed to be this kid's mother.

She said to me, "Good morning Jimmy, you better get ready quickly or you will be late today."

"Well I guess I'm Jimmy today." I mumbled to myself.

"What's that, Jim?"

"Oh nothing... mom." I didn't want to be Jimmy or Billy or Tommy or anybody. I wanted to be me.

On the other hand, at least I was a guy again. There's something reassuring about being your own gender. When would this finally end? I quickly took a shower, although whatever kind of place I was in didn't even have decent conditioner. I grabbed what appeared to be Jimmy's stuff and headed out with whom I thought was Jimmy's father to this guy's old car. As we were getting in the car, I noticed the sun wasn't up and exclaimed, "What time is it! Why are we up so early?"

"Don't you remember you have PSAT practice today before school, so we have to leave by 6:15?" I was flabbergasted at the thought that Jimmy needed practice for such an easy test. Well, at least it wasn't church again. After about forty-five minutes in the car we finally arrived at Jimmy's school, and I headed in.

Luckily this kid kept a map of his classes in his backpack, although I didn't know what kind of human wouldn't learn their schedule in the first week of school. Now I just had to sit through a boring PSAT prep until actual school started. This was great; these "rent-a-teachers" were telling me how to use English like I hadn't spoken the language for the past sixteen years. And then off to practice math, so they could show me how to use a calculator.

When that finally ended, I hoped I might be able to go to some classes for smart people. No such luck. I sure hoped all this wasted time wasn't aging my *real* body and only affected Jimmy's. As I sat down in Jimmy's AP calculus class, I noticed he sat near the back. He's probably some slacker who doesn't know anything. "So can anyone tell me the derivative of $5X^6$?" the teacher asked. As I sat there investigating Jimmy's backpack, I saw no one even attempting to answer the question. Was everyone in the class stupid, or did no one want to talk? Like I usually did after waiting a little while with no one answering, I jumped in and said "$30X^5$," and yet no one gave me any recognition. The teacher didn't even seem to care. Whoever "Jimmy" is, he must have set a pretty low standard for himself. I opened his notebook and saw some of the worst handwriting I'd seen in ages. It looked like an eight year old decided to spell half the words wrong. Most of this class must thought I was a poor student just because I was stuck in his stupid body. I thought I heard the bell, but I didn't really care that much. I headed off to Jimmy's next class anyway.

After spending six minutes trying to read Jimmy's terrible handwriting, I finally was able to decipher that his next class was AP Physics. Because of that I got a tardy slip, but whatever, this Jimmy kid would be stuck with the tardy. It's his fault anyway for having such terrible writing. At least it was just a lecture class and I didn't have to pay attention at all. I already knew how gravity worked, and even if I wanted Jimmy to do well, paying attention wouldn't help him. It is crazy how long fifty minutes feels when you're sitting and just daydreaming. Then out of nowhere this short kid that sat next to me, poked me and pointed toward the teacher.

"So what's the answer, Jimmy?" The teacher said frustrated. He must have noticed I was daydreaming. Oh, well.

"The Kinetic energy is equal to one half the mass times the velocity squared," I replied.

The teacher, looking surprised, responded "Very good." Teachers can be so stupid, they never seem to notice that when they ask a question during a lecture the answer is usually on their power point directly behind them, but they still think you're a smart kid for reading it. Then the bell; I headed over to Jimmy's homeroom.

There went 10 minutes of my life; off to Jimmy's next class already. "Hmmm what's next" I wondered. There it was: Room 103, Japanese 4. Nap time for me. No use wasting my time on a language I didn't understand. As I woke up half way through class, I saw the teacher shouting at me, but I had no idea what she was saying. I just shrugged it off and went back to sleep after she left me alone. Some days I cared, but that day, I couldn't care less what she thought of Jimmy.

As I headed to Jimmy's next class, Interdisciplinary Writing, I started to think about it again. What was going on? Why did this keep happening? While trying to ponder all the different possibilities, I accidentally took a wrong turn. When the bell rang, I realized I hadn't been paying attention and sprinted over to the writing classroom. I burst in the door late, with every other kid already sitting down, looking at me. All of a sudden I noticed all the kids I'd been were in front of me. Sophie was in the corner not listening, Zach was talking to his buddies in the other corner, Lea wasn't looking like she's that happy even though she had just gotten into college, and sitting next to Augie the swimmer was that kid whose name I didn't know. Glad he was out of jail. Well, that was good news. But then it hit me: "There were 30 kids in this class. Oh, my God, did that mean I'd have to go through all of them? Was that it, or was there more to it?" For the entire class we were supposed to be working on the laptops, but I couldn't stop trying to connect the dots in my mind. I may have been late and not had the best day, but I'd take a victory when I could get one.

After that class ended, I made my way to Art 1. What a joke class; I remember having taken this for the credit when I was a freshman. I just did other work or slept during that class. No art teacher actually grades you on doing work well; I would always just scribble something up at the last minute, put on a straight face and say, "I'm not very good at drawing, this is the best I could do." I would always get full credit. My memory was correct. As usual, we were doing nothing in this class. Our teacher was lecturing us on different types of lines; I *definitely* understood why the school required us to take this. "Can someone name a type of line?" the teacher asked. This question I didn't even bother to answer, it was simply not worth my time. The bell then rang and I headed off to Economics.

At least this was a class that was useful. I could imagine myself handling money in the future a lot better than I could imagine me counting lines. So far, the class seemed to have students who talked a lot. Either the teacher was really lazy, wanted to help the whole class, or both. I didn't even get to jump in as the smart kid because the teacher was calling on students randomly; apparently there was no raising of hands there. The only question he has asked me was, "If the supply of an item goes down what would happen to the demand?" to which I quickly answered, "It would go up." I hated when teachers did this and if you got a question right, they wouldn't call on

62

you again because they wanted the dumb kids to do better. Then when one kid didn't know the answer we just all sat there wasting time while the kid *slowly looked* through his lack of notes until he found the answer or someone gave it to him.

Then I was off to Jimmy's lunch period. Unfortunately no one in his family made me a lunch, but I had Jimmy's wallet so I decided I might as well go somewhere and order large. All of a sudden a bunch of kids approached me and said, "So, where do you want to go to lunch?" Pausing because I had no idea where his people generally went, I got lucky because some other kid jumped in and suggested "How about Billy Goat's?"

After the group wasted five minutes discussing whether or not Billy Goat's would do and finally agreed to go there, we ended up at Subway. While we were at lunch, Jimmy's friends talked about the most obscure topics. Most of the information was useless but at least they were tolerable. I added a few jokes and nods to the conversation. We headed back to school with roughly no time left in the period. When I realized Jimmy's next class was ping pong, I didn't care how close to being late we were. This "Seminar" on ping pong seemed like a waste of school resources: you didn't get any information, you didn't get any grades, and you didn't get any credit for it. At least the teacher didn't think it was very crucial either because he didn't seem to mind me lying near the window in the sun the entire class.

When the school day ended, all of a sudden I realized I had no idea how to get back to Jimmy's house. As I was about to panic, two kids walked up to me and said, "So Jimmy, you taking the train?" Having no better idea of where to go, I replied, "Sure." After twenty minutes of following those two on the train, one of them left, but I decided to stick with the remaining one because of how long it took to get to school. After another fifteen minutes or so we boarded a bus, and then twenty minutes later we got off and started walking. I hoped I was going the right way, but I never asked because it would have seemed weird. Luckily we walked by my house and the kid that was with me said, "Jimmy, we just passed your house, you know," and I replied, "Oh, yeah, I wasn't paying attention." I headed into Jimmy's house and decided to explore the place a bit.

Looking around I saw his house was kind of a circle, with the rooms meeting together. There was an upstairs and a basement that wasn't well furnished. Overall I guess it was a decent place, but by no means did it compare to my own. As I found his refrigerator, I decided to grab an extra lunch. It wasn't like I was paying for it. With my newfound knowledge from English class, I didn't think I'd be Jimmy the next day. In that case, there was no need to do his homework. But you know what, compared to some of my other days this one hadn't been too bad. I figured I'd do his assignments just to help out and then headed off to bed. A week and a half ago, that would have been the strangest day of my life; but now I know better.

CHAPTER 9
The Tutor

I woke up to the sound of an obnoxious alarm. I reached for my alarm clock but instead all I found was a phone where my alarm clock would have been. I thought to myself, "I guess I should have known that I wasn't going to wake up in my own room." I rubbed my eyes to get a clearer view but I couldn't see anything. "I guess this person doesn't have 20/20 vision like me," I muttered under my breath. I squinted and looked around the room until I saw a pair of glasses on the desk next to this bed and reluctantly put them on. All I could think of was, "Whoa."

Everything in sight became clear. I observed the room and noticed the excessive amount of female clothing and accessories. I thought, "Well, I guess I'm a girl today. At least it's a change of pace from being Jimmy. Hopefully the people in this person's classes won't be so dim." I was getting tired of having to deal with their stupidity. I got out of bed and stepped over various pieces of clothing and shoes and walked slowly out the room, hoping that I wouldn't run into anyone from this family. I saw a door at the end of the hall and pushed it open, hoping it was the bathroom. Luckily, it was. I looked at myself in the mirror and I realized that I recognized this girl. She looked so familiar but I couldn't place a name to that face. She sat in the back of fifth period but I never talked to her, so I never bothered to learn her name.

I noticed the array of cosmetic products ranging from foundation to eyeliner to contacts. Fortunately for me, it wasn't the first time I'd been a girl so I picked up some skill practicing with these products. Being a guy, though, I didn't need anything to look nice. It was all natural good looks for me. Since it wasn't even my body,

I didn't really care what this person looked like, so I just attempted to brush my hair, grabbed the first outfit I saw, and walked downstairs to grab some breakfast. Or at least I hoped there was. To my disappointment, there was no breakfast waiting for me at the table. I rolled my eyes in annoyance at how disappointing this family turned out to be. I guessed I'd just grab something on the way to school since these people seem well enough off for me to assume I'm driving. I was thinking about all the choices I could get for breakfast when a loud, booming voice distracted my thoughts.

"Amanda, hurry up! If you don't, you're going to miss your bus."

I listened attentively and assumed that since I didn't hear anyone else in the house that Amanda was the name of this girl. Forgetting myself for a moment, I spoke for the first time and protested back, *"but I'm going to drive to school myself."*

This man approached me and laughed while, saying "In your dreams, kiddo."

"Are you serious? I have to take the public transportation? Again?" I thought to myself.

Begrudgingly, I dragged myself towards the door and looked at the choice of shoes that I had. There were so many options but they all seemed so uncomfortable. I had zero knowledge of girls' shoes. All I knew was that they all were ridiculously designed for walking. I grabbed the shoe with the shortest heel (which was probably about 2 inches) and walked to the nearest train station that I could see from this house.

I dug through Amanda's backpack and found a gold wallet. I hoped there was either money in there or a bus card or something. I tried the bus card and luckily, it worked. I walked up the stairs and saw an Asian girl waving at me but I didn't know her, so I just stood further away from her. When I got on the train, that same girl sat in the seat next to me and poked me. "Why aren't

66

you sitting with me today? We always sit together." Still not knowing who she was, I just coughed and said I was sick and that I didn't want to contaminate her. I quickly searched Amanda's book bag for headphones and found them, fortunately. I stuck them into the phone jack and blasted whatever music I could find just so I wouldn't have to listen to this girl talk. Eventually, I guess she got bored or something and got up and moved to another seat. "Thank God." I just sat in silence for the rest of the train ride and prayed that no one else would talk to me.

All I could think about was getting to school so that I could be one day closer to being done. My inner voice started to ramble on. The faster the days passed, the faster I could officially say that I'm done with high school. But what then? What if I was stuck with all these people forever? What if I never got back to my own body? What if this great wheel of misfortune stopped spinning and left me forever inside someone with a great lack of intelligence? How fair would that be?

Finally, I arrived at school. I took out my ID and flashed it at the security guard. I glanced at the back of the ID and apparently I was supposed to go to 2nd period Seminar, wherever that was. After an intense amount of searching, I found out that it was located in the Writing Center and that it was a College Essay Writing Seminar. When I found this out, I couldn't help but roll my eyes. "Why would anyone sign up for this in January?" She should have begun the process a month and a half ago. I walked in and sat down and ignored everything the teacher said. I looked at the schedule on the back of the ID again. I was supposed to go to AP Biology next. I took that class last year so I just decided to skip it. Feeling like I was losing it, thinking about the scary possibilities ahead of me, I decided to hide out in the library. I didn't want anyone to talk to me like that girl earlier on the bus.

I entered the library and was greeted by the librarian. I guess this girl spent a lot of the time in the library. One point for her. I quickly waved hi and speed walked towards the comfy looking couches. I basically lay there for the next period and then the bell rang. Not feeling like getting up, I decided to just lie there until I felt like I should get up. I considered going to my 5th period Interdisciplinary Writing Class to see how that would go. At least I could catch a glimpse of Nia. Meanwhile, that same librarian kept calling Amanda's name. I didn't answer at first, but realizing she wouldn't let up, I looked up and she gestured me to this seat. Then, she said, "Okay Division 321, we have some announcements today."

I guess this was my Division. I didn't even know that you could have Division in the library. This was such a horrible location to have Division. You couldn't eat or talk loudly or anything. After listening to that librarian drone on and on about all things irrelevant, the bell rang again. I didn't really feel like staying and since this is probably a dream, I decided to just ditch. What's the worst that could happen? They can't give *me* a cut or anything. So I grabbed what I assumed to be Amanda's jacket and her book bag and headed straight out the door.

Suddenly, I felt something vibrate. It was that same phone with the girly case. I guess I got a text message. I didn't know whether or not to open it. It said 'Mom' so I figured it might be important. It said, "Don't forget to tutor Justin." *Hm, tutoring.* That should be easy enough. How hard could it be to tutor this "Justin" person? I looked through the notes in search for an address to his house. Luckily, it was actually there on the phone. I quickly typed it into the Google Maps app and headed over there. I walked slowly towards the door, hoping that I was at the right house. I rang the doorbell and this Asian grandma came and opened the door. She seemed to have recognized me and started speaking in

68

Chinese. I had no idea what she was saying but I assumed it was something along the line of "come inside." I took off my shoes and looked around. It was a really nice house. It was almost as nice as my house.

I looked at the grandma to see what I should do next and she gestured towards the stairs to go upstairs. I didn't know which room I was supposed to go into but I walked up the stairs anyway. I just decided to knock on the first door but there was no response. I moved on to the second door and said, "Justin?" The door opened and this small child came out. To my surprise, he wasn't at all what I expected him to look like. He had Down syndrome. I didn't know if I was even capable of teaching him.

After an hour of struggling and doing my best, I decided it was time to go back to Amanda's house. I reflected about that hour and realized how impatient I was and how easily frustrated I can get. Maybe I should be a little more patient. It's probably not such a great quality that I am so impatient. I quickly left the house out of frustration and looked around at my surroundings. It looked really familiar and I realized that Amanda's house was only a block away. I walked towards her house and opened the door. Fortunately, there was no one else at this house, so I ran up the stairs. I lay in her bed and dozed off, hoping that I would get back to being good old me, but thinking, at the same time, that it probably wouldn't happen.

CHAPTER 10
Getting Dissed by My Boyfriend

"Here we go again," I groaned, as I realized that I had once more woken up not only in someone else's bed, but also in someone else's body. Ironically, I began to expect it. As if it were normal for this to be happening. I felt strands of wild, unkempt hair brushing against my face and sighed. Girl again. Yesterday's prediction was right—I was quite obviously no longer Amanda. How long was this going to last?

I sat up and surveyed my surroundings. To the right of me was a closet with a floor length mirror hanging from the door; I wiped the sleep from my eyes and saw that today, I was Olivia Walsh.

Olivia was in my AP French class—I'd never held a legitimate conversation with her, so I didn't know much about her besides the fact that she was passionate about the language and asked the most questions in class. She was definitely worth sharing a conversation with, but I'd never gotten around to it. Some days she appeared alright, and others the buoyant spirit in her usual demeanor seemed absent—every once in a while I'd allow myself to wonder why this was. I didn't care too much about it, though; whether I knew or not, my life would continue on, as would hers. I figured that I would find out today. Surprisingly, this excited me.

I glanced at the alarm clock on the small bedside table; the numbers read 6:00 a.m. I yawned and stepped out of bed. The house was quiet, but a soft glow from light downstairs illuminated the hallway, so I figured that someone had woken up already.

I didn't know what part of the city I was in, so I hadn't the slightest clue how long it would take me to get to school, or even how I would get to school for that matter. That's what I'd come to hate about this waking-up-in-somebody-else's-shoes-everyday thing—I had to navigate my day blindly, with no idea how these people normally carried out their lives.

I scanned the bright, green-walled room and sighed with relief upon spotting a set of car keys on the desk in the corner of the room. *So, she drives,* I thought. *Plus one for Olivia Walsh.*

Quickly, I threw on some sweats and a bright green Northface jacket and headed downstairs.

I assumed that the woman brewing tea in the kitchen was Mrs. Walsh.

"Good morning, mom," I said hurriedly, slinging my backpack over my shoulder and heading for the door.

"You don't want a bagel or something? Here, take a vitamin," she said, pulling a small jar from the cabinet over the stove.

"Thanks. See ya."

I didn't want to stick around and possibly create an awkward situation—after all, I knew nothing about this family or their daily habits. I had to confess, though, this place was nice. I could tell that Mrs. Walsh preferred that things were kept tidy and in order at home.

Stepping outside, I realized that I was in Beverly—usually the homes in this neighborhood were older, but Olivia's house had a more modern feel that I was admittedly fond of.

Olivia's shiny silver sports car was parked out front. I climbed in, revved the engine, and pulled off.

My first class was a breeze.

It was Probability and Statistics, a simple but useful class. I could never figure out how anyone could possibly struggle with this course, but then again, I had to remember that everyone didn't think on the same level that I did. Students these days were lazy; they did what they had to do to skate by. I chuckled at the thought of what was to come for them in college.

In study hall I managed to type a paper and finish two homework assignments. I hadn't realized how useful a free period could be, and thought that perhaps having one my sophomore year when I took four AP classes would've been vastly beneficial. I shrugged the reflection away; it didn't matter now.

I shuddered when the fourth period bell rang.

Olivia had AP French, and so did I. This wouldn't be the first time I saw myself in the halls, yet it was still so creepy. I considered myself a fairly logical and sensible person, and I had wracked my brain trying to formulate an explanation for being here and there at the same time. I had nothing.

I slid into Olivia's seat, scanning the room for myself. As usual, there I was in the front row, slumped lazily in my chair, my hands clasped together on the desk in front of me. My expression was bored; I was uninterested because I could recite the material in my sleep if I'd wanted. At this point, I was simply going through the motions. The real me was counting down the minutes until the bell, but the me inside Olivia Walsh was attentive and involved.

Every couple minutes, I glanced over at myself, fascination and puzzlement coursing through my veins like a wildfire. I wanted to talk to myself, to really figure out how I was in two different bodies at once. Was I even in my real body? If I wasn't, then who was? Goosebumps rose on my skin at the thought.

When the bell rang, I leapt from my seat and started towards the front of the room, hoping to catch myself before I disappeared into the sea of loud, busy students beyond the classroom door.

Crap, I thought, cursing myself as the real me slipped just beyond my reach. I wasn't fast enough.

I sighed, gathering my belongings.

Next was class with Ms. Glass, and I'd be there again. As I walked into the room, the foundation of a thought flitted through my mind and rested on the edges of my consciousness; as class wore on, it became a solid hunch. I watched myself as I was as quietly arrogant as ever, answering my daily one question quota. It was hard to watch, so I switched my attention to Ms. Glass. She poured her opinion of Magic Realism onto the class, as if she were pouring a frosting of interest and excitement onto a disengaged and indifferent cake. She was always so passionate about the material she taught us, and that really made me appreciate her class.

When the bell rang, my heart jumped into my throat. I swallowed it back down and crept to the front of the classroom, waiting until the last of the students dispersed into the hallway before asking for a moment of Ms. Glass's time.

"Olivia! What can I do for you, dear?"

I hesitated. "Well...I don't really know how to say this without sounding completely insane." I paused, gathering my thoughts. "Something weird's going on and I think you know it."

Ms. Glass stared, waiting patiently for an elaboration. She seemed completely unaware of what I was talking about, which made me reconsider my decision to bring it up again in the first place.

"I mean...I don't know how to explain it. I'm not...I'm not *me*."

The corners of her lips twitched upward ever slightly, but in a quick moment her solemn expression had resettled on her face.

"What do you mean, Olivia? Are you feeling ill? Would you like a pass to the nurse?" Her expression had become one of confused concern.

I shook my head rapidly. "No, no." I sighed. "I remember you talking to me—to Jake, that is—about a week ago. About empathy or something, do you remember that? And the next day, I woke up, and I wasn't me—I wasn't Jake. I was Tessa, and the day after

73

that I was Sophie. And now I'm Olivia, but I'm not *really* Olivia. I'm Jake. I thought you'd know something that could help me figure this out."

I stopped, watching Ms. Glass's face carefully. If she was freaked out by what she was just told, she did a damned good job concealing it. I figured she was processing what I'd said—or maybe she wasn't, because she already knew what was going on. At least, that's what I hoped.

"I'm not sure I can help you on that one," she said softly, finally. "You think it might be better to see the nurse?"

The corners of her lips twitched again, and her eyes seemed to dance with excitement. I could tell that she was amused by my story; frustration and embarrassment surged through me as I felt my cheeks grow warm.

"Forget it," I muttered. "Just—forget I said anything."

I turned and sped out of the room, feeling Ms. Glass's eyes burning into my back the entire way.

Lunch was next.

I walked slowly, trying to sort out the conversation with Ms. Glass in my head. There wasn't much to work with, really—I had foolishly let her in on specific details of this bizarre situation, and she seemed to have no clue what I was talking about. Yet something in the back of my mind told me that she *did* know what was going on—in fact, I couldn't help but maintain the feeling that she had something to do with it. I tried to shrug the thought away; it was clear that she was as clueless as I was. Or was it? The glimmer in her eye; the twitch at the corner of her lips—was it innocent amusement or mischievous knowledge?

The conversation faded into the back of my mind and the gears switched as I got closer to the Red House lunchroom, a feeling entirely unfamiliar to me swelling in my stomach. Was it fear, anxiety? Hope, maybe? I couldn't tell.

Why did Olivia feel this way? I guessed that the answer to this would be the cause of the melancholy, less cheerful Olivia that I sometimes noticed, too. I surveyed the hallway. My heart skipped a beat when I spotted Joey Henderson, and I instantly understood that this was Olivia's boyfriend. Months of raw emotion flooded over me—pure, wholesome ecstasy and sheer pain, all at once. I wasn't used to passion this elaborate and profound, but Olivia, without a doubt, was. In the moments I stood watching Joey from across the room, I felt a tireless yearning and unconditional affection, but looming not too far off was a foreboding cloud of hopeless despair. It was almost too much to handle. Once more, I allowed myself to wonder.

With timid apprehension, I made my way towards Joey. Still, I questioned why I was so anxious.

"Hey, babe," I whispered.

"'Sup."

"Is something wrong?"

Joey shrugged indifferently, then shook his head. I was staring into his eyes, but he was focused on something elsewhere—beyond me. Finally, his gaze settled on mine. His eyes were a scorching gray, a portal to dark secrets and unsolved mysteries just beyond the surface. They burned into mine when he looked at me; my heart raced.

For a few short moments we stood there, silent and unmoving. Before I could form a coherent thought, he broke the spell and wordlessly trudged away. Just like that, I was left alone, in a throng of chattering, laughing students—students completely oblivious to what just happened. I envied them. Joey had been detached and uninterested; he had cast a cold shadow over the both of us, one that crushed me a little more underneath its bearing every step in the opposite direction that he took.

Suddenly, the emotion that I felt earlier was fading, replaced by something more powerful, more urgent. A whirlwind of hurt swirled in my chest, breaking me down from the inside. I hugged myself, biting back tears. These couldn't possibly be my feelings; I couldn't possibly be capable of it—this was Olivia, and I couldn't help but feel what she felt.

A moment passed before it clicked. Struggling to place this strange, unimaginable emotion, I now knew what Olivia Walsh was feeling.

I stood in the hallway, in the midst of the seemingly happy, carefree faces, helplessly, hopelessly, as my heart broke.

That evening I sat in Olivia's room with the door closed, contemplating the day's proceedings. I couldn't imagine feeling the way that I felt earlier day after day; I marveled at Olivia's ability to do so. At the same time, I wondered why she stuck around if Joey brought her that much sorrow.

Girls really don't make sense, I decided, letting myself fall back onto a fluffy green pillow. The magnitude of the emotion that I'd felt earlier had dwindled slightly since I'd gotten back to Olivia's house, but I no longer had the capacity to deal with it. I applauded and reproached Olivia at the same time; she was a strong, yet silly girl. Tomorrow couldn't come fast enough.

I studied the bedroom. It was vibrant, but cozy. A strand of Christmas lights hung above the bed, washing the room in a soft, warm glow. Large black block letters were cut out of construction paper, forming the quote "life is better lived" above the white wooden desk across from the bed—but this is no way to live, I thought sullenly. One wall was covered with photographs; memories of homecomings, birthday parties, and unforgettable moments all in one place. Near the top of the wall was a snapshot of Olivia and Joey—they both

76

wore wide, genuine smiles, and I wondered if it was all a façade.

I glanced at the clock: 9:45 p.m. I guessed it wasn't too early for bed; the sooner, the better, anyways. I pulled Olivia's iPod from a small pocket on her backpack and tucked myself in.

I regarded sarcastically the iPod's shuffle feature's ability to perfectly complement my mood with its music selection—somehow, melancholy, passionate music always seemed to soothe and depress me at the same time. Once again, I realized that Olivia's emotions were overwhelming mine—that was the only way that I could possibly feel the depth of her despair. After all, this was something that she was going through, not I; yet, I could feel what she felt as clearly as if the feelings were my own.

I brought my fingers to my cheek, brushing away wetness. I hadn't realized that I was crying. This seemed to be just the push I needed to send me over the edge—suddenly and uncontrollably, I began to weep. I stifled my cries in the pillow, sad and soulful melodies still playing softly in my ears. I didn't know how long this lasted or if I ever even stopped, but when Olivia's body decided that it was too tired for consciousness, I let the tears carry me to sleep.

CHAPTER 11
Looking At Love

For some reason, waking up to a dark room makes sense. I lay there for some reason. Staring into the darkness, I wondered why my nose was so stuffy and what made my lips so chapped. As I moved my lazy tongue to moisten my top lip, I tasted salt.

I assumed I fell asleep crying and wondered if they were new or old tears. Whether they were the same tears from my previous body or freshly dried from the eyes of my new one, I wasn't sure. If I had to guess, I'd say they were from my new body, seeing as though I was overwhelmed with a gloom I knew nothing about.

I turned to my side. Although I couldn't see it, I felt long strands of hair cover my face. I was a girl again.

Explains the moodiness.

I got up and turned on the light. I looked around a room filled with earth tones, and a soft carpet reminiscent of cotton. It wasn't a small room, but it wasn't big either. It was similar to the size of mine at home. Greens and browns covered the bed, while a light tan covered the walls. It was neat. I saw a door filled with pictures and my jaw instantly dropped.

Long, curly, brown hair and beautiful, dark brown eyes that I loved to look into everyday during my fifth period Interdisciplinary Writing class. I was Nia Gray. The brown skinned girl I have had a crush on for the past year.

Nia was wonderful. She always had a smile on her face every time I saw her.

"Guess what?" She would say to me every day before she told me a new story or a funny joke. I never really listened. I would always be too busy staring at her. I would come back in on major parts and the end where I chimed in with a laugh and smile inferior to hers.

Her eyes glowed when she talked. They would show her excitement and passion in her heart. She never seemed sad or mad. This confused me and sometimes frustrated me. I wanted to know she wasn't perfect so that this embarrassing child-like crush would go away as fast as it came. It happened the moment when she first asked for my name. Somehow I never had the nerve to ask her out.

All of a sudden I got confused. Why did Nia fall asleep crying?

I instantly got upset at the idea of someone hurting her feelings and balled my hand into a fist.

The door slammed open and I quickly turned away from my reflection.

"Get ready."

That was the only thing said before the woman walked out of the room and left the door open.

I knew nothing about Nia's mom. She never really talked about her. She was a hip woman who looked young for her age. I still stood staring at the door stung by the coldness of the words that left her mouth. From the sharp tone I guessed she was mad at me. I refused to believe Nia could have done anything that bad for her mother to be that cold. I did what her mother said and walked out of the opened door into more cold darkness.

The whole house seemed kind of gloomy.

I brushed my hands along the dry walls trying to find a light switch. As my fingertips found one, I flipped it up and blinked ferociously as the light lit the darkness. I looked at Nia's smooth legs as they walked and guided me into a nearby bathroom. Turning on the water, I again began the awkward process of getting ready for school in someone else's body. This time, it was someone I liked.

After an interesting and exciting thirty minutes of cleaning and dressing Nia, I walked down the stairs of the small house into the kitchen.

Her mother was waiting. As soon as I settled myself in a chair assuming I was about to be handed breakfast as usual, more emotionless words came out of her mouth. "Let's go."

I quickly got up and grabbed my book bag to follow her to a green Honda CR-V. The car ride was long and awkward. Our eyes never met and we didn't talk. The strange sadness I woke up with came back. I couldn't help but wonder what had happened between them and if I could somehow make it better.

We pulled up to the school and I reluctantly said goodbye. She didn't respond. I was instantly enraged by her cruelty towards Nia. I got out of the car and closed the door with a slam.

I entered the school, unlike the Nia I usually saw. I was sad and couldn't bring myself to smile. I still didn't know why.

"Hey, Nia girl!" Olivia said smiling.

I only responded with a smile to match hers and quickly avoided any further communication by walking faster and more to the side opposite of where she was walking.

"Nia! Hey!" said another smiling face. I responded the same as the last. I walked up the stairs and was greeted by another grinning face. I couldn't escape. I just didn't feel like talking. I didn't know how to talk. I didn't know how to be 'Happy Nia' when I felt so sad.

Periods passed and I drifted by, easing through each class. Well, until I got to fifth period.

I knew I would see myself. I walked into the class and immediately met my eyes with Nia's or Nia's with mine. It wasn't that weird but it's hard to explain. It'd happened before, but this time I could see that "I" was giving this new body a different look. I saw my pupils grow as I looked into the eyes of Nia. So this is how pathetic I look when talking to her.

"Hey, Nia," I said to myself.

I spoke for the second time today.

"Hey, Jake."

We were still looking at each other smiling. It was nice. For the first time today, I wasn't as sad. Maybe Nia liked me, too. I immediately snapped out of it and climbed back into my funk. I walked to my seat and didn't turn around to talk to myself like Nia usually did. The class went by slowly.

The entire school day was filled with awkward goodbyes and hesitant hellos. But once I got home, well to Nia's home anyway, it wasn't much different. I dragged my feet up the same stairs I had reluctantly come down earlier and landed my body heavily on top of the bed.

I closed my eyes and felt slow trickles of tears roll down my cheeks. Nia's cheeks. It wasn't me in pain. In fact, I had no idea why I was crying. A sharp pain stopped my tears for a moment as I felt around for the culprit.

It was a journal.

It was a small, brown diary embedded with blue lace and green beads along its side. There was nothing on the front or the back. Just a smooth, brown cover. I just looked at it for a while. Deciding whether or not to open it. I knew I would be invading her privacy. But then, I thought, I *am* Nia.

I opened to the first page.

I traced the elegantly scripted handwriting with my finger and read the neatly written black words: PROPERTY OF NIA GRAY. As I turned to the next page I found a poem.

> *Have you seen the moon wait for the sun?*
> *It patiently longs for its touch all evening,*
> *Only to meet then be turned away.*
> *I am afraid to be your naïve moon.*

I looked up from the diary and wondered who the poem was about. Could it be me? My curiosity guided my fingers to turn from page to page in a quest to finding my answer. What I found gave me hope and a grin. A small heart engraved with "N + J" excited me and I immediately started to plan my next move. I anticipated returning to my body to express my feelings to Nia and imagined all of the possibilities while my stomach fluttered. I quickly returned to flip through more pages hoping to find more. With each page I saw a new side of Nia. I smiled as I skimmed through her feelings and glanced at each little doodle, short poem, and diary entry. I stopped as I came to one from two days ago.

> *He left a week ago and hasn't called me. It's getting worse. She yells at me every day now. I miss the days when we used to play board games and laugh about everything. I miss talking with her. Now everything is an argument. I told her I hated her today. But it was only a response to being called a "bitch." Got called an idiot too, but that one I'm used to. I guess everything she wants to say to him she just shouts at me. She says we're just alike. But I'm mad at him too. Who can I yell at?*

That explained it all. I started to cry again, but this time I knew why. They weren't Nia's tears this time either; they were my own. I didn't want Nia to cry anymore so this time I took the pain. I wish she knew she could tell me more than jokes. I wanted to know everything and I wanted to make everything right. Then I realized, I might never get the chance. I looked down at Nia's body and tears fell down heavier and more frequently. I feared I would be stuck and never be able to be myself again. Never being able to lie in my own bed again; never getting to tell Nia how I felt. My eyes grew heavy as each tear fell and I soon found myself falling asleep in the same position I had awoken from that morning.

CHAPTER 12
Getting Used To It

Today I woke up to the alarms of a phone and alarm clock, one after the other set for 6:30 AM. I pulled off the covers and immediately began to shiver, realizing why I had slept with two blankets that night. I climbed to my feet and brought my attention to the window above the bed. The blinds were drawn already to reveal the sunrise. The clouds were a warm pink color as the dark blue sky began to concede to the golden light of the sun.

I yawned as I rubbed my eyes in attempt to wake them. Still standing on the bed, I turned around to observe the room around me. It wasn't the cleanest, but it seemed to be an organized mess. The walls were painted a light green and the computer desk was white. I eyed a rack full of makeup products in the corner of the desk and realized that this was a girl's room.

I looked down to find myself wearing a tie dyed shirt and a pair of Christmas-themed pajama pants. I shrugged and trudged myself down the hall to the bathroom. I yawned as I walked to the sink and when I looked at myself in the mirror, I saw that I was an Asian female. I thought about my fifth period English class and placed her in the back of the room. I thought her name was Melissa, and that's what I decided to go with until I heard differently. I had slightly curly brown hair and dark brown eyes.

After I had brushed my teeth and washed my face, I came back to the room to find myself facing the closet with absolutely no idea of what to wear. Girls' fashion isn't exactly my forte, but the body I was in seemed to know what to do. I pulled on a sweater, a pair of black skinny jeans, and a pair of black rain boots lying on the floor. My body sat itself down at the desk and my hands immediately began working its magic and fifteen minutes later, I had applied eyeliner and what I think was foundation onto my face. I was getting better at it.

I grabbed the backpack lying on the floor and made my way down the stairs. I brought myself to the kitchen to find a woman sipping tea at the table while reading the morning paper. I presumed she was the mother of the girl. My stomach growled and so I grabbed the tub of French vanilla-flavored yogurt from the refrigerator and a box of blueberry granola from the counter. I poured the granola into a bowl of the yogurt and took a bite. I was surprised at how light and tasty this breakfast was and finished the bowl quickly.

When the mom heard the clang of the bowl entering the sink after I had finished, she got up and handed me the car keys and proceeded to put her shoes on. She opened the front door and I followed suit. She walked over to a red minivan parked in front and that cued me to unlock the doors with the key. I slipped into the driver's seat and started the car. Without thinking, I turned on the radio to 90.1FM, which I presumed was a Christian radio station. The talk show hosts discussed a somewhat stupid case where an organization named "Freedom from Religion" complained about some signs that cheerleaders from a Texas high school made which said something along the lines of "In Christ, We Can Do All Things." The principal of the high school banned the signs, but in court the judge banned the ban. I wanted to comment on the case, but wasn't sure how my "mom" felt about it, so I left it alone

I arrived at school with barely any time to get to my locker. I handed the keys back to my "mom" and pulled out my ID to enter the school. I zipped through the Arts Building, went across the bridge and through the Blue House lunchroom to my locker. I quickly grabbed my notebook and headed to my first class. Since it seemed as if I knew all the answers in class, I spent most of the period on my phone surfing through Twitter and Instagram.

Before my 4th period class, I had Division in the library. The library was probably the gloomiest room in the entire school. The floor was carpeted with an ugly brown color and all the furniture was a dull, faux wood color. I'd always hated it. The windows were also covered with blinds that eliminated any natural light from coming into the library. As soon as I walked in, the gloominess of the room seemed to suck all the life out of me and I slowly trudged to the back of the room where my Division met. A classmate read announcements concerning the school from a bulletin and when senior nominations were asked for, my peers rushed up to the front to give their input on whom they wanted to nominate for 'cutest couple', 'best smile', and so on. In my opinion, this whole thing was extremely trivial and pointless, but everyone else seemed to take it very seriously.

As the day went on, the classes got progressively more boring. However, what was interesting was that the person whose body I was occupying seemed to be a rather friendly person. There were many underclassmen as well as upperclassmen that waved to me and without even thinking, my hand returned the wave and a smile came upon my face. I realized a new perspective, as I was a very short person and every time someone waved to me as they walked by me in the hallway, I had to look up to them. It felt odd but somehow illuminating.

The last class of the day was a college application process Seminar. I logged into Melissa's CommonApp account and looked at the list of colleges she had added. Most of them were private colleges such as Grinnell, Wheaton, University of Southern California, and Washington University in St. Louis. Judging from the tuitions of these schools, I assumed that Melissa came from a rather well off family.

"Oh honey, you need to check the box for need-based financial aid," informed the counselor.

"Oh really? Even if my family makes too much for financial aid?"

"Oh yes. It's almost mandatory to check that box. Even if you don't think your family qualifies, they still need the check to be able to give you merit-based scholarships."

"Alright, thank you for telling me!"

The bell rang signifying the end of Seminar and the end of the school day for me. I waved to a couple of friends whom I was conversing with during the Seminar and walked to my locker. I swiftly opened the lock and grabbed the coat I had left inside this morning. It was rather chilly that day, so I grabbed the beanie and scarf as well.

I then proceeded to Blue House to talk to some people and eventually was found by presumably my best friend. We shared stories of what happened to us during the day and laughed all the way to the door. We exited the building the same way I had entered in the morning. When we walked outside, I could feel the biting wind blow through my hair and pulled up the scarf around my neck to protect my mouth. The two of us continued to talk about everything from homework to the latest gossip.

When we arrived at the train station, my body again acted on its own and went through the train commuter's process of reaching for the train card and entering money onto it. I found the transit card in between the phone and phone case, which I thought was quite convenient and fast. I walked through the turnstiles and mentally patted myself on the back for starting to think like Melissa. I felt as if I were starting to "understand" the people I was inhabiting just a little bit better.

After transferring modes of public transportation and being jostled around on the bus, I arrived on the street that I had driven on in the morning. I surveyed the street since I had not paid attention to it in the morning. There was a bar on one corner, a Caribou Coffee on the corner across, a Jamba Juice on the next, and finally a rather expensive-looking shoe store on the last corner. It was quite an interesting mix. Past the Jamba Juice and Caribou Coffee was what looked to be a park with a baseball diamond. I began walking back to the house and allowed the body I was occupying to follow its instincts and guide me home.

I arrived at the house and this time went through the back door instead of the front. Their backyard consisted of a wooden deck and brick ground instead of the traditional grass that the houses next to this one had. I entered the house to find Melissa's mother sleeping on the couch covered in a Hello Kitty blanket and went straight for the refrigerator to get something to eat.

After I had eaten my fill of TV dinners from the freezer, I went up to the girl's room and pulled out the homework she had. Thankfully she didn't have much and I finished it up in only two hours. After studying for an AP Psychology test the next day, I got into pajamas and curled up in the bed. Before falling asleep, I processed my day in my head. The girl seemed to be rather likable and judging from her house and conversation with her counselor, she lived a privileged life. Her life was simple, but rather comfortable. I decided that though her life was comfortable, I preferred to have a slightly more spontaneous and wild lifestyle. However, it was interesting to live a peaceful life of a privileged Asian girl. Her warm personality seemed to almost rub off on me. Sweet dreams, Melissa.

CHAPTER 13
Saturday With The Kids

I woke up from a dreamless sleep in a warm bed. When I opened my eyes, I examined the ceiling above my head. A light blue. I suppose at this point, I shouldn't really be surprised that it's not my normal ceiling. Light slipped through the shafts of the blinds. It was a lot brighter than the past days. It must be Saturday, at last! I could make out a bed on the other side of the room. Hmph. They share a room. Suddenly, a cell phone blared with a screeching alarm. 'Ugh, where is the darn thing?' I got up and groped a desk for the source of the sound. 'Ah, got it.' How pathetic. A first model Blackberry. Practically a brick by the sleek standards of today's phones. How horrific. If only I was in my own home.

I went about my morning as usual. At least, I tried to make it seem as normal as possible. 'Hmm, which toothbrush should I use?' Based on my appearance, I'm going to go with the pink. I entered the kitchen where a man was cooking breakfast. After eating in silence while he read the newspaper he asked,

"Ready?"

And off we went into the car. Where were we going? It's a Saturday! *'Well, at least I'll get a ride,'* I thought. As I convinced myself that this day in a stranger's body would not be that bad, he brought the car to a halt outside the Kimball Brown line station. *'Ugh, not the train.'* Another long train ride of coffee breath, homeless stench, and blank stares. I shuffled out of the car and searched my backpack for some sign of a train card. *'Aha, in the pink wallet.'* I stood on the train platform, waiting for the train to come, unsure of my final destination.

Waiting for the train, a boy with glasses spotted me from across the platform and walked over. I hope he knows this girl and isn't being a freak.

"Hey, Lindsey, are you helping out today?"

Ah okay, I guess he knows her. Er, me.

"Umm"

"I thought you told me you were."

"Well…"

"Do you, like, not want to anymore? I thought you loved kids?"

Children?

"Like, babysit?"

"No silly, you help out for the church's children event. You know with the big bouncy house and games?"

Oh, this is church related…I'm not really a church kinda guy but I guess she is.

"Yeah, I'll help"

"Great! I am, too! We can work together!"

Grrrrr. This kid seemed nerdy, annoying, and much too talkative for my taste.

The train pulled into the Western stop and the boy, who I learned was named Jonathon asked, "Aren't you coming?!"

I sighed as I followed him off the train and walked towards a red brick church. In the parking lot of the church was a huge bouncy house that was still in the process of being blown up. In the basement of the church tables were set, and the floor was littered with a plethora of toys, candy, decorations, and crafts. A girl from the corner of the room waved to me. I went to her and learned we were going to work one of the tables together. We set up a ring toss game for the kids. I had never really been one for children nor hosting games or activities for them. How would I get through this day? I sighed deeply, contemplating how boring the day would be. Then the children began trickling in.

The once empty basement soon became a scene of perplexing pandemonium. Grimy children ran about, falling and wailing. Their shrieks pierced my ears in addition to their loud waves of laughter. The kids were wild and filthy. Their faces quickly became streaked with frosting and grease. They had mud on their shoes, snot running from their noses, and stinky diapers. Then, the little devils started walking towards me.

"Me! Me! I want to play! Can I play?"

They were closing in on me. I was going to be attacked! Help! Ah phew, the girl came to the rescue. She didn't seem scared at all. In fact, she dealt with the kids with such ease, she could have been their own mothers. She knelt before them and talked with them. She easily organized the children into a single file line and gave out rings for them to toss one by one. After every throw they got a reward -- a lollipop. *'Oh sure, they listened to her because she's a girl. Oh, wait, I'm a girl too. Sort of.'* What did she have that I didn't? The girl then motioned me over. *'Oh, no.'*

"You have to bend down, they need to see your face, not up your nose"

Ah. That's reasonable I suppose. I knelt down. The kids were even grosser up close.

"Now you have to show them how to play."

Deep breath. You can do this.

"Hi, do you want to play?" I asked. A boy with wide blue eyes nodded.

"Here, take this ring, and toss it onto that cone over there. If you get it, you can get a prize," I said in a strained voice: my attempt to sound kind.

The child's eyes lit up at the word "prize."

Sticking out his tongue and furrowing his brows in concentration, he tossed the ring. It collapsed pathetically to the ground in front of his feet, nowhere near the cone. I sighed aloud in exasperation.

Suddenly, the child's eyes welled up. Oh no. Tears. Panic.

Instinctively, I bent down, eye-level to the child like the girl taught me. I tried to hold his hand and somehow reassure him with my facial expressions that it

90

was okay.

"It's alright, it's a hard toss; not everyone gets it the first time." Where did that come from, didn't I just scoff at him for missing?

The tears welled from his eyes and flowed down his cheeks. His mouth opened and out came the most hideous, ear splitting cry known to mankind.

"Ahh, okay, okay. It's all right, hey kid, it's okay. You want some candy?"

The girl ran over and scooped the boy up in her arms. She rocked him and tried to calm him.

"Did you try your absolute best?" she asked. The little boy nodded over his subsiding cries.

"Then you deserve a prize. Anyone who does his best can get one. I think you deserve one."

And with that she grabbed a candy bar and placed it in his palm. The boy gave a watery smile and waddled off contentedly.

Ugh. I so had the situation under control. What a show off.

"Come on, Lindsey, you gotta soothe them. You need to reassure them."

It took all my strength to restrain myself from rolling my eyes. But she had a point, I suppose. I mean she did manage that situation well.

Over the course of day, I became more prepared. The crying children came by and I mimicked the girl's method of comfort. I tried to rock the children and asked them if they did their best. It's really not such a bad idea.

By the end of the day, I was the baby master, if I do say so myself. Kids really aren't that bad I suppose. Yes, they're messy and stinky, but they can be very sweet.

By the time we had to close up, several kids ran over and gave me a hug before they left. Their unexpected embraces surprised me. So *this* is what it feels like to be a loved babysitter. I smiled and waved, surprisingly, out of genuine happiness, when they left.

91

As I walked outside I found my father, or Lindsey's father, who drove us home. Exhausted from the day and thankful for silence, I flopped onto my bed. How do mothers do it? As I drifted to sleep a new appreciation blossomed for children and the mothers and teachers who care enough for them. As I was drifting off to sleep, I considered changing my mind about the little shorties.

CHAPTER 14
The Perfect Nightmare

I woke up to the sound of an irritating noise. The sound was so loud that I almost rolled off the bed. I opened my eyes slightly, and I tried to figure out where the noise was coming from. It was coming from the brand new, shiny iPhone 5. The alarm was scheduled to ring at 4:45 A.M., and it was titled "RUN."

As I got out of bed, I saw a pair of running shoes placed along the bed. The floor was covered with running clothes. I looked around the room and saw a very neat, organized schedule. It was a Sunday morning, and I was already awake before 5:00 A.M! On the iPhone was a notes page. I read in horror. I was supposed to go on an easy ten mile run. Afterwards, I was to take a shower and eat breakfast with the family. In the afternoon, I was supposed to clean and work on homework. The last event on the schedule was a party, however it had a question mark next to it in parentheses.

I went to the bathroom and got the chills as I stepped on the cold tiles. As I brushed my teeth, I thought about the ten mile run. It was still dark outside, and I had no clue what the neighborhood was like. I quickly ran a comb through my hair.

As I walked out of the bathroom, I saw a man come up the stairs. In a quiet yet serious tone he said "Good morning, Josh."

"Good morning," I replied. I realized I was Josh, a guy who sat two seats behind me.

The father asked, "How long is your run today?"

"Ten miles," I said.

He replied, "Good luck," and walked into a separate room. It seemed to be filled with books, like a miniature library.

When I got back to the room with the bed, I quickly got dressed in the running clothes that were spread out on the floor. Then I slipped on the pair of shoes. I left the room and headed down the stairs.

When I made it down the large flight of stairs, I realized the house was massive. As I wandered in search of an exit, I realized the house contained expensive furniture and fancy decorations. The hallways were long and each doorway led to a new room. I was relieved when I saw the front door. I quickly left the house in need of some fresh air.

As I walked down the steps, I looked around at the other houses. They were equally large and beautiful. I was almost positive they were worth a few million dollars. In each driveway there was a Mercedes-Benz or a Ferrari. Although the neighborhood lighting was bad, I did not feel frightened as I started running. The area seemed too safe.

Surprisingly, I had run for about an hour and I did not feel tired. My legs were pounding against the cement, and I felt a rush go through my body. I knew I had to run ten miles, but I was not exactly sure how long that would take me. I assumed that an average mile could be run in seven minutes, and realized my run should take seventy minutes. More than an hour into the run, I decided to turn back and run towards "home."

When I returned, I knocked on the door. An older lady wearing an apron opened the door.

"Good morning Josh. Your mother says to take a shower quickly and come down for breakfast," she said.

"Thanks," I replied. So she wasn't my mother.

I found my way to stairs, and went back to the bathroom I was previously in. I undressed and stepped into the shower that was large enough to fit over six people. I remember the older woman telling me to shower quickly. I rapidly washed my hair with shampoo and washed my body. I got out of the shower, put a towel

94

around my waist, and walked back to the room with the bed. I looked through the closets and drawers for a pair of jeans and a T-shirt. However, I only found polo shirts and khaki pants.

I put on a light blue polo with gray khaki pants and headed down the stairs. In the dining area, there was a long table with all sorts of breakfast foods: pancakes, cereals, Belgian waffles, juices, eggs, sausages, etc. A woman sat on one end of the table, while a man sat on the opposite side. He was reading a newspaper.

"Finally, you're finished," said the woman.

"Sorry I'm late," I replied.

I sat down at the table and we said a quick prayer before eating. "Josh, you have a lot of chores you need to do today. You better work on homework and those college applications. Also, I want your room clean," said the woman.

I nodded and the rest of the time we ate in silence. The man did not say anything during the whole meal. I could tell there was something going on between the woman and him. When we finished eating, the older woman wearing an apron came and cleaned up our dishes.

When the woman left the table, I also got up and went to the room with the bed. I sat in the desk next to the bed and opened up the laptop. There was a post-it note next to the desk with three schools listed: Harvard University, Yale, and Princeton. Next to the name of each school was a website, a username, and a password. I decided to pull up the application for Yale University. I quickly skimmed the basic application and then found the essay. The topic of the essay was to write about a specific hobby, how you would continue participating in that hobby in college, and how a Yale education was going to benefit you. I could tell the essay had just been started because there were only two short paragraphs. However, they were the worst two paragraphs I ever read for a college application!

In the two paragraphs, the hobby of running was mentioned. He loved running because he could run away from life. Running was a way to escape from his family, his friends, his school, his home, and his neighborhood. He mentioned that he would continue this activity at Yale because he disliked the university and he would like to run away from it. The last sentence said, "A Yale education would not be beneficial to me, it would be beneficial to my father."

I continued to log into the other applications, and I was shocked to read each essay. It seemed like this kid hated his life. However, he had a family, a huge house, shiny cars, new electronics, and tons of money. His only chore was to clean his room because the older lady took care of everything else. As I studied the post-it note, I wondered what was happening to this kid. I held the note in my hand and then turned it around. On the back, there was one more university listed: School of the Art Institute of Chicago.

I quickly logged into the application and went straight to the essay. It was over a page long, and I was excited to read it. My heart pounded as I read each paragraph. About five minutes later, I almost had tears in my eyes. It was the most touching story I had read. It talked about his dream in life, which was to become a graphic designer. However, his parents did not approve of his decision because he was supposed to become a lawyer. They forced him to apply to the top Ivy League schools. He loved expressing his emotions in the form of art, yet his family did not allow him. Additionally, his family never talked anymore. His parents were filing for a divorce. He may have had all the money in the world, but inside he was hurting. He wanted someone to care about him and care for him. He wanted to follow his dreams.

After "working on the college applications," I quickly organized the room and put the dirty running clothes in the laundry bin. I wanted to sit down for a minute because I was too overwhelmed with what I had read. The moment I sat down, I heard a woman yelling a name. I went down the stairs into her office.

"Josh, is your room clean?"

"Yes," I replied.

"Did you work on homework and college applications?"

"Yes," I replied again.

"Then you can hang out with your friends and go to that party. But you need to be back by midnight. Do you understand?"

I replied "Yes" one last time and went back upstairs.

I looked for the neat schedule and thankfully I found the address of the party on the calendar. I wrote the address on a piece of paper, searched it on Google Maps, and went downstairs. I was about to leave, and as I was putting on my shoes I heard the sound of yelling and screaming. I immediately heard the serious voice of the man as well as the cries of the woman. They must have gotten into an argument. I left the house as quickly as I could because I did not want to get involved in any more situations.

The party was only two miles away so I decided to walk.

I found the address. The house had a full driveway and the whole block was parked with cars. I already could hear the sound of music. I pulled open the door and entered. A large boy in a football jersey came up to me, patted my back, and said "Hey, what's up man?" I did not respond, but instead I was handed a cup of beer.

There were so many thoughts in mind that I kind of zoned out at the party. I was still thinking about the kid's family, college applications, and money. Without noticing I had drunk a few cups of beer. I sat down on a nearby chair and slowly my eyes began to close.

CHAPTER 15
Life Of A Quarterback

I woke up in a small apartment in Lakeview. As a loud alarm clock rang, I looked around the room and realized that I was still not myself. The sun was shining off of this orange wall. For some reason, I was in a room dedicated to the Chicago Bears. The sun was almost blinding me as I tried to reach for the off switch of an annoyingly loud alarm clock. Frustrated, I grabbed the alarm clock and tried to find the off switch. The more and more it rang, the angrier I got. I finally found the button to turn the alarm off, but not before involuntarily attempting to choke the alarm clock. When I realized that I was futilely trying to choke a mechanical object, I set it back down and tried to get my bearings.

I finally was able to stumble into the shower, after a few minutes of dazed meandering around the room I was in. I turned on the water, only to realize that for the first few minutes there was no hot water. I then spastically attempted to escape the tyranny of the cold water. After about five minutes, I was able to take the long awaited shower. I returned to my room from the shower, only to find a massive mess of random assortments of clothes, papers, and boxes impeding my way to the dresser. I thought that I should start cleaning the mess, but I had no time. I managed to get dressed, finding some clothes that seemingly matched.

Immediately after getting dressed, I heard a shrill voice yelling, "Scott, hurry up! Your breakfast is getting cold, and you'll be late for school!" I walked out of the room and saw two small breakfast sandwiches. The sandwiches consisted of sausage patties between flaky pieces of bread. I took a bite into the first one and discovered that it was cold in the center. Because of my apparent tardiness, I just suffered through it. I went into the bathroom and put some contact lenses in and brushed my teeth. I found a massive gym bag next to my backpack. Suddenly I realized that I was on the football team. Now, all of the posters and random football related items around the room made sense. I tried to quickly grab the gym bag but the weight surprised me. When I was finally able to leave, I hoped to find car keys. I looked for a few minutes, until I realized that I don't have access to a car. Begrudgingly, I got a ride to school.

I arrived at Sojourner Truth and looked at my schedule. I found out that I started off with AP Calculus. It surprised me that a football player would be in the BC class, because I just could not imagine anybody that likes such a barbaric sport would want to take a class that covers the first two semesters of college calculus. Anyway, I went to the class and suffered through a boring lesson about derivatives.

The next class was even more boring. It was U.S. History, which is a class most people take as sophomores. Apparently this kid likes taking classes later than normal. I just got into class as the bell was ringing, and found a random seat. The teacher was droning on about the colonists, while I decided to open up a good book. After about thirty minutes of reading, he scolded me for not participating.

I then said, "Studying this type of history is futile, because we are not learning about how this affected anything. We are just simply learning that this happened."

He replied, "That is true but this knowledge is required to graduate."

"That's crazy," I responded, "Why?"

He exclaimed, "Because the government wants you all to know the necessary knowledge to be Americans!"

I then replied, "That's ridiculous."

He quickly answered back, "That may be true, but you have to learn it anyway."

So after that little conversation, I went back to my book for a few more minutes. I realized I probably didn't help Scott's grade with my little outbursts. The bell rang and then I made my way to the most pointless time of day, Division. Division: the time of day when the school makes meaningless announcements and hands out stuff nobody cares about. As an added bonus, once a week, there is something called long Division, which is even more pointless. Long Division is about half an hour, and sometimes certain grade levels meet in the theater for some worthless presentation.

After ten minutes of pondering about the pointlessness of Division, I made my way to the fourth period class, AP Physics. Now I would commend this kid on taking this class, if he wasn't taking the B class. Here's the deal: there are two classes for AP Physics, B and C. The B class does not use calculus for any calculations, but the C class does. So anyway, I somewhat listened to the lesson about power and work, which you also learn in Honors Physics by the way. Boring!

The bell rang, letting us know that fourth period was over. All I was thinking about was seeing myself again in the English class. I walked into the room, and saw Ms. Glass. When I was about to go up and talk to her, the bell rang and I had to sit down. I opened up a notebook and started journaling, while trying to keep an eye out for myself. My normal body walked into the room. I was just about to say something to myself, but then I was interrupted by Ms. Glass's sudden introduction, which she does every day. She was still talking about empathy. I just thought to myself, if she only had any idea what I was going through now. I listened to her for about twenty minutes, but then I got bored again. I was starting to get a little hungry, because my normal lunch period is during fourth period. I checked my schedule, and saw that Scott's lunch was sixth period. I was going to try and wait to talk to myself, but Ms. Glass called my normal self over after class. I waited for a couple minutes, but my hunger took over and I had to leave.

I decided to do my usual lunch routine, and go to Starbucks. Today, I decided to come back to school and sit in Red House for the remainder of the lunch period. I sat down and found out that this lunch period is mostly filled with freshmen, meaning that that lunch period was the most loud and annoying of all. I had to sit through about twenty minutes of kids screaming about utter nonsense. The bell could not have rung fast enough.

The bell rang and I checked my schedule. Sports Management was the next class. I was hoping I could get some sleep in that class. My plans were ruined, when I found out that basically the class was comprised of people who only like to yell and make jokes. I did not know if I should also contribute to the jokes or just sit there quietly, so I just sat there and observed. I started to feel bad for the teacher, as I watched her try to maintain order. I would have tried to help her, but I didn't feel like doing too much work at this point. So I sat through fifty straight minutes of laughter and general rowdiness, until class was over.

The next class was Beginning Guitar. This was a worthless class for most. I was really hoping that anybody who takes this is just looking for a graduation requirement. The class was filled with kids who could barely grab the right string, much less play the correct note. Now I am not a good musician or anything, but I could at least follow the simple instructions of playing the strings in order. After listening to some painful guitar playing, I was again saved by the bell.

The next period was a Seminar. The Seminars are all new, because some guy in CPS decided that we need more time in school. I found that absurd. Anyway, I walked into the Seminar a minute late, and the football coach was telling me how being late will not serve me well in life. He ended up giving me a tardy slip, but he did it somewhat expecting some response from me. When I showed my complete apathy about being tardy, he seemed to disappointedly walk back to his chair. He started some video of another football team. He talked about different positions and stuff that I didn't quite understand, and didn't care to either. Everybody was nodding their heads, like they knew exactly what he was talking about. Although Seminar is the shortest period of the day, it felt like the longest.

The bell rang. Right when I was about to go home, I was told that we had practice. In January? I thought the season was over. I panicked, thinking back to my day as Augie and the double swimming practices. This was the first sport that involved some major contact. I went down to the locker room, threw on some sweatpants and looked around for football pads. When I asked one of the guys where the pads were, he laughed. It was the off-season and we were in the weight room.

Weights! I hated the very idea of lifting weights. What was the point? Pick them up, put them down. Wasn't life hard enough without adding unnecessary weight to our personal burdens? But, after a few minutes I realized that I was actually really strong. I started to use my strength, and I was not too bad at that. The training lasted until 6:15, and I was exhausted. I went back to the locker room to change back into my regular clothes. I looked around for my ride home, but it was not there. I called home, only to find out that I was not getting one. I was disappointed to have to take the train home so late.

I slowly followed the other kids to the train. I had to take the Brown Line. I transferred to it and waited in a crowded train car, as the train slowly traversed the path to the north. I realized when I got to my stop that I also had to walk about a mile home. This further frustrated me, because after practice I felt like I could barely walk. I staggered the mile to the apartment. When I got home, it was nearly 8:00.

I walked in the door, and smelled that dinner was ready. I ate the dinner, which was pretty good. I then started my homework, which I did not think would take too long. I ended up doing it until 11:30. I realized if it weren't for the practice, I'd be in bed a lot earlier. If I had to do this on a regular basis, I'd always be exhausted the next day. I then realized that nothing I did on any given day while I was "body-changing" seemed to have a physical impact on me the next day. Although I felt somewhat responsible for Scott while I was in his body, part of me was still upset at my wasted effort. I probably should have gone to bed, but I realized I didn't need to.

So even though I was tired, I watched "Two and a Half Men" for about half an hour. I thought about how the day went. The day went all right, except for the fact that the practice was exhausting. Halfway through a second episode of "Two and a Half Men," I passed out.

CHAPTER 16

The Sting of Not Being Seen

A loud beep sounded and I opened my eyes groggily. Groaning, I reached in the direction of the noise and fumbled with a phone, turning it off clumsily. I squinted at the phone's screen, noted that it was 6:45 am, and promptly went back to sleep. Around fifteen minutes later I woke up again, this time to someone's voice speaking through the door.

"Get up; you're going to be late," said someone whom I assumed to be my father. I had woken up as someone else, yet again, but that was not the part that I was shocked about. My "father" just spoke to me in Chinese, and somehow I managed to understand every word of it. Amazed at my newfound understanding of a foreign language, I got out of bed and stretched, noticing the pile of clothes spilling out of the hamper.

"Looks like I'm a girl today." I thought to myself when I saw a dress at the top of the pile. "Too bad, I kind of liked being that guy from yesterday. Minus the long hours of football practice, that is. " I muttered to myself, wondering how easy it was for Scott to wake up this morning. I looked at myself in the mirror and thought that she didn't look like the sporty type.

"Glad I won't have to suffer through another day of weight training," I thought. I walked towards the closet doors and pulled them open. I did a quick whistle when I noticed the amount of clothing stuffed inside the closet. Hanger after hanger of tank tops, shirts, sweaters, blouses, and a multitude of other clothing items that I could care less about the names of. I grabbed a black sweater and a pair of olive skinny jeans, gave them a once over, and deemed the outfit safe enough to wear to school without embarrassing myself and potentially ruining whomever's social life I was about to live. I glanced at the clock and saw that it was nearing 7:30 a.m. and decided that I should probably hurry before "I" was late.

I raced downstairs, wondering whether I should eat breakfast or not when my "mom" shouted, "Hurry up and eat something!"

"Well, that answers that." I said to myself. I shuffled my feet towards the kitchen and sat down, staring at my breakfast. Dumplings, pot stickers, or whatever they were, piled high on a plate. "Is this what she has for breakfast every day? Where are the eggs and bacon?" I thought to myself. I gripped the chopsticks clumsily and managed to get a dumpling onto my plate. Before I could change my mind I quickly popped the dumpling in my mouth, chewed, and swallowed. "Hm, that wasn't too bad. I should try this kind of food more often," I thought as I drank a cup of water. I glanced at the time again and decided to quicken my pace.

I walked towards the door and saw my dad waiting for me holding car keys, and I assumed that I was going to get a ride to school. I followed my dad towards a Corolla and climbed into the car. The drive to school didn't take long; good thing the girl lived in Bridgeport. I walked into the school, showing the ID of "Cindy" to the secretary guard at the front door. "This girl needs to set her alarm earlier; she's probably late every day," I thought, when I saw the empty halls. "Where to now..." I wondered as I checked the back of her ID and skimmed her classes. I quickly memorized her schedule and headed towards her second period class.

Class time passed by quickly and before I knew it, it was the end of the school day. I walked absentmindedly, wondering if Cindy had any after school activities that I should attend. "Cindy!" yelled someone from across the hall. I spun around on my heels as if my own name was being called and searched for the owner of the voice. A girl a few feet away started walking towards

106

me. "Hi…" I said hesitantly. I was hoping to avoid as many people as possible today.

"Going to ping pong right now?" said the girl.

"Is that what I normally do after school?

"What are you asking me for, shouldn't you know?" the girl said, chuckling.

"I guess I am then."

"Let's go." The girl said with a smile. We walked towards the ping pong area and I let Cindy's friend do all the talking as I nodded along.

Multiple people waved when we arrived at the ping pong area. One guy that I knew by the name of Ryan motioned me towards a ping pong table and handed me a paddle.

"No, um, actually, I don't really play." I said instinctively.

Ryan gave me a strange look and just laughed. He served the ball and I quickly hit the ball back, surprised by how natural it felt. We rallied back and forth and soon I began to use all sorts of side spins, top spins, and under spins. I looked back at the times that I walked past the people playing ping pong and scoffed, thinking about how silly they looked playing in the middle of the school. I mean, mini tennis, really? After playing ping pong myself, I decided right then to take back my thoughts of what geeks they were. Maybe I'd even try playing ping-pong in my own body when I went back to it, *if* I went back to it…

"You seem to be playing differently today," said Ryan, interrupting my thoughts.

"Really?" I said. I didn't notice how much I was enjoying myself with my new ping pong skills. I continued playing but decided to tone down my excitement a bit to avoid any suspicious thoughts from arising.

"Let's rest a bit," said Ryan after rallying for another fifteen minutes or so. We sat down at a small table with the ping pong tables nearby so that we could continue watching people play. I glanced at the girl who I walked to ping pong with and saw that she was watching me with a knowing smile. She gestured her head towards Ryan when he bent down to tie his shoes and mouthed the words "get to it," while exuberantly motioning towards him. When he finished tying his shoes he looked at me and smiled. I looked back at the girl and quickly glanced towards Ryan, confused. Suddenly it hit me. Cindy must have some sort of romantic interest towards Ryan. "How interesting," I thought.

He noticed me looking at the girl and back at him and said, "Hey, you know Kathy right?"

"Um, sure." I said, assuming that the girl whose name I didn't know was Kathy.

"What does she think of me?"

"What do you mean?" I said, hoping that the conversation wasn't going where I thought it was going.

"Like, do you think she's into me or something?" Ryan said, looking slightly embarrassed.

This was definitely going the way I thought it was going to go. "I don't know, dude." I automatically said. Oops, I accidentally reverted to guy mode for a minute.

Ryan continued talking without noticing my small change in personality. "You're her best friend, think you could find out for me?" I stared at the guy in disbelief. Did he seriously just ask me that? "Well?" said Ryan.

I reverted to full guy mode and said, "Sorry man, you're going to have to figure that out for yourself." I got up and walked towards Kathy without looking back.

"Ready to go?" said Kathy. She grabbed her backpack and we walked towards the train station.

"So, how was your little love fest?" said a grinning Kathy.

"Um, fine?" I said unsure of what else to say. This was the most awkward I've felt talking to a girl.

"Oh, come on, I saw you guys over there. You two looked so cute!" squealed Kathy. She continued to go on and on and how great we looked together. I tuned her out in the first two minutes of the conversation and thought about what Ryan had said. So I'm guessing that Cindy has a romantic interest in Ryan but he just told me, or at least hinted that he is interested in Kathy who is apparently her best friend. Normally, I could care less about other people's relationships and high school gossip, but it felt a little different this time. Perhaps because I'm currently living through this girl and she's somehow influencing me. I wasn't sure why I wanted to help her but I just knew that my current feeling towards her was empathic. On a whim, I took out a sheet of paper and scribbled a short note about the conversation I had with Ryan.

I folded the note and handed it to Kathy. "Don't read it, and give it back to me tomorrow, but don't mention anything about this exchange, okay?" I said.

"...Sure." said a confused Kathy.

"Thanks. Well, this is my stop, see you." I got up and stepped off the train and proceeded towards my home for today. I thought about the note that I had just written. It was so unlike me, butting into other people's business. Really, I couldn't care less. But for some reason this girl's situation reminded me of the times that I blew off girls who I knew liked me. They just seemed so silly and immature at the time. Now, I felt a little badly about the way that I had treated them. I actually admire the ones who continued trying to befriend me.

I found the house that I had left this morning and opened the door with a key that I found in my bag. Exhausted after a long day of new experiences, I headed towards my bedroom and fell onto the bed, face first. "Not this again," I said to myself. "I thought being in Olivia's body meant that it was my first and last time as a heart broken girl. I bet no other guy can say they got their

109

heart broken as a girl. Twice." I chuckled at the thought of saying that to Ms. Glass someday after I somehow discover a way to tell her what's going on. In the midst of thinking about how badly I wanted to return to my own body, I fell asleep, but not without making a mental note to myself to treat girls, and people in general, a little nicer if and when I returned to my normal self.

CHAPTER 17
Getting Along Swimmingly

The alarm clock rang. I opened my eyes, and I was surprised to see that it was still dark. I glanced at the alarm clock and noticed it was four-thirty. What the hell was I doing up so early in the morning? Running, swimming, what was going on? Who had set my alarm clock to ring so early?

Before I could answer any of these questions a woman flicked the light switch and told me to get up. I remembered her face, earlier this week she had come to school and dropped off some homework for Matt. It was Matt's mom, meaning I was Matt. All right. I assumed I was getting up for swim practice. I knew Matt was on the swim team, Ms. Glass occasionally referred to him as the swimmer. This actually explained a lot.

I shifted myself to a sitting position on the bed. It wasn't long until I fell back onto the bed with a sigh. I didn't know how much more I could take. Realizing my options were limited, I gave myself a little pep talk and sent out a prayer to whoever might be listening.

"This is only another day that I'm going to have to fight through. If the universe is listening, I've learned my lesson! I've learned my lesson. I was wrong. Not all of the kids in my class are idiots. I want to be home again, and by that I mean in my own body. I don't need to go through this anymore." I don't know what I was expecting, but nothing happened. I was still Matt and I still had to go to swimming practice.

I got back up, dressed and quickly washed myself. I stumbled downstairs to the kitchen, where a nice breakfast was sitting on the table. It consisted of a toasted bagel, scrambled eggs with bacon, as well as a cup of coffee. The coffee was black, probably the worst way it could be consumed.

111

"Hey, could I please get some cream and sugar, I really don't like my coffee black." I said.

Matt's mom looked at me with a confused and angry face, as if I just asked her if she was a man or a woman.

"Are you feeling alright? Last month you told me you hated the taste of cream and sugar in your coffee. Can you please make up your mind," she said snapping at me, "I mean, you made an entire argument about how sugar and cream masks the true taste of coffee. How can you go back on that and tell me you want sugar and creamer."

"Right....." I said, feeling caught off guard. "Well, could I just get some cream and sugar today? It'd be nice to have some once in a while." It's not like I wanted to be a total asshole and screw his relationship over. I felt a sudden need to put some greater effort into living some of these people's lives.

"All right, if you say so." she replied, pouring Dean's half and half slowly into my cup. I took a quick glance at the coffee, and became hypnotized with the cream's diffusion throughout the coffee. The cloudy mixture of the cream and coffee slowly merged, the cloud of cream slowly spreading throughout the cup, forming a nice light brown liquid. Perfect, just how I liked my morning coffee.

I made a connection to my current mental state. It seemed that as I sipped the coffee, the dim thoughts and cloud of confusion within my mind slowly disappeared. I wasn't sure if it was the coffee waking me up, or if I had quickly adapted to who I was, where I was, and what I was doing. I felt bummed out after I realized what time it was, but this life wasn't bad at all. Half-decent. Too bad tomorrow this could all change and I wouldn't know whom I would end up as. The circumstances I would be under could be completely different and certainly far less pleasant. For the time being, I was lucky to be where I was.

Just as I had summed up my thoughts, I had inherently finished eating the delicious breakfast. I was definitely becoming accustomed to this very bizarre feeling. Everything was flowing very smoothly, as if I had been doing this for months. This was my schedule now.

I stood up and thanked his mom while I grabbed the plate and cup and dropped off the stuff at the sink. I ran over to the door, where Matt's mom as well as two bags and a sweatshirt were waiting for me. I slipped the sweatshirt over my neck, feeling surprised at how thin but how warm it was. I put on the cyan-gray backpack and tossed the black sports bag over my left shoulder. We opened the door, entering the darkness of the night.

From the little I could see I could tell that someone really cared for the outside appearance of the home. The grass was cut, flowers were planted, and bushes were trimmed. Still, only the dim street lights and the luminescent moon were illuminating the area, and it was hard to see much other than the general shapes of the objects, which appeared to be very neatly laid out.

We walked over to the silver Camry sitting under one of the few streetlights on the block. The car I could see in much more detail. I could tell that this vehicle was really cared for. The car was very clean and polished. We hopped in and drove off. This neighborhood seemed strangely unfamiliar, but that didn't really matter, as Matt's mom was driving the car. Right turns after left turns followed by another right turn led us to Archer Avenue. We followed this road for a few miles while I examined the environment I found myself in. We passed numerous stores along the four-lane road, many of them containing signs promoting their Polish products. It was very strange seeing these signs. I didn't speak Polish or know much about the culture and language, but I was able to understand what these signs meant. It was second nature to me.

For some moments I wondered what this would all be in the future. I started with some specific questions about the near future. These questions I could attempt to answer, but I couldn't be certain. Would I be able to keep this culture with me and continue to understand it in the future? Probably not, but it would be great if I could. Then I began to ask myself more general questions. These I could not answer, but they worried me about my future. Will this ever end? Will I ever be myself again? If yes, when? What does all of this even mean? I became extremely aggravated and annoyed with the fact that I couldn't answer these simple questions. I came back to reality, realizing we had arrived at the long awaited destination, the train station.

Exchanging our "byes" and "so longs," I got out of the car, grabbing the two bags from out of the back and closing the doors behind me.

I couldn't even take a few steps before I was interrupted by some guy's voice.

"Yo, what's up? Long time no see! I didn't know you took the train so early."

I looked to my left only to see a chunky Mexican kid sipping on some iced coffee from Dunkin Donuts.

"Hey what's up, Chunky," I had no idea who this kid was but somehow knew his name. That was new. "I wish I could talk but I actually have to run to get to swim practice on time. Need to get there on time or my coach will kill me, you know?"

"Alright, that's cool. Hit me up sometime, we should chill and catch up. You could see Julian." he responded.

"For sure, my schedule is pretty hectic right now but I'll try and figure something out." I was getting better at this, encountering all of these people wasn't even that bad anymore.

"Alright, later, bro," the stranger said as I began walking towards the train turnstiles.

I popped out my wallet and took out the student CTA card. I inserted the card into the turnstile. The small black screen which would usually display "Thank You!" now displayed "Error: 1343. Please Contact Attendant." I glanced at the clock. It was five-eighteen. I had forgotten that the student card didn't work before five-thirty. To avoid further conversation with Chunky I decided to just pay the full fare and hop on the train a bit earlier. Before reattempting to cross the turnstile a second time I looked back at Chunky. He was staring at me with a strange look on his face. I felt that he could sense that something was up; maybe I wasn't playing the part too well.

I heard the bell that indicated that the train was about to leave. I rushed to try and catch the train; it was the least I could do to try and play the role of someone who was trying to make it to practice on time. I entered through the train doors just as they closed behind me, and I decided to sit down in one of the isolated singular seats.

I took a quick glance at the station's sign as the train was leaving the station. I learned that I was at Midway. I was here once when I took a plane from Midway Airport to Baja for a marine biology course last summer. I thought about how I would get to school, but I came to the conclusion that it wasn't worth the effort. This was largely due to the fact that the train's maps were missing, probably stolen by some kids who thought they were anti-government anarchists because of their "mischievous" actions. I decided to just fall asleep, using the backpack filled with towels and swim gear as a pillow.

I woke up to the pre-recorded sound of "This is Jackson. Transfer to Blue Line trains at Jackson." My luck couldn't be any better. I jumped from the seat, grabbed my stuff, and ran for the door. I walked down the pigeon-poop-ridden station stairs towards the Blue Line, and managed to catch the train just as it got to the platform. After the three stops I got off the train and made my way to the school.

I started the short journey by using the Loomis exit, and then I made my way for the gym building. I was worried that I wouldn't be able to get into the school because all but one of the doors to the school was locked to prevent intruders from trespassing. However, to my delight I found that the door to the building was propped open with a black rug.

I located the boys' locker room, which I remembered from the dreadful "swimming" classes we had for a semester of gym class. All we had done during this class was learn how to blow bubbles underwater while performing bobs. Oh, and we learned how to define swimming terminology that we would never use in our lives. Mr. Parnell found enjoyment in making our lives miserable.

I entered the boys' locker room and was greeted by some shouts.

"Humbertooooooo, whaddup brooooo!!!" screamed someone who looked like a California douchebag with his bleached hair.

"Sup," I replied.

I didn't pay much attention to anyone. I quickly changed into a swimsuit, which only went a few inches down my thighs. It felt very awkward, but after I saw everyone else was using the same suit, I decided I was going to be able to survive these few hours.

I grabbed a pair of goggles and walked out onto the pool deck through a thick metal door. After taking a few steps onto the deck I heard the loud smack of the door shutting behind me. It sounded like I was entering an inescapable prison, trapped by its heavy concrete walls. My attention turned to some of the kids diving into the pool from the starting blocks. I grabbed one of the workout sheets that was left out on the diving board and made my way for lane three. I jumped in the pool feet first and examined the workout sheet more fully. I flashed back to Augie's workout, which had almost killed me, but I was still surprised and impressed to see how organized and planned out the practice was. The workout was made up of many drills that totaled up to four or five miles. Although there were many abbreviations and words I didn't fully understand, such as "sculling" and "d.a. back," I recognized some of the terms from Mr. Parnell's assignments. Those terms that I thought were stupid were about to come in handy, at least for one day in this life.

I put my goggles on and began the workout in lane three. My body took over, and my brain fell into a sleep-like state. I wasn't thinking about anything, my mind was blank and I just continued to swim. This workout was a series of repeated movements. Despite the difficulty, I continued swimming.

Right arm, left arm, breathe. Right arm, left arm, breathe. This pull pattern coordinated with the kick pattern, right leg, left leg, right leg, left leg.

After about two hours of this, morning practice finally ended and I was allowed to leave "the prison." I took a quick shower in the swimsuit and then changed back to the jeans and t-shirt I originally arrived in. The freshman class, which had to suffer through swimming for gym class, began coming into the swim locker room, which meant that second period was about to start. I quickly threw my things into the locker and locked it up.

I continued through the classes of the day, trying to give my best attention and learn, but all I wanted to do was sleep. We did a bit of class work, listened to the teachers lecture, from Calculus to AP United States History class. I got a few tests back. I was pleased to see that Matt had received an A on all of them, except for an annoying B in history. I didn't really care for now, because even after that coffee all I really cared for was to get some sleep. I was able to take a quick nap on the couch in the library after telling some kids I wouldn't be eating lunch with them today. I was lucky enough to be able to take a nap in my Seminar without any problems from the teacher. She seemed to be very empathetic and understood my situation. The final bell rang, and I was finally released, or at least I thought I had been.

I had forgotten all about afternoon practice, and I made my way for the boys' locker room, remembering those boring gym class days and the dreadful morning practice. Once again I changed into the swimsuit. This time I was ready for it, and it was a lot less awkward changing into the small suit. After changing, I walked out onto the pool deck, letting the steel door close behind me. I dove into the pool, and began the boring strokes, letting my mind go to sleep. Left arm, right arm, breath. A few thousand repetitions of this while I thought about random things and I was done. I got out of the pool exhausted. I took a good thirty-minute shower and got ready to leave the school. I couldn't stand the stench of the chlorine sticking to my skin throughout the school day. After trying my best to cleanse myself of the chlorine, I dressed and left for the Blue Line.

I got outside and saw that it was already dark. I took my phone out of my pocket and looked at the time; it was seven-thirty. I hadn't even been able to see the sun today. I made my way for the train station and took the same exact route home as I took to get to school. After I transferred to the Orange Line, I called my mother and asked her if she could pick me up. I fell asleep after the call and woke up just as the train pulled into the Midway station.

Matt's mom was already waiting at the train station for me, and we drove back to the house, where Matt's mom made dinner.

The dinner was so simple, but it was one of the greatest meals I have ever had. I wasn't sure what was in it. It was some sort of a pork cutlet with some Greek potatoes and a salad, but it tasted great.

Unfortunately, I couldn't savor the meal because I had to complete the homework assigned for the next day. Luckily, there wasn't too much, only an hour of concentrated work. I finished the work and headed upstairs for my room, completely exhausted.

I fell onto the bed, and thought about the day. This was not a life I wanted to live, but now I understood how some people had to sleep and valued it so much. I hadn't thought too much about this, but before I knew it, I was out.

CHAPTER 18
Learning to Deliver

Dun da da, dun da dadada. Dun da da, dun da dadada. I hit the snooze button and closed my eyes one more time. I still had enough time to get ready. Nine minutes later, dun da da, dun da dadada. It was 6:54 a.m. and no surprise it had happened again. I was lying on a really tall full-sized bed and the first thing I saw was a giant poster of a Minnesota Vikings helmet.

"Gross," I muttered under my breath.

"Logan, come grab the keys," the mystery mother shouted from upstairs.

I walked to the stairway, looked up, and a middle-aged brunette woman, dressed only in her nightgown, looked down and dropped car keys.

"*Riiiiing,*" my phone sounded on the bed.

I went back into my room, and saw a text from Casey Ford. It read, "I'm on my way." Well, looked like I gave him a ride to school. I was nowhere near ready, but he was already on his way. I threw on jeans I found on the floor, opened his closet and grabbed the first shirt on the giant pile: a white t-shirt with a map of the Washington D.C. train system. Interesting. I grabbed my backpack and a sweatshirt just in case it got cold later. I finally made it to the bathroom, looked in the mirror, and saw an average-sized brown-haired boy. Not bad. Threw on deodorant, brushed my teeth, combed my hair, and headed downstairs to the kitchen.

I made my way to the pantry, and it was nothing like I had ever seen before. It was a giant walk-in closet full of snacks and food and appliances. I saw on one counter Reese's Puffs, Frosted Flakes, and Raisin Bran. Not enough time for cereal, so I grabbed two Nature Valley bars.

"Riiiiiing," another text from Casey. This time it read, "In the alley."

I walked out the back door, got to the garage but got stuck when I opened the keypad to get in. I tried 5290 and it miraculously opened. That was weird. I saw an old, silver Toyota Prius, unlocked it, and opened the overhead door to the alley. Casey, a tall kid with curly brown hair, stepped in.

"I hate school," he said.

I only nodded in agreement.

We both got in the car, and I put the keys into the ignition. I put the car in reverse, backed out of the alley and pulled onto the first street.

"Are we getting Willie today?" Casey asked.

"Uhhh, yeah," I said, hoping I could magically figure that one out, too.

I was heading south on Paulina, and I took a left to head east on Addison. Next, I took a right on Lakewood, and another on Roscoe. A short, dark-haired kid came running out and hopped into the back seat.

"What' up, guys?" Willie said

"Chillin'," Casey and I both said in unison.

"Do you have work tonight?" Willie asked again.

"Yeah," I said.

I just went along with what he said so we didn't get lost in conversation, but somehow I needed to sort that out.

For the rest of the car ride I tuned them out and focused on my thoughts. This transformation was becoming routine and I needed to try and stop it. I was afraid that if I became too comfortable with the transformations, one day I would be someone else and never get back to being me.

We finally got to the school parking lot, and I took a spot near the back. I got out first and walked ahead of the group to the back of the Arts Building. All I wanted to do was get to school so I could sit in class and not have to worry about anyone else speaking to me. I was walking to Blue House and I heard the first bell ring. I guessed I didn't really need to go to my locker. I walked to my first class, British Literature with Mr. Sanders.

The entire class Sanders just sat behind his desk and talked about things that happened to him or things going on in the world. I adore this kind of teacher, because I could just sit in the back of class and put my head on my desk.

Third period I headed to Mr. Key's American Literature class. I sat in the back of class, and pulled out my notebook to work on the daily journal. I took down the word of the day, the fact of the day, the quote of the day, and began writing. I wrote about my experience over the past couple of weeks, and I reflected. Of course I hate waking up every day in a new person's room, where I had to figure out everything that was going on, but I will say it has been a learning experience. I got to the end of the page and the thoughts stopped there.

Fourth period with Mr. Suma went by like a breeze; he likes to sit at the front of class and crack jokes with funny impersonations. Again, I got to sit in the back and just listen without having to interact with everyone around me.

Then I got to fifth period with Ms. Glass. There are about 30 kids in the class, and I had already been in over 15 of their bodies. It seemed a bit strange to me that I became a new person in this class every day. I still wondered if the teacher had anything to do with it. "No," I thought, "it couldn't be Ms. Glass; she is way too loving. Then again… If I ever get out of this, I'm definitely going to confront her; well, maybe not."

I hadn't had much to eat, so I put my head down and tried to doze off. Twenty-five minutes later the bell woke me up, so I drowsily stood and walked out of the classroom.

I went through my next two periods, then finally I had lunch. It really sucked to have 8th period lunch. I went to Blue House where Casey and Kleave were waiting there for me to go out into the car. I did not have enough time to make a lunch that morning, so I agreed, although I wasn't very enthusiastic about the whole idea. I would much rather have driven somewhere alone, but I had to manage. We went to Jim's Vienna Beef by the expressway, and I got a delicious cheeseburger with grilled onions. We did our eating in the car parked outside the walk-up grill, and when I was done with the burger we headed back to school. I enjoyed the fries on the ride back, and we talked about what we were doing after school. Casey had football, Marc had soccer, and I guess I had to go to work.

Upon arriving at school, the bell immediately rang so it was off to Seminar. It was really unfortunate that I had to stay through my lunch period just for a thirty-minute Seminar. It was a college application Seminar where all anyone ever did was work on essays or apps. However, that day we were in the cinema listening to an admissions representative from Missouri University. I tuned in and out of the presentation since it didn't matter much to me since I would be a new person the next day. Finally, after the bell sounded, signaling the end of school, I walked to the car to make my way to work.

After driving for about fifteen minutes, my phone rang in my pocket and it read "I Monelli." I answered, and a male Hispanic voice said there was a delivery waiting for me and I needed to come in pronto.

This was a little hard after all. Upon arriving at work, there was a delivery bag stuffed with food and a receipt in the flap. I pulled out the receipt, checked the address, and made way to the car. I drove to the appropriate address and rang the doorbell. A young, fat woman with short orange hair answered the door and I handed her the food. I drove back to the restaurant and this time I actually got to walk inside. It was a small Italian restaurant where all the workers spoke either Italian or Spanish. I was reminded I got one meal a day, so I decided on a margarita pizza. When it was out of the oven, I grabbed a Sprite from the fridge and went and sat at a table. I took my first bite and was instantly hooked. The sauce was delicious and the crust was to die for. Now that, I could get used to.

After I finished eating, I got my next delivery. I packed it up and took it to the car. I arrived at the apartment and stepped inside. The receipt had no last name, so I had no idea what bell to ring. I took out my phone, and called the customer.

"Hi. Your I Monelli's delivery is out front."

"Great thank you, I will be right down," a woman responded.

She came down, and I handed her two half pizzas. She signed the receipt, and when I walked back to the car I checked the tip. $12 for two pizzas?! Nice! I drove back to the restaurant, and there were three more deliveries waiting.

At the end of the very busy night, I signed out with the owner who didn't speak English. I earned $74 for 6 hours! All I can say is it was better than working at Potbelly's or being a waitress. Come to think of it, I'd gotten quite a bit of job experience in the last three weeks. Not that I would have chosen any of it if I'd had the choice. Still, these low level jobs do give me a different perspective. Whatever.

I left the restaurant at 10:00 p.m., drove home, and walked in the back door. My temporary parents were already in bed, so I just walked upstairs, brushed my teeth, stripped down, and climbed into bed. It had been a great day: school went by with ease, and having a job was awesome.

I wondered what tomorrow would be like.

CHAPTER 19
My First Girlfriend

"BRRRRRRRING BRRRRRRRRING!" I wake
up to a screeching alarm clock that I furiously look to
shut off. All of a sudden, my head is pounding with pain,
and I can't think straight. I intrinsically understand that
this is going to occur for quite some time, but I can't help
but feel angry. Being infuriated, I'm about to scream at
the top of my lungs to show my angst, when I hear
someone bellowing my name to wake up and get ready
for school. This person, who I guess was supposed to be
my "mother," then proceeds to open my door and says,

"Mijo, its 6:20 already, how late do you plan on
entering school today?"

Puzzled, I realized it was a rhetorical question and
decided I needed to do my usual routine, to figure out
who the lucky guy is today, and how I'm going to get out
of this one. "Here we go again," I said to myself.

As I got out of bed, I noticed this room was not
too big, but very colorful and surrounded by artwork. "At
least this guy doesn't have a giant poster of the Vikings
on it," I laughed. I then saw a piano and a guitar on the
opposite side. Feeling curious, I walked over and checked
out some of this guy's stuff, and something caught my
eye. I read to myself, "James 9/02/12," which was on the
bottom of a portrait of a really pretty girl. I was
impressed, but then reassured myself that he couldn't
draw anywhere near the quality of the artwork and
disregarded it. I walked out through the door, and
conveniently, next door was the bathroom. As I went into
the bathroom to brush my teeth, I realized I was exactly
who I thought I was, and said "Oh brother, now I know
why I was so angry in the morning."

As I brushed, I noted that he had very white,
bright, and straight teeth. I washed my face with this

125

scrub he owned, and went back to my room to change. I looked inside his closet, and found that he surprisingly knew how to dress. I remembered speculating about him being gay so this seemed reasonable. I picked out one of his preset outfits and dressed, then fixed my hair to what I thought looked decent. If only everybody had my hair, that'd be a huge blessing! Next to the mirror, I found glasses, which I put on and immediately saw better.

I left the house, following pursuit of three curious kids calling me "brother," and followed our mother to the garage. We got in their green Astro van, and we were off. This lady had tried talking to me, but I pretended to sleep so I wouldn't have to say anything. I secretly observed the scenery and tried to make out which neighborhood I was in, and quickly saw that Midway Airport was right by, so this had to be Clearing. The ride took no more than forty-five minutes, but it was SO unbearably annoying and boring because this woman listened to the news on the radio and these kids wouldn't stop fighting until we dropped them off at their school.

Afterwards, it wasn't too long until I realized where we were. As we approached Sojourner Truth, I decided to be polite and say thank you and good bye, secretly hoping good manners *might* lead me to a better place, like my own body.

As I whipped out my ID card and entered the school building, I remembered I didn't know where to go. I looked at the ID card and noticed that he was in Blue House, while the locker number was written on the top in black sharpie. As I approached the lockers, I found my locker, and also my alleged locker partner, Jozay Franklin. Jozay was a tall, muscular dark-skinned junior, who was actually really fast. I know this because I ran against him in the 400 meter dash at a track meet last year, and Jozay ended up stealing the show. Despite this, he's one of the few people I would consider "above a bone head level" at this school. I greeted him good morning and opened up my planner to see if I had anything due today or if I'm supposed to dip out of every class. As I scanned for today's date, I noticed the organization of the agenda was decent, but I reorganized it to make it better.

As I read, I found out exactly what I needed and thought, "Hmm, maybe if I do everything right today, whatever continues to go on with me will *finally* come to an end…A guy can dream, right?" I decided I'd give it a shot; I don't enjoy unwillingly immersing my soul into the body of unintelligent sloths. Afterwards, I realized what I said, and said to myself "Wait, NO, I didn't mean that, I meant there are many unique different individuals who have a hard time living life because they aren't as brilliant as I am!....umm wait, scratch that, I mean…Oh, forget it." This might take me a while to get used to. As I cleared out of my locker, some sort of female specimen attacked me. I wasn't quite sure because I only turned around and then was tackled by a full bundle of hair, which flew right into my face! I felt something weird; it's as if I have some sort of close connection with this person, despite never having seen her in my life. Her amber-hazelnut eyes darted into mine, and then she sang with a bright smile, "Goooooooood morning honey, how are you feeling?" I didn't know how to reply, she'd paralyzed me.

I replied with a smile and tried to sing, "I'm confused because I don't know why my life is still succumbing to this affliction, but other than that I feel OK."

As I said that, I didn't know if my mind was deceiving me or if this was actually my singing voice. I then remembered that I'm supposed to be involved with operatic arts, so I supposed this is the result of all that. She told me, "I'm sorry baby, I hope you figure out what's bothering you."

She then gently tried to hold my hand, and then I jumped. She asked me if everything was all right, but I assured her that I was fine, just surprised. I think this kid actually has a girlfriend. Wow, I was way off.

As we walked towards Blue House, I noted her personal features, and then became unsure if she was supposed to be "my" girlfriend. She's a skinny crazy-curled brunette who was around 5' 5" in height. I had to admit, although I used to think the majority of the girls were sort of trashy, she actually looks pretty, and now I'm in disbelief; a guy like this *can't possibly* go out with somebody like her.

She joined her group of friends, while everybody was greeting us with "Good morning James & Bonnie!" They all called us cute, while I stayed looking like a lost puppy. Unsure of what to say, I decided to say as little as possible and be as agreeable as possible. In the end, they were all right, even though they looked like people I would, in my own body, avoid. Nothing like my crowd, at least. But then again, I didn't have a crowd.

Out of nowhere, the first bell rang, and everybody was scrambling to get to class, while I tried to figure out where I had to be. My supposed girlfriend walked me by the stairs, and said, "This is where I leave you to go to French IV, have a great day" and then came awfully close to my face and kissed my cheek. Giggling, I walked towards the classrooms looking for Honors US History, and once I found it I was unsure if I was in the correct classroom, as there was a meatball sitting where the teacher usually sat. I approached an empty seat, and she quickly remarked, "Hey son, you're in the wrong seat, did ya forget where you sit?..."

"Wait, don't answer that, do you see that seat over there? That is where you sit," an inner voice abruptly said to me. A little shocked that I knew where I sat, I decided to follow my inner voice and sit. All we did during this class period was watch a film on how the American States were formed, and before I knew it, the third period bell rang. Then it was time for a class that might offer some small amount of knowledge: AP Bio.

I went to AP Biology, and learned that it's more difficult than what I had expected. I would've struggled if it wasn't for this Indian kid who sat next to me, and it hit me that there are smarter students in this school than I had previously thought. I left AP Biology for Division, which was with Mr. Salidor, an art teacher whom I had heard had earned lot of notoriety with his art pieces. Afterwards, I headed to Art, which I figured was a blow-off class, but today turned out to be highly instructive.

I went to my fifth period, and saw that Ms. Glass was absent and we had a sub for the day, and everybody was leaving. I watched as a number of students asked to go to the bathroom and never came back. I saw myself reading a book. I walked over and saw that it was Herman Melville's *The Confidence Man*, a book on my personal reading list because a famous author wrote it and I knew almost no one had ever read it. I scoffed at my pretentiousness, then sat down in James seat and started to read. Nia was either absent or had left before I got there. I thought to have a conversation with my real self, but I just couldn't stomach it.

I had choir after this, which I sort of actually enjoyed, because I cannot sing at all in real life, yet this guy could! Calculus turned out to be a nightmare, not because of the math, but because I had a hard time understanding Mr. Tzsu. Finally, lunch came by. I didn't know what to do during this period, but then the same girl that I was with in the morning came around and asked me what I wanted to do.

I wasn't quite sure, but we went outside and stood under the autumn trees, and we talked. She seemed like an interesting person, and has similar musical tastes as me, which I do find neat. We spent the whole period talking about our favorite musicians, and it turns out we're *really* similar. I told her she was amazingly cool and that I think I'm in love, and she reacted ecstatically! I probably shouldn't have said all that, inasmuch as James is the one who will have to deal with the consequences, but it sort of came out and it's actually what I felt at the time. I couldn't tell if it was James or me who was feeling it.

I ran off to guitar, and I've always wanted to learn how to play "legit-ly," so this was going to be fun. I got there and played as if I'd been playing all my life. This guy James has skills. I was almost jealous of him.

Then came cross-country practice, something I assumed would be doable. I should've realized I was in for some serious hell. This muscular dark-skinned man that went by the name of "Gipson" told me to get dressed and meet the boys in "Billy's office." I got dressed and went downstairs, and found the group of guys. Lanky high school boys surrounded me as this man told us what our workout was. He said we would have 5 one-thousands at 2:55 and 6 two hundreds at 28 seconds afterwards. I understood him although I'd never run cross-country before in my life. The intensity of the workout reminded me of my days in the pool as Augie and Matt, but also my days as a waitress as Lea. I had to give credit to this guy for being able to keep a good physique and such a great amount of endurance; otherwise I would've died out there!

When I got home, I showered and dressed. I was exhausted, and I sort of fell on my bed, planning on getting up after a couple of minutes, having some dinner and doing a little homework.

CHAPTER 20
Things Get Graphic

All my awareness seems to stem from a buzzing noise. All of a sudden, I have vision: a tiled ceiling in a very dark room. The vibrating alarm comes from a phone on the floor next to me, and as I slowly make moves to turn it off, I notice I'm on a mattress on the floor. For a second I'm a bit surprised, this isn't my bed yet again, but I feel too tired to even bother with the thought. Next to me, through foggy eyes, I see the lumps of someone asleep on a bed. The darkness is due to the only window being covered by wooden grating. This looks like a basement.

The time reads 7:12 a.m., a strange time to set an alarm for. If I haven't fallen off the standard chronology of things, today should be Saturday. The alarm must mean something then. Maybe the phone will hold some clue? There's two new messages, one from some 'Richie' saying "so how was it?" and another from 'Mr. Cage', reading "UIC 8:30! Wake up!" Okay. So there's a destination for me.

As I exit through the door into a small, messy kitchen, my eyes begin to itch. I take a hand to them, only to remove chunks of gunk. The house is small, with a living room to the left and a short hallway to the right. There's a pit bull sleeping at the end of this, seemingly guarding the far door. Through the living room window I see stairs leading up to a sidewalk - this whole place is a basement.

I find the bathroom to the right, and look in the mirror. There's scraggly hair, a hint of a beard, and reddened eyes with darkened skin under them. Around each iris there're light blue circles – this idiot fell asleep in his contacts. This idiot I recognize, however, as Melbourne Dorrisey. He seems like an all right kid, and

I've heard comments that he's smart, though I usually see him sleeping in AP Physics C. I suppose I can relate on some level… I wonder what his Saturday has in store for me.

After a quick shower, I don't really know what to do. I notice my shirt smells like… smoke and alcohol. Whatever's happening at the University, I should probably come off a bit fresher. I go back into the bedroom and grab a shirt from the closet, and head outside. The way the houses on this street have ditches instead of lawns, it seems I'm on the near South Side, maybe Bridgeport. Trusting this body to direct me, as the others have, I instinctively turn to go to the backyard, and there I find a bike locked up. I search my pockets and there's a keychain with a little black lock key. I find it works. Thanks, instincts.

I've been to UIC before, on a research opportunity last summer, so I figured I'd know the campus once I got there. A text to 'Mr. Cage' asking which building we're in yields "Science and Engineering South, Taylor & Morgan." Okay. Destination. I bike around the block and see Halsted. That should take me right up there. I've never biked in traffic, but how hard could it be? The kid's got an iPod, so once again I shuffle it to get a sense of the guy. As I navigate the speeding cars and trucks, the songs that come up are all over the place: some sort of metal/electronic fusion, an indie rock band, some white rapper, probably Eminem, and… Tchaikovsky?

On campus, I realize I'm hungry and very tired, yet full of a subtle energy. I look into Mel's wallet to find three bucks and… no. I'm not sure what I'm looking at here. I wonder if Richie was talking about… "how was what?" I text him back. Well, as there's three bucks here, I buy a coffee. After a few more blocks I pull up to the science building, with all its strange angles, and find a sign that says "CCML -->." This is my best bet, so I follow

132

the arrows to an auditorium. There's a bunch of kids in the navy blue and orange of Sojourner Truth, their shirts emblazoned with a net of shapes and "Sojourner Truth Math Team 2012." So this is a math competition. Shouldn't be too hard. But if the thing in the wallet was what I think it was… and the smell of that shirt…

I realize my stomach's feeling really shitty. These two Asian twins come up to me laughing, reaching their hands out for handshakes. I oblige, and quickly excuse myself. I run down the hallway until I see a Men's sign, and puke into the first toilet I find. My stomach feels much better, but the tiredness is still there.

I don't want to interact with people.

I go back, and try my best to look exhausted, which isn't very hard. The twins laugh some more and talk in the strangest mix of heavy Asian accent and "yo dawgs" that I've ever heard. A few more people give me handshakes and hugs and I respond to some "hey, Mel's" with a weak "hi." There's a box of munchkins, and I eat about seven. Needing some space, I sit a row above everyone, and open up the wallet again. Richie's an early riser too it seems, as he texts me back with – something doesn't add up here. Yet there it is on the screen, the name of the substance, and in the wallet, just as before, is the little bag of white powder. And yet here I am, at a math competition. After going through eighteen bodies, I shouldn't be fazed, but… How do people pull this stuff off?

I grow a bit concerned, but before I can decide what to do, it seems the contest is about to start. The proctors tell us to sit in such and such places, and they hand out a turned-over test. The guy up front – whom I recognize as the math teacher Mr. Cage – tells us we have 50 minutes to complete the exam. I turn it over to find 20 questions on precalc. They're not the kind most classes go over and for a bit I just stare at them. Something in Mel's head and mine clicks, and all of a sudden I find myself zooming through the thing, whipping out obscure formulas and theorems I read about maybe once in my life. I've always liked math, but never really explored it past what I have had to. When I finish, the clock up front says only 30 minutes have passed. I begin to double-check the test, might as well give it my best after all, but find that everything seems to be in order.

After the contest comes grading. As I look at the kids on the team, I realize most of them I've at least seen in some AP class or another. Two of them got perfect ACT scores, which isn't any big feat but they're definitely not morons. If I weren't so tired, I'd consider starting some intellectual conversation. Instead, I sit in the back and listen to the iPod. It seems any sort of music I can think of has found its way into this thing.

My peace is interrupted by another round of problems going around, and this time the whole team seems to be working together. These are from all areas of math, and I find myself greatly entertained by them, not like the plug-in-numbers problems in my math classes. Before I know it, I'm joining the quick demands for the collective answer sheet and heated arguments over the solutions to a polynomial of trig functions. Soon, the results are in and to my mild surprise, I get second place with one point off a perfect score. At least I haven't mucked up this person's day, so far.

It's now noon, and as I wonder what to do with the rest of this Saturday, some texts rush in from a few people about going to "the silos." The victory put me in a good mood; I'm feeling a bit adventurous, so I agree to go. The bike ride should be enjoyable. I ask for the address and get some texts like "how could you forget?" but eventually I get another destination. Before I depart, I get a call from 'Tata', and answer to a new language. No, that's not right, it's… it's Polish! Awesome, I thought I'd never understand it again. Tata means dad, I realize. 'Dad' asks me about the competition, and laughs when I tell him the simple mistake I made. *"Jak zawsze"* (as always), he says. I guess simple arithmetic must be Mel's bane.

The parts of town I'm biking through look very industrial, full of factories and scrapyards. I've never been here, but it's no surprise that Chicago can still hold something new for me. Eventually I come to the intersection specified, which leads up to a massive overpass, to the side of which are what look like huge, derelict grain silos. That... must be where I'm headed. I'm suddenly a bit worried. Melbourne may be smart, but he associates with some shady people. Who knows what I'll find in there.

I bike up the bridge, which is quite an effort. This thing is much longer than it looks, and the top seems to be moving away faster than me. Eventually I see the ramp that leads down to the silo complex, which is fenced off. It could be a park, I suppose, if the things didn't look like they've been abandoned for years. Going down the ramp, I realize how flat most of Illinois is. The wind's rushing past... Tentatively, I release the handlebars... the bike immediately swerves to the right. Not a good idea.

The fence has "No Trespassing" signs all over it. I lock the bike, and look at the barbed wire up top. There's got to be a hole or something; I'm expected to make it in there. Beyond are tall reeds and a series of decaying buildings. Eventually I come to a ditch that leads under the perimeter. I crawl under, something I'm not sure I'd do in my own body, my own clothes.

There's a dirt path in front of me, so this seems to be the common point of entry. I follow it, not sure where I'm headed.

A text: "where you at?"

"I'm in."

"Come to the back, by the basement entrance."

It's really quiet here, not even the chirping of crickets. The overpass and highway lightly resonate, but they sound like a distant wind. As I walk, to my right is a rusty warehouse of sorts, on the edge of the Chicago River. The windows on the second floor are all broken, and every surface is covered in graffiti - words, pictures, strange abstractions in all colors and styles, covering the old bricks while nature slowly takes the place back. I've never been to a place like this. I spot the entrance, an industrial-sized door, and I have an urge to go in and explore. Another time, maybe.

As I walk in between the two groups of silos, I look up. There's a rickety wooden bridge, also covered in paint. My first thought is "so the roof's accessible." The thing looks like it could collapse at any time. I look back down, and – wow. In front of me is a small hill. On the top there's a big wooden cross. Next to it is a rusting combine, sunk into the ground. It looks like a scene straight out of... a dream? Literature? It's the sort of thing a survey of lit teacher would spend a day analyzing.

Around the back of the silos is a path leading down to a rotting dock. Near the end there's a hole into the silo complex; it looks like it leads into the basement. It must, for there are three figures standing around it. I get a good look at them as I come near, not sure of what to say just yet. The one nearest me is a brown-skinned guy, about my height, with messy black hair that almost conceals his inch-wide earplugs. A necklace of neon blue skulls hangs comfortably around his neck. The middle kid is taller, white and blonde, with a red San Diego State sweater on, a blunt in one hand and a handshake from the other. Then there's a black kid with a yellow plaid shirt, a faint mustache and below it the friendliest grin I've ever seen. "Hey Mel."

"How's it going, man?"

The group talks, initially about their jobs. Hank, the blonde, works as a student teacher on the south side. He tells us about a joke the kids play on him:

"Mr. Luckton, why they always hangin' together?"

"Who?"

136

"My nuts."

Crisco, with the neon skulls, works, perhaps fittingly, at a slaughterhouse. "The thing is, the goats are eerily silent. You know, silence of the lambs? I never thought that was a real thing. And when they do make noise, it sounds like children laughing."

Davis, the happy kid, came from downtown, where he's a sale clerk for some clothing store.

At some point the blunt gets lit and we pass it around. I find myself entranced by the silos even more, and am glad when we step into the basement. It's darker here. There's a thick layer of dust and grain over everything: the floor, the walls, and the giant cones on the ceiling that are the bottoms of the massive storage bins. This place is covered in graffiti, too. There are bits of machinery here and there, and the far wall has caved in. We take a walk around, and I notice holes in the wall, doorways leading to dark tunnels. We've got flashlights but the beams don't reach that far. The others have started whispering, so I too lower my voice. With the high I can't stop thinking about the history of this place, from when it was operational to all the explorers who have been here before us. I imagine ghost images of all of them, walking and working and painting and scheming. It strikes me that someone may have died here, though I dismiss the thought.

We enter a room with a chair bolted to the ground, the spinning kind with the foot rest you find at a barber's. There's a pipe jutting out of the cone above and from it hangs some cloth. I turn around to see Crisco pulling bottles of paint from his backpack. He tosses each of us one, pours some on his hand, and starts drawing a curve on one of the walls of the octagonal room. I look at my own bottle, an electric teal. I pour some color on my hand and attempt to draw a line. The dust is killer; it smudges the line and sucks up the paint in a second. This'll be tough.

We start talking once again, about books. Crisco starts ranting about his most recent, *A Scanner Darkly* by Phillip K. Dick. He tells us of a cop who's hunting himself because his brain's been split in half by some drug... hogwash, in short. Though my own brain's been split twenty ways by now, I still don't like wasting time on straight science fiction. My only attempt had been Aldous Huxley's *Brave New World*, a supposed classic. The character development was horrid, the plot a ramshackle frame for the author's alarmist ideas.

In response I mention *Slaughterhouse-Five*, by Kurt Vonnegut. It might be weird enough, darkly humorous enough for these friends of Mel's. Not only that, but I'm thinking about Billy Pilgrim, the protagonist. He became unstuck in time, not knowing which part of his life he'll end up living next. I too have become unstuck, from myself. For the first time I wonder... what if my classmates have been going through the same thing as me? What if we're all destined to live a day in each other's lives? Maybe not, we'd all notice if everyone were acting weird for nearly three weeks now. Perhaps this is an alternate universe, and after going through everyone I'll wake up three weeks ago, nothing having changed. Come to think of it, the experience would make an interesting book...

Some unfathomable time passes, I find myself clear headed once again. Our pictures are finished. Crisco painted an orange tribal-looking face, the lines all clean. It's got an expression of... agonizing pleasure. Davis and Hank collaborated on a piece, a red-purple cowboy shouting "Get a grip!" It's a bit messy, but the chaotic splotches give it artistic zest. My own attempt was at a guy looking through a kaleidoscope, which is how I feel, but it mostly looks like a bird shitting teal. Crisco takes out two more bottles, black and white, and starts throwing paint all over his tribesman.

"Why?" I ask.

"Fuck it."

The classic answer. Okay. Hank comes over and we pour some on our hands. Fuck it. I smash my palm into the kaleidoscope man's face. We start smashing just about anywhere we can. Hank makes a leap and smashes the cone above us, which lets out a deep thunk and sends off a cloud of dust. I find a painting of a cartoon cat's face, with a toothy grin and black holes for eyes. Smash! It's got handy pupils now. My hand hurts from all the smashing, and as I pick up my backpack I get paint all over it. Fuck it.

It's nearly dark as we climb out of the place. We find the dirt path leading back to the ditch, but they walk past it. Near the river the fence ends, and I see I could've simply swung around the last post instead of crawling. I get the bike and meet the others. "Show's in an hour." says Davis as we're walking up the ramp. Show? I'm feeling exhausted, the weed has drained me. "Aight, you gonna bike it, Mel?" I have no idea where or what this show is. "No, too tired." I'm considering going home for the night, but here's a Saturday night in another body. We walk on, back to the other side of the overpass. I look down on the endless traffic and marvel that none of these people will ever know that above them, Jake and Melbourne are defying everything we know about reality.

We get on the Orange Line, and I awkwardly stand with my bike, taking up way too much space. The trip lasts over an hour with a transfer to Blue Line to boot, so I'm relieved when we finally get off at Western. We start walking up Milwaukee. The streets are filled with a disproportionate amount of scantily clad people for this time of year. Detouring through an alleyway, we end up in the far reaches of a CVS Pharmacy parking lot. We have a seat against a wall behind a big white van. Crisco's to my left, Hank and Davis to my right. They're discussing shows they've previously been to, and I jokingly mention my only concert experience: a Chicago Symphony

Orchestra viewing. "We should go tripping," replies Davis. He pulls out some folded papers: "here are your tickets, by the way." I look at the name, 'Die Antwoord + Many More!' Never heard of 'em.

Crisco has pulled out a notebook and is shaking his hand over it. A small pile of white powder gradually builds up under his fingers, and he tosses an empty baggie like mine to the ground. "Mel?" "Right..." I slowly pull out my own bag, and my phone starts buzzing. It's 'Tato'.

"Jesteś na koncercie?" (Are you at the concert?)

"We're almost there."

"What time's it get out?"

I glance at my ticket, a bit surprised at the late time.

"Two."

"Coming home?"

I'm not sure where Mel's house is, but I don't know the alternatives. I suppose I can go home with one of Mel's friends.

"I'm not sure."

"Dobra, bąć bezpieczny." (Okay, stay safe.)

"Of course."

Crisco, having mixed the contents of my bag with his, lets out a chuckle. "I wonder what he'd say to this," he tells me as he pulls out a twenty. I do too. I think back to the night in Sophie's body. Her father told her he expected the rent, Mel's told him to stay safe. I felt weary being her, that craving to escape the troubles of life. The loft that night was full of seeming junkies, falling over each other, drugs and sex abundant. This is different. These kids don't seem self-destructive at all, and I realize I haven't felt an urge like in Sophie's body. Crisco finishes his line and hands me the notebook. Taking it, I realize I'm shaking in nervousness. "You alright, man?" he asks, "You know you don't have to."

There it is. No expectation. No pressure. I'll never have the chance to do this in my own body, or rather I

140

never would. I take the twenty, lower my face to the notebook, and inhale...

Ow. It doesn't hurt as much as I figured, but there's still a sting. My nose gets runny, but the nervous shake has subsided. One by one the lines disappear up our nasal cavities. We walk back to the street and join the mass of scantily clad strangers migrating north. The venue is only a block away at the Congress Theater, and I realize this is the cause of the decrease in clothing. Inside, the foyer is packed with people. Many are wearing summer wear or less, but a few have elaborate costumes and I notice a group of men in suits. There's electronic music emanating from the auditorium ahead. I'm no longer tired. I'm not full of energy, either, but I feel like I can manage just about any level of activity.

In the hallway outside the auditorium, Mel's friends find people they know and our little group grows. We step into the auditorium. The music's loud as can be, and all of a sudden I have the urge to *move*. There's no band on stage, naturally, just a figure with a track board and laptop. Behind him a ring of light pulsates and shoots electric beams across a giant LCD screen. Everyone's looking excited and I find myself grinning. "This is gonna be a face-melter," says Hank. We walk into the crowd, and everyone around us is dancing or putting on a little lightshow with glowing fingertips. Half our party's grooving in some way or another. What the hell, I join in.

No one, as far as I could tell, stops moving for a second. At some point a kid named Alex, who has greeted me with much gusto, hands me a little green pill with a smiley face on it. Apparently having no inhibitions, I take it without hesitation. About twenty minutes later, a wave of euphoria suddenly crashes into me. I bring my hands to my face, amazed at how awesome having hands is. I rub my face, and damn did rubbing my face feel incredible, too. Just about everything feels.. *ecstatic*. My heart might as well have exploded from the pounding, but doesn't.

During the first three acts I need to use the bathroom. There is a security guard in there with a jar full of peppermints, handing them out. I take a handful and started sucking on them incessantly. They are so deliciously sweet and minty, more so than any peppermints I'd had before. An unconventionally tall man in a wedding dress is rubbing himself against a wall, which nobody seems to mind. In the spirit of inquiry I ask "how's that wall, bud?" He turns and his face is extremely feminine, almost too much. His voice I can't even describe, but it too has some feminine qualities. I think that maybe he's a transvestite. He starts walking towards me, telling me we should get acquainted as he brings his face dangerously close to mine. I realize that despite my newfound friendliness, I'd really rather not and leave.

There's a shimmer over everything, like a thin layer of sparkling liquid enveloping the world. The stage gets dark, and the crowd gets louder than seems possible, the whole place is about to collapse from these people's screams. I join in and soon a glitched vocal sample starts playing, at which point Crisco shakes my shoulders in anticipation. A high-pitched, dominating female voice starts rapping, and the stage lights up with two figures in orange hoodies pacing around aggressively. The present rapper's a short blonde chick, while the other is one pissed-off looking blonde guy. In the back is a DJ with some kind of mutant-looking mask on. The pissed-off guy starts rapping too, and they've both got these... *raw-ass* accents that sound like Middle-Eastern mixed with French. So this is Die Antwoord. It may be... it has to be the drugs, but in this moment there's nothing I'd rather be listening to. The music just pumps the whole crowd *right the fuck up*. Excuse my crass language but no other words come close to the right meaning. Everybody's

142

jumping like they're trying to cause an earthquake up in here. I don't know any of the words but what chunks of choruses and hooks I can pick up I yell at the top of my lungs, just like the hundreds of strangers dead-set on raising our collective body heat to lethal levels. After a cornucopia of ultra-frisky beats coupled with hilarious, rapid-fire rapping, the finale demolishes the room with one of those dub step bass drops that are to the present day what ridiculous synth lines were to the 80s. I think in this moment I comprehend the primal exaltation of sharing such a ridiculously intense experience with a room full of people, people who are all letting themselves loose. Here under the influence of music and what has to be a generally shared altered state of mind, everyone seems equal, as much parts of some super-organism as antelope running in a herd of thousands. Goddamn, my brain's pulling out some fine word choices, choices I'd feel fruity about any other day. But now I'm loving every bit of it.

As a group, we've survived the sensory overload, the onslaught on our self-control. I look around, and see that Hank was right; people's faces have indeed melted as their makeup couldn't handle their facial waterfalls of sweat. The main lights come on, and people start moving towards the exit. Our group trudges along, discussing the kick-assery of what we just experienced. Once outside, we split off, with the majority walking north somewhere, while Crisco, Davis, Hank and I head back toward the Blue Line. I feel sympathy with the drivers on the street: the crowd has spilled onto the road at a comfortable pace showing no concern for nighttime traffic.

Walking to the train, we pass a group of people, and overhear that it's one of their birthdays. Congratulating her enthusiastically, we begin a collective chant of Happy Birthday, and by the time we sing *dear*, about twenty more people join in. On the train platform and during the ride downtown to Hank's apartment, this

143

sense of community continues, with conversation and laughter blind to any group boundaries. This is such a contrast to the ride here, where the default mindset seemed cautious detachment, everyone trying to keep as much to themselves as possible, acting like sharing a commute is only a chance to accidentally create social discomfort. Perhaps I'm reading too much into it, perhaps those folk were just happier taking a break from people. It's almost as if I forgot that I myself would gladly sit alone. At the moment, however, this is much more preferable.

We get off at Monroe Blue Line, and walk to Hank's high-rise, nicely situated a block from Millennium Park. The doorman inside gives us a nod of recognition; I'm guessing he's used to this group's late nights. In the elevator, we go up over forty stories, and the elevator does its elevator thing of inducing weight change, which makes me giggle with appreciation for physics. The change in altitude is big enough that my ears pop.

At Hank's, the four of us head to Hank's room, the one nearest the windows. Davis pulls out another blunt and we head onto the balcony adjacent to Hank's room. It's rather spacious, with a bench and a cart of flowers. Down below is a view right on to the 'L', straight ahead is the top half of the Sears (or, rather, Willis) Tower, and in the distance is a plane of lights, the enormous grid of Chicago streetlights and homes lights lit for their inhabitants, enjoying their various Saturday night activities. As we smoke, we discuss these people, in all their homes, in the thousands of windows in the skyscrapers before us, in all the cars travelling down the thick luminous veins that are the highways, and all their complements in all the cities around the world. We are in awe at the amount of peers in the world, at the unfathomable number of lives unfolding, of people's stories being written.

We spread our sleeping bags and Melbourne's friends fall asleep in rapid succession. Perhaps it's the novelty of this whole new flavor of thought, or the fact that I've got three weeks of other people's lives filling up my brain, but I just lie there for a long time, riding these philosophical trains of thought. I find it surprisingly easy to think of people without criticism. That all those billions of lives are being lived with their own strengths and weaknesses. Hell, even the kids in my own class have lives I couldn't imagine handling for more than a day. And they're all better than me at something, aren't they? I'll never be able to run ten miles with seemingly no effort, to play a guitar as well as James would probably take me years of practice... hell, I can't even claim to fully know a language besides English. The quiet folk on the train, lost in their own thoughts. What are they dealing with?

Throughout this, my eyes are getting closer and closer to shut. My thoughts slow down and get more abstract, start going off on nonsense tangents. When I awake, I'll be someone else. I drift off, genuinely excited for tomorrow's experience.

CHAPTER 21
The Poet In Me

The sounds of ambulance sirens and loud noises awaken me. Mel, what have you done? I rub the crust out of my eyes lazily and become aware of the most annoying sound I've ever heard. I stumble out of bed and closer to the screeching noise. I stop at the speaker system installed in the wall. My eyes adjust to the emerald glow of the screen as I read it. *"Prince . . . .Do Me, Baby (Live) . . . One Night Alone . . . .Live."* flashes across my eyes. I quickly turn off the music, if it can be called that and slowly venture out into a familiar unknown.

In the quiet darkness of what seems to be the wee hours of the morning, I find the bathroom. I feel my hands around for the light switch. "Not Mel," I think. As the light brightens the bathroom, I am enlightened. "Oh shit, I'm Ashanti" I clumsily blurt out loud. I look down at the black-and-red Mickey Mouse pajamas I am wearing in shock, my eyes bulging out of my head.

"Damn, this chick is built." I exclaim. I mean I've been a girl before but none of those girls have bodies like hers.

I stretch before I enter the shower. To the left, to the right, down the center and back up again. I slip out of the pajamas, one article of clothing at a time. I pull back the glass door and turn on the showerhead. My body jerks from the frigid liquid meeting my skin. I adjust the temperature to a lukewarm setting and exhale.

While in the shower, I begin to think about where my life will be in the next week or so. Nine days to be exact. Today is Day twenty-one, I have just nine more days to go. Nine more days until Sojourner Truth Magnet High School is a distant memory in the recesses of my brain. I had planned on forgetting all of the people in this school, but now that seems impossible. Nine more days until I face the inevitable, the future. Unless I'm wrong and the body jumping keeps on going. Please, no. Let this end, please!

What does the future hold for me? Will I blaze my own trail or become just another one of society's clones? Before I get too deep in my thoughts, I take a nearby loofah and bottle of body wash sitting on the windowsill and begin to cleanse my body. As the water rushes over my body, my nose is delighted by the faint scent of strawberries and champagne. I lean down to turn off the showerhead, pull back the sliding door and step out of the warm chamber of solitude. My body shivers as the cold air meets my warmth. I quickly scan the bathroom for a towel to wrap my body with. A purple, cotton one catches my eye amidst the amber and burnt orange tones of the bathroom. There's only one thing separating me from getting it, my 5'4" frame. I walk over to the towering shelving unit and reach, up on my toes, for the large purple towel. I retrieve it with concerted effort. Even small successes are great.

I return to her bedroom and turn on the speaker system. I begin to sing along to a song that contains walking bass, gentle guitar strumming, double-time drumming, and a wash of euphoric vocal reverb. I am instantly hypnotized by the simple yet meaningful lyrics. "*Do you like drugs? Have you ever felt alone? Do you still believe in love? But do you like drugs, do you like drugs…Well me too, me too, me too babe Me too, me too Do you like hugs, Do you like love Well me too, me too, me too babe Me too, me too It's what we gonna do.*" Searching through drawers, I find the bare necessities: a black lace brassiere, black satin pair of underwear and heather grey trouser socks. I look to the closet for the actual outfit. As I glance over the organized closet, a stark contrast to her actual bedroom, a pair of dark wash bell bottom blue jeans paired with a crisp white button up shirt complete with a pussybow catches my

147

attention. I scan the floor of the closet for the completion of any outfit, shoes. I settle on the first pair I see, red booties. I can't help but wonder, what does this girl have to hide? She has a clean closet but a dirty room; what a paradox.

I slip on the seemingly fashionable items and head downstairs. I turn the corner and scare the hell out of myself. I was *not* expecting that glass mirror to obstruct my path. I jump back and scream out, "Aaaaaaaah!" With my heart racing and chest pounding, I am greeted uneasily by my echo. I'm all alone in this house. I ponder the possibilities of what I could do, what I should do and what I will do. I walk into the kitchen and open the fridge. I pull out eggs, fresh herbs, butter and cheese…the ingredients to a perfect omelet. I peruse the tall shelves and cupboards for pots and pans. I grab the small, black skillet, a bowl to mix the ingredients in and a whisk to mix. I place everything out in a straight row on the counter and proceed to turn on the small radio next to the toaster. "*So Amazing*" by Luther Vandross calls out to me and pulls on my heart's strings as I incorporate all of the ingredients. I really don't measure anything, just add every ingredient in the quantity that I see fit. I place the skillet on the front right eye of the stove and turn it to medium low heat. After seven minutes in the pan, I grab the rubber handle of the skillet and flip the omelet. "Perfect." I say to myself. I ransack the cupboards for a plate and fork and eat my yellow crescent at the counter.

I look out the window and notice the sky. I wonder what a bird feels like soaring through the sky without the slightest notion of falling. Can I ever get to that place? Will I ever get to that place? So high in the sky, far away from the doubts I place upon myself. I mean, what if all this continues? Can I endure it?

I place my dirty dishes into the sink and almost race back to her room. I grab a purple damask journal on her dresser and run outside. I race down the stairs, through the living room to the front door. The warm sun kisses my face and I embrace her warmth, walking into her enveloping arms. I sit down on the porch and write until my doubts flooded the pages. Here's what I came up with:

Secrets

banished to a place dark and deep in my head,
isolated from the thoughts that swirl and spread
locked away tight in maximum security,
a place where no one can coerce them out of me.
when my secrets are safe I can breathe, I can sleep;
I can relax, live life, and sleep in peace.
I visit them occasionally when I wander too far,
and find that my doors sit slightly ajar.
if these were to escape
I could make do with the rumors, the critique, and the ache.
but I would rather them go away,
where they're safe to stay.
where I can keep my emotional relapse
at bay...

Time

silhouettes of dreams had
hidden in the shadows of the past
searching,
trying to find blue skies
Dear God, show me your light.

      Are these her thoughts....or are these my thoughts? I close the journal abruptly as I come to realize that these are my thoughts and more importantly, that someone could feel the same way that I do. I thumb through her journal and stop randomly at a page near the end of it. My eyes skim the page as my heart reads it.

Lost

stairway of heaven leads to the door of hell
tripped on an angel and down you fell
eyes of loved ones cast like a shadow on the wall
keep on blinking like you found a way to stall
palm to the door, you feel no heat
palm to your heart, you feel no beat.

    I have begun to feel emotions again; it's okay I
guess. I need to find something to do to pass the time. I
enter the house and head to the kitchen, my stomach
guiding me to it. I look up at the digital clock on the stove
reflecting in the stainless steel exterior of the refrigerator.
It reads 6:15 p.m. I didn't even notice it had gotten this
late. I open the refrigerator, open the compartment
labeled "Fruits and Vegetables" and pull out a large bag
filled with kale. I place the leafy greens on the counter
and locate the necessary materials and ingredients: extra
virgin oil, garlic cloves, salt, pepper, a garlic press, a
colander and a sheet pan. I wash my hands at the sink and
place the colander in the sink. I take the kale out of the
bag and begin to rinse it. I set it on the sheet pan in an
even layer and douse it lightly with the olive oil, salt and
pepper. I turn the dial to 350 degrees and wait twenty-five
minutes. The heavenly aroma of the earthly green fills the
kitchen; the kale chips are ready. I graze on the chips as I
return to her bathroom and prepare a bath, not before
turning the oven off though. Once the water is scalding
hot, I pour in bath salts and bubble bath. I grab a loofah
and bar of soap and drop them into the water. I remove
all articles of clothing and submerge my body into the
tub. "Aaaahh." I shallowly exhale and relax myself. I sit in
the tub until my hands and skin are wrinkly. I lather the
loofah with the soap and cleanse my body thoroughly.
Judging by the dark abyss outside my window, I am aware
it is nightfall. I exit the bathroom and retire to her
bedroom. I find pink Minnie Mouse pajamas and clothe

myself. After putting on lotion, deodorant and under garments, I retire to the kitchen to put up the kale chips and pour myself a glass of wine.

I retire to the bedroom, glass in hand. As I sip on the crimson liquid, I realize that I'm feeling just fine. Whatever's going to happen is going to happen; nothing I can do about it. As the liquid courage takes effect, I slide into bed and pull the covers up around me. I am comforted by the sound of the peace my heart is radiating and I fall asleep.

CHAPTER 22
Bitter With A Smile

I woke up with an attitude, far more bitter than I had felt previously, specifically to the vibration of an iPhone screaming one of the most vulgar alarms I had ever heard. "Wake the fuck up, wake the fuck up, wake the fu…" I managed to silence it, before it became too embarrassing to bear. I laughed to myself; "It woke me up didn't it?" I looked around at the light green and yellow walls around me, the strategically placed dark mahogany furniture, and the gray and black spotted cat stretching at my feet. I crept out of the room, and walked down the hallway, peering through the cracked door of a room with an empty bed, two cats sprawled at the foot, fast asleep.

"Great" I thought. "Home alone."

I moseyed to the bathroom and looked in the mirror. Like when is this shit going to end? But really, another girl? Curly haired, caramel skin, large eyes. Ugh, what's her name? Natalie? Yeah, Natalie, that's it. She always has a snarl in class and today I'm feeling it. I have no choice, so I might as well get it over with. I brushed my teeth and showered. Clothes, shoes, water bottle, car keys, and I was out the door. I matched the logo on the car key with a shiny silver Nissan sitting in front of the house. My attention moved to a chirping sound, it was coming from her, well, my iPhone. I checked a text from "mommy" saying "Did you leave yet? Don't forget to pick up Melanie."

And she's right; I've almost forgotten to pick her up. Again, I am surprised. I have some intuitive knowledge of who Melanie is. My ability to be and feel like the people I inhabit seems to be growing. Is it better for me in the long run that I'm getting better at this, or is that a bad sign? Doesn't immediately make a difference, but I'm wondering how much today's attitude is Natalie's and how much is mine. Whatever. I pop a U-turn on Jeffery…

"Call Melanie," I command Siri, my iPhone personal assistant.

One ring, two rings, "Come out, I'm up the street."

"Okay be out in a sec," she says, but I know that a sec is never a "sec" with Melanie.

It's painstakingly annoying when I have to wait for someone. Especially when I'm doing them a favor. Particularly when they know to be ready. But that's exactly what she does, thirty-nine seconds too many for her to come out of the house. I'm hoping patience isn't part of whatever it is I'm supposed to learn from all of this insanity.

I try not to act too annoyed when she gets in the car for her free ride to school, all at the cost of my patience and our friendship. What a wonderful way to start the day.

I pull into the parking lot, amongst the entire parking permit lacking, hand-me-down cars belonging to my classmates.

It's time for yoga. Yes, yoga. I'm guessing it was the least stressful and pathetic of the Seminars Natalie was offered as an alternative, yet mandatory attempt at a uselessly longer school day. Thanks "Mayor" Rahm.

Yoga was terrible; I sweated unnecessarily and nearly broke my wrists being a downward facing dog. What on earth was she thinking signing up for that? I'm hoping the next class isn't as pointless as the first.

I stroll across the Arts Bridge, fully aware of the dwindling gap of time allotted to get to my next class. I find my way up the stairs and peer through the window into the class, pleasantly delighted to see whom my next teacher was going to be. It was Mr. Suma, the Polish god of imagination, figuratively speaking. To say the least, I

153

really liked Mr. Suma, and gained a bit of respect for Natalie for taking his class. He's one of those teachers who remember what it was like to be in high school, contrary to all of the instructors who magically catch selective amnesia and can't possibly seem to understand why one might hate high school.

I open the door, and I'm thrilled to see that everyone is doing exactly what I expected... not a damn thing. Sure, we talked about psychology, and sure I actually grasp the general concepts, and sure we might veer off into a tangent about what drugs are best, or whether Godzilla or King Kong would win in a cage match, but I appreciated this class the most. I'm not badgered with some nonsense a teacher tries to spring upon me, hoping to catch me off guard; it's simply not going to happen here.

The bell rings, and I'm not surprised to learn that I have, in fact, not learned anything at all. I'm quite content to walk to Division knowing that my lunch period is only fifteen or so short minutes away.

I couldn't fathom how much I would hate Division until my shadow graced the corners of the doorway. The highly anticipated and repetitively annoying voice of Jenny, screaming "Natalia!" as I walk through the threshold; Mr. Mousin's inaudibly monotone voice noting that I'm obviously on time, Rebecca's overly perky stature, and Michael's annoyingly cocky face, are a lethal combination... I want to shoot myself in the foot, just to have an excuse to leave class.

There are two types of boredom. The enjoyably tolerable happiness of a free mind, i.e. Mr. Suma's class, and the horrifyingly, soul-sucking boredom of being surrounded by people you hate with no tangible routes of escape. That's Division.

1.0353476789 milliseconds from suicide, the bell rings, freeing from my bond to the ten minute pointless gathering of students, in various rooms, separated by

"Division number," to which we were all randomly assigned. I leap out of my seat as I, overwhelmed with joy, rush to the door, secretly battling myself on where I would like to spend the next forty plus minutes of my lunch period.

I walk to Blue House and Sophie, Fabio and Linda, apparently my "usual" posse, approach me. Everyone else clusters around like little hungry fish, seeing whom they can latch onto for a ride out to lunch. Linda mumbles something in her lucidly fabricated kind Asian voice, and leaves us to attend to her NHS (National Honor Society) mandatory tutoring session. What to do, what to do? We sit at our table, looking at each other, all knowing what we want to ask but not saying it.

"Not today," I say, "let's start the week off right."

Sophie looks at me disappointedly "Why? It's not like were aren't going to do it eventually."

"Nope, wait until the weekend, its only Monday. Plus, we don't have time."

"Let's get fries and smoothies."

"Okay, let's go get fries," I say, knowing I just opened up the door for so much more than fries and smoothies on our short road trip to Jubilee Juice, a small juice bar on Halsted.

We get back to school, seven minutes prior to 5th period, car keys, smoothies, and fries in hand, feeling and looking like the seniors we are. We prop ourselves in Blue House, obnoxiously ignoring the numerous posted signs warning us of "NO FOOD AND NO DRINKS." We've never been caught, and never will be. What's the harm in a little rebellion? The bell rings and no one budges, acting as if they've heard nothing at all. It's as if we all don't have to be seated in a classroom, seemingly halfway across the world, in the next two or so minutes. We each peel off, one by one, anticipating just how far we can push the envelope of Ms. Glass's tardy slips.

I get to the bottom of the staircase and the siren

like bell screeches across the intercom. I secretly hurry into the maze and around the corner, leap through the door, and slip into my seat. I made it. Or so I thought. I turn back around from pulling my notebook out of my bag to find a bright yellow slip of paper sitting on my desk awaiting my attention.

"Great, another tardy," I thought. I glare at Ms. Glass through her thick bifocals. Yes, yes I do realize that murder at this point is uncalled for, but it's still a credible option. I slump into my seat, annoyingly centered in the front row, irritably awaiting the start of class, with not one bit of intent of actually filling out this stupid form. Ms. Glass gives the class that look which means that there is probably an assignment due, so everyone rustles through their book bags, many pulling out crumpled pathetic excuses of bare minimum essays. Idiots.

I reach into my perfectly organized folder, and display a neat, college level, well composed, 100 plus percent essay on Magic Realism in Latina feminist literature. We pass them up to the front of the class like third graders and my boring teacher starts her boring lesson with-

"Today we're going to review "Magic Realism" as it relates to current literature. The question I'd like to begin with is this: How absurd do you find stories where events happen that seemingly could not happen in real life?"

Of course no one answers. I check my phone continuously, well aware that the time has yet to change. I look to my left and am stunned to see that I have my hand raised. Good old Jake, trying to rescue Ms. Glass. I'm almost intrigued as to what he has to say when I'm even more stunned when Ms. Glass calls on me.

"Natalie?"

Oh, please. Why me? I don't know, and more importantly, I don't care. I smile sweetly at Ms. Glass, then unload, "I find these kind of novels extremely tedious. What happens in them can't possibly happen in real life so what's the point of reading them?"

Ms. Glass doesn't even flinch, but there's a stillness about her that suggests she's not impressed with my opinion. I don't care.

"Jake? Can you give us your perspective?

Oh, no, she didn't.

"Novels that contain Magic Realism are important because they add grist to the mill. They challenge us by challenging our perception of reality and forcing us to consider that we have become too jaded and perhaps too fossilized by our current notion of reality."

"Fossilized?" Am I for real? The bell rings and I can't believe how irritated I am with myself.

I run to my sixth period class, Accounting, knowing that I would have absolutely no tasks to perform. We sit in class and listen to "the hen" as I like to call the teacher, whose name must not be mentioned. You're probably thinking "how rude to call a teacher a hen." But trust me, if you laid eyes upon her, you couldn't possibly not note that she talks, gestures, and resembles a plump little hen. So like I said, we did nothing, and I couldn't help but sleep to pass the time.

I go to the library for seventh period, study hall, and skim through a thick, medieval looking book that I had randomly selected from the shelves. I enjoy the next forty minutes engulfed by this wonderfully crafted masterpiece, not having to look at or be bothered by anyone that I didn't find fit for a glance. Is it bad that I prefer books over people? Disappointed that the bell cut my solitude short, I prepare myself for my next and final class.

I walked into my eight period class, and am immediately annoyed to see Mrs. Ellsworth sitting at the front desk. I cringe remembering her from my sophomore year of geometry. You can quote me when I say that I learned absolutely nothing from that class. I force myself to throw a weak attempt of a smile her way, and find my seat, grateful that a much larger student sat in front of me, blocking her view of me. Good one, Natalie, good one. "You get a brownie point for teacher evasion" I say mimicking an actual conversation with the person whose body I've stolen for the day. Slightly satisfied with Natalie's ways of thinking, I put my head down waiting for the bell to alert me that it's time to leave and go home.

I hop in the car not a second later than 3:40, relieved that I am freed from such a wearying day. I was beyond tired of the numerous, exasperating teachers, all of whom, for the most part, had some aspect that I detested. I was just happy to go home and go to sleep to erase them from my mind.

When I arrived home, I skimmed through my homework, and pushed most of it back into my bag, knowing damn well that I wasn't actually going to touch it again for the rest of the night. I'd much rather prefer to lie back on my bed and try to assess the events of the day. As I start to drift off to sleep I can't help but notice how much I've come to feel the emotions of Natalie.

CHAPTER 23
Hard Work And Family

I woke up to this little girl screaming "NeNe!" Obviously a nickname, I have no clue who I am today. Oh, well. Time to start our day I guess.

"NeNe, it's time to get up. Come on, you're going to be late."

"What? Who are you? Where am I?"

The girl let out a slight giggle and whispered, "I see you're really tired," and then she left out the room. I jumped out of the bed and looked around the room. I saw a little blue mirror on the closet door and went over there to see myself. "Whaaaat?" I wasn't looking back at myself. I reached up to my face and began to feel it. The reflection was doing the same thing. "Wait! This is me? Or her? This is that girl, umm, umm, what's her name?" I thought for a second, "First row on the left side, Jones, De, De, Denise!" That's her name, Denise Jones!"

"NeNe! What are you doing? Hurry up!" A motherly voice yelled through the walls.

"Uh, okay."

I was surprised at how much higher my voice was. Well, her voice. Higher than Natalie's. "Well, I guess this is supposed to be some type of life lesson or whatever," I thought. "Or! Maybe I'm supposed to do some type of charity thing and somehow better her life." I looked at the window and realized I was on the South Side.

"Oh, Lord! She definitely needs some help, especially living out here." I rumbled around the room just to get a feel of it.

"They must not be as financially stable as my family and obviously she doesn't have any type of cleaning services."

I went over to the old looking dresser and picked out any shirt and pants. There wasn't much that I would

159

like, but I had to remember "you're not yourself right now."

I walked back to the closet and opened it to find a mess of junk. "Where are her shoes?" I looked around for a bit, dodging all heels until I found some decent Ed Hardy's. "This will have to do." I walked out the room into a long hallway.

"Good morning!"

"Good morning, NeNe."

"You're gonna be late."

All of these little girls, four to be exact, were scrambling around getting ready for school and constantly talking to "NeNe," well, me. It was weird.

"Good morning guys, I mean girls," I replied to them. I went down the hall slowly, so I could figure out where the bathroom was. Once I found it, I looked around to try to guess which toothbrush I could use. "Umm, I am not going to use any of these used toothbrushes."

The mother walked past the bathroom so I decided to ask her, "Uh, mom, where are the extra toothbrushes?"

"Girl ain't nothing wrong with your toothbrush. Y'all just got them from the dentist last weekend."

"But..."

"No, hurry up and finish in there, I need to do my hair."

"Okay."

"What?"

"Okay?"

"NeNe, you know its "yes, mam" and "no, mam," don't act brand new."

"Sorry, yes, mam."

She then gave a little smile and reached over to kiss my cheek. "Ewww." This family was strange, too strange for me.

I decided to use my fingers instead; I couldn't

160

bear the thought of using her toothbrush in my mouth, well her mouth, well, whatever. After I was done, I decided to walk downstairs and see what new things I would come across.

Surprisingly, they had a very nice house. Everything was clean and put in place, but still not even close to how nice my place was. I still had to give them credit; for the South Side, in my head, this was good. "Okay, I do have to go to school. I should go back upstairs to the room to get her book bag." I walked back upstairs, careful not to cause too much of a scene so I could just get the bag and get out of there.

"NeNe, you still here? Aren't you supposed to been gone?"

"Uh, yeah. I'm just, uh, I forgot something in my room."

"Your book bag?"

"Yeah. I'm leaving now."

These kids were too nosey for me; I don't know how Denise handles it. I rushed into the room and found the book bag right by the door. Just as fast as I got the bag, I was out the door into the cold winter weather. "Okay, now, since everything in my life is different, I'm guessing she has no car." I looked on the street, which was not as bad as I would have guessed and saw no car parked in the front. "Well, that's a no." I had taken CTA before from this area, so I knew I could get on the train and get out on Jackson. Since this is the South, I probably am going to be getting on the Red Line. "Ugh." I walked over to the nearest busy street, which was 87th and I scoped around to see where the bus stop was to take me to the train. "Okay, across the street." I walked over there right before a bus came. "Hold on, how am I supposed to get on this bus with no money." I mean, I have money of course, but does she?" I reached into the book bag and found a little blue wallet. I crossed my fingers and opened it to find a CTA student riding permit. I put it into the machine and we were on our way.

The ride to school was a hard one. I never had a seat on the bus nor train, and there were a lot of cranky people all over the place. When I got to the Blue Line Jackson stop, I felt a little sense of relief. I finally was in a place of familiarity. This short black girl came running towards me and gave me a hug.

"Hey!"

"Hello?"

She let out a giggle. "I love you girl. So how was your night?"

"You would never guess." If only someone knew what really was going on.

"Tell me! Tell me!" She laughed again.

This girl is too energized, too early in the morning. "I'll explain later, right now, I'm tired."

"Oh, okay." She seemed a little disappointed. But oh, well, she didn't feel as bad as I did at the moment.

As I walked into school, the anxiety kicked in. I took out her ID and saw that she had second period Work Study class with Mrs. Lewis. "Work Study? Ah, shit. I have to actually work, especially like this? What's next?" I walked into the room and saw a few people that looked familiar, but no one I could socialize with. I took a seat up front and was quickly moved by a guy because it was his seat.

"Where's mines?" I said.

"Right back there?" I could tell he thought I was dumb, because I should've known where my seat was, well, her seat, whatever.

I didn't do anything in class and just told people that I wasn't feeling like myself today, so to not bother me. I guess that these three girls Nakiya, Alex, and Ashanti are very close to her, because they kept trying to talk to me and ask what was wrong. I've never really had people be that interested in my well-being. The only thing my parents worried about were my grades.

Next, I had Contemporary History. It kind of was an interesting class. All we, well, they did, was have a lot of informative discussions. For a moment, just a slight one, I forgot all about my "situation" and just thought I had walked in on an interesting discussion. Division was Division and then I had art. That flew by, too. My last class was Ms. Glass Inter. Writing class. This is the class that I had with Denise. This is the class I was most familiar with. "Whew. Some type of break." I began to walk over to my normal seat, and then realized "you're not normal right now." I did know where Denise sat so I just went over to sit down. As I began to slouch down in the seat to avoid anyone, Ashanti came and sat next to me. *"Please don't talk to me."* I thought. I hoped she wouldn't say anything, but hopes do fail.

"Hey." She said to me as soon as she sat down.

"Hi."

"Why are you so dry today?"

"Dry?"

"You bland as fuck, my nigga!

"What!?"

She let out a small laugh. "I love you Denise. You be having me dying laughing.

"Right." I said with the straightest face I could.

"What are we doing today?"

"I don't know. I don't feel good today, not like myself. So I'm just going to sit here."

"Girl please, you betta get that shit together. Niggas got work."

"Can you stop saying that word?" She laughed again. So after that I just tuned her out. I pulled out one of Denise's notebooks that was titled "Writing" and wrote down the word of the day and definition and quote. Ms. Glass started talking, but I was too consumed into my own thoughts. I had Ashanti rambling on to my right and I knew after this class I had work. As soon as 11:50 hit, Ashanti was ready to be on her way to work.

163

"Why is this girl so energetic? Why are all Denise's people so crazy?" Ugh.

I guess Ashanti and me ride to work together, so I just let her take the lead on our route.

"Where do I get off again?"

"Have you not been doing this shit for the last four months?"

"Right, but, I, uh, am, confused tight now. A lot on my mind."

"Clark and Lake, dumb ass."

"Yeah, right, thanks." She was getting very irritating to me. I can see Denise and I can't have the same friends.

I got off at Clark and Lake and asked one of the CTA attendants where Kirkland & Ellis was. He led me in the right direction and I began walking. "I hope I don't get this girl fired."

I looked into the book bag again to look for some type of ID to let me into the building. I found it in her black purse. "Here you go, don't screw up." I got in and figured out I had to go to the 9th floor. When I got there, I had no idea where to go. I had to get my ID back out to let me into the doors where the cubicles were. A guy walked past me and mentioned they fixed my computer.

"Thanks. Um, wait, where again?"

"Where what?"

"Is the computer?"

"Right down there, where your office is."

"Yeah, yeah, I know, thanks."

I walked over to where he pointed to and just sat in the chair. I had no idea what I was supposed to do. So I just sat. A fairly old man came by and asked what I was doing.

"I forgot my login for the systems, sir. He laughed. "It's been quite some time you've been with us Denise. How could you forget your login?"

"Um, I'm sorry?"

"Well don't worry about it; username is smithdam and the password you wrote down by your desk. When you do get settled we have meetings all day, so bring your laptop and meet me in room 920."

"Okay." This was going to be a long boring day. I still had homework, too! Well, technically I didn't, she did, so I was confused if I should do it or not. "Okay, you're at work, not school." The meetings dragged and the few times they did ask for my comments I just rephrased things other people said. It seemed to be working. I got off at five; I learned that from Ashanti earlier. So after I got off, I followed my same route to go back to Denise's place. I hated this. I felt a buzzing sensation coming from my bag and realized her cell phone was in there. When I looked at it, a person named Mari was calling. I picked up.

"Hello?"

"Yeah, NeNe, choir rehearsal is cancelled. Ma just said go straight home and clean up and make the kids dinner."

"Ohh kay?"

"Alright, bye."

Before I could even get my goodbye out, she had already hung up. By this time I was back on the train heading south. I began to wonder and feel nosy, like her annoying little sisters. So I pulled the phone back out and decided to go through it. She had a lot of texts. The ones that stood out to me were the couple from a person by the name of "Boopie." I'm going to guess and say that is her boyfriend. "*Boopie*"? What kind of nickname is that? See, that's why I don't have time to be in relationships, especially if a girl is going to call me that." From the looks of the texts he sent, it seemed that he was pretty upset he hadn't heard from Denise, well, me, whatever. So I texted him back and just said I was a friend and that she didn't have her phone with her. He quickly responded with

"Okay, thanks, I'll try her sister's phone." I didn't want to cause a breakup, so I felt as if I had really done a good deed. Once I got back to the house, after knocking on the door for what seemed like hours, I went upstairs and put all my stuff down. I tried to lie down because my day seemed too long, and Denise is a very busy person. "I don't know how she handles all of this." As I climbed into the bed slowly, I heard footsteps running up the stairs and I hoped they weren't destined to come to the room I was in.

"NeNe, when you gone make us dinner?"

"Oh shit!"

"Ooh, I'm telling mommy." She let a smirk run across her face as if she had the biggest secret to tell.

"Ugh. I'm sorry." I began to get tired of apologizing to everyone. "Just make you guys something fast. I'm tired."

"Okay!" She seemed thrilled to be given the power to cook for herself.

I don't know exactly how it happened. I knew that all I had to do was go to sleep and I wouldn't be in this mess anymore. All I do know is that I was woken up again to screaming in my face. I knew it was the mother and it was only 9:27 PM. "What else?" I was too tired for this.

"What are you doing!? Why didn't you do what I told you to do? My house looks a mess and you're just up here laying down, not doing shit."

"I'm sor..." She didn't even let me get my words out before she rudely interrupted me.

"No! Get your ass up and go clean my house!"

"Okay."

"What!?"

"Oh, yes ma'am." This was beyond horrible. I felt as though my body couldn't even find the strength to get out the bed, but I was too scared of the mom to try to keep lying down. She stared me down all the way until I started walking down the stairs. I asked the girls what did

I have to clean and they just told me to straighten up the living and dining rooms. And so I did that. After all of that I wasn't even thinking about food, and I realized I hadn't eaten all day. There wasn't even any time in her day to eat. I don't know how she does it.

I went back up to the room and laid down, clothes on and all. I didn't care. All I was thinking about was to sleep, and hopefully waking up in my bed. And if not mine, anybody else's.

I thought about this day and how weird it was. The many different types of people I encountered. How people acted towards me and treated me. How much I had to juggle today and maintain. I never would have known all that she has to deal with by just looking at her in class. I mean, I saw her with her dressy clothes every day, but didn't know she worked downtown at a law firm. I thought that was just her style. I had heard that she was kind of goofy, but wouldn't have thought she had skills to get such a prestigious job and juggle it with school and home. This was crazy. Denise, well me, whatever, had a life that would kill most people.

CHAPTER 24
Bullied

I wake up by the alarm endlessly ringing 'til I am able to drag my body across the room to turn it off. I'm hoping this body-switching nightmare will end soon. I mean, seriously, of all people, why do I have to go through all this? Why not Natalie? Why doesn't she have to go through this? But, then again, maybe she is. Maybe I should ask her. Maybe I shouldn't. Yeah, forget it. I'm not doing that. Too big a risk. Just get through today. Today should be better than yesterday; yesterday was pretty close to hell. At least I'm a guy.

I scan the room and see blue walls, textbooks all around the floor, some candy, a black and white desk with a laptop sitting on it, and I find some clothes that are thrown onto a chair that looks as if they were preset for today. I grab the clothes that are lying out and as soon as I exit his room I see the bathroom just to my right. I turn on the lights and I am temporarily blinded until my eyes are able to adjust. I see my face in the mirror and think about whose body I am actually in. After a while I finally recognize that I am Frank. I don't really see this kid talk much in class, but I occasionally see him in the hallways talking to his friends.

I hop into the shower and cleanse myself. The water is refreshing; by the time I get out I am more alert and awake. I get out of the shower, dry off, and then put on my clothes. I don't really like what he has put together for today, but I guess it will have to do. I mean it is just for a day. I turn to the sink about to brush and then I realize something is on his teeth. What is it? I look in the mirror and see that he has Invisalign on his teeth. I try to take them off so I can brush but it is a lot harder than I thought it would be. There are attachments making it harder to come off and it hurts. I can't imagine having to deal with doing this every day. After about two minutes of trying, it finally comes off. I can now brush to get the nasty morning breath feeling out of my mouth. Once that's done I grab his backpack and head downstairs. His body guides me to the computer to check the bus times for the bus.

I miss the first bus and I have to wait about ten minutes for the next one. When I see the bus tracker says that it's about five minutes until the bus reaches my stop, I leave. It takes approximately seven minutes until I have to get off and transfer to the Blue Line stop, Belmont. I walk to the other end of the station because that side will be closer to the school and I will not have to walk as much when I arrive. I have to wait for the UIC train to pass and then wait for roughly ten minutes so I can get on the train that will take me to school. While waiting, I look up and see how long until I reach Racine. It is quite a long ride. *"Another kid with a long commute,"* I thought. It's not the longest commute I've had but it is still something I don't really like doing.

There are few seats open and there are more people boarding the car than there are seats open. I want a seat because I am tired from staying up all night doing homework. Also there is nothing to do on the train so sleep is the best option. Frank's body has adjusted to naps on the train, so when I'm close to the stop I wake up and stay awake until we arrive. I get off the train, walk up the ramp and head towards school. Since I am at school early, I am able to listen to music. I look into his backpack and find a book to read. When the bell rings I go to his second period class, Anatomy.

Anatomy is an easy class. It is a basic review of Biology and Chemistry with some relation to Anatomy. The class right now is not a challenge to me and it is not a challenge to him, either. The teacher hands out a worksheet and tells us to read through it before we start.

I get to the instructions and I find out we are coloring in this worksheet. Is this a joke? A high school class where you have to color in a picture to get a grade that isn't an art class? In a way, I feel sorry for Frank because he probably expected to actually learn anatomy.

The next class I go to is AP Environmental Science. It is the only class that has a direct relation to Frank's interest. We listen to the lecture our teacher gives for the whole period. Before I know it class is over and it's time to go to Division.

I am slightly worried because Division is mostly socializing so I need to be careful to make sure people don't suspect that I'm not Frank. On the other hand, I've been able to act as if I was another person for the past twenty-three days, so today shouldn't be too hard. I seem to know Franks friends; we have a short conversation and after ten minutes fourth period begins.

Frank's fourth period class is AP Physics. Our day in that class seems pretty typical. It is a short lecture and then some practice AP problems that we do in groups. The people who I'm working with joke around half of the time. Only one other person knows what they're doing so the other people of the group mess around and then copy our work. I didn't mind.

My fifth period class is my writing class with Ms. Glass. We begin by doing a journal. I look through his and see that he rants about something in it every day. I see that Frank has some small troubles with his parents and with some of his friends. He seems to be troubled by them constantly and is irritated by them. After about ten minutes the time to be writing journals is over and Ms. Glass says, "Take out *Like Water for Chocolate*."

She begins the class discussion by saying " Yesterday we ended class with Jake suggesting that it's important that we read novels that include Magic Realism in them, otherwise, we might become fossilized by their current perception of reality. Would anyone care to comment?"

Surprisingly, a couple of students raise their hands and she calls on Zach in the back corner of the room, who says, "I think Jake is a fossil." The room laughs and I look over and see myself shaking my head, not out of anger but of chagrin. Almost as if to say in body language, "Who are these people and how am I required to sit in the same room with them?"

I'm disappointed in myself. Why did I use the word "fossilized" yesterday and why can't I just appreciate Zach giving me a little grief for it?

Ms. Glass redirects the class. "Let's go back. Can anyone give me a good example of Magic Realism in *Like Water for Chocolate*?"

There is a short silence and the students look around at each other and then a daring hand goes up by a student who is a bit nervous about answering. "Well… there is this time when the character Tita cries tears of sorrow while making frosting for a wedding cake and her tears fall into the frosting mix and uhhh when the people at the wedding eat the cake they feel sick and sad."

"Yes. Now how exactly is that magic realism?"

Another student says "If someone were to cry in real life and have their tears fall into the frosting, at most the frosting will just be a little salty. The tears are nothing that will make a person sick or sad. But in the story the tears had sadness and sorrow and that made the guests sick. We know that it would not happen like that because it is unrealistic, but as we are reading we accept the fact that things like that can happen."

Can they? I'm beginning to wonder. We continue to talk about *Like Water for Chocolate* for the remainder of the period: coming up with more examples, talking about the plot of the story, and Ms. Glass answered any questions people have. Although I couldn't understand why there were any questions. I thought the concept was simple and the story made perfect sense.

171

The next class is AP Calculus. This class is quite challenging because it is hard to pay attention. Frank generally gets very sleepy in this class. The teacher's tone is soft and he has a pretty strong Chinese accent, which makes it harder to understand what he is saying. He is very good at math, but he is not good at being able to simplify how the math should be done for students to understand. By this time it is twelve o' clock and I have been up for roughly six hours and I haven't eaten a thing. I am starving. I look into my backpack desperate for something that I can eat. I find some candy and eat all of that while listening to the teacher. It isn't much, but it is all I have.

To make my math class even worse there is a big student named George who bullies me. He messes with my papers just enough to annoy me and have me lose focus, but he never does anything that would ruin my notes and homework. I'm thinking it would be fine, but when the class is over and no physical harm has come, I get up and my feet can't really move much. I find out he has tied my shoes to the desk at some point when I didn't notice. I am angry with him for that, but my host body instinctively takes over in a panic to get to the next class on time. I dig into his bag and grab a pair of scissors and cut the laces. I check his watch to see that there is enough time to make it to his next class by power walking. I find out that he was trying to make sure that he maintained his perfect attendance. That is actually somewhat impressive: being able to make it to school every day and on time to every class.

After that, I have lunch. I look into Frank's wallet in hope that I can finally eat, but to my disappointment I see that he doesn't have any money. I end up going out to lunch with his friends anyway. The topic of human cannons is brought up and people aren't really sure what shooting mechanisms are used to launch the person. We all know it can't be gunpowder like a typical cannon so we come up with the answer of either a spring or a pressurized cannon. Someone takes out their phone and finds out the answer can be either of the choices we came up with. We leave fifteen minutes before the bell for ninth period and then play some ping pong till the bell rings.

Ninth starts and I find out that art class is the last class of the day. We spend the whole day working on an art piece. We have to use the concepts of value scale into a drawing of an object that was preset on the table. I am not artistically talented, and neither is Frank, so the drawings we ended up with were mediocre.

The school day over, I am relieved that I can finally go home. Frank's body doesn't take me to go to the train, however. He goes to Asian American Club. The members of the club are practicing the dance for the show that I always hear about, but never attend at the end of the year. I find out he is the head of one of the dances and in another. I am the head of the flag dance. Sounded simple enough. Just wave around a flag. Turns out it was harder than it looks. Turns out there's spinning and tricks to do with the flag. I don't know how the dancers do it. Luckily Frank knows how. I'm impressed. Halfway through I leave my dancers to practice on their own and go to practice another dance I'm in. Around 4:30 the Club is over and I head to the train to go home. I arrive at his house around 5:30.

I am incredibly hungry, so I rush over to the kitchen and grab some dinner that his parents have cooked before he got home. I take it upstairs to eat. It doesn't look like they ever eat as a family. That's sad. Not eating with your family and not really being a family at dinner time. They just grab their bowls and go separate ways.

Because I cannot do my homework while eating, I log on to Facebook, and then YouTube to watch some videos. Once I finish eating, I return the dishes to the kitchen and begin to do my homework. My homework includes physics problems, calculus problems, an anatomy worksheet, a reading for environmental science, and finishing *Like Water for Chocolate*. Right as I pull out my homework to begin working on it, I hear a shout from a little girl, who I am assuming is his sister, "FRANK!!!!!"

"Yes?"

"Can you help me with my math homework again?"

"Alright!" I say intuitively.

I head downstairs to see what she needs help with. It's basic algebra that I have been doing for years now. I think that this will be fast. Algebra is easy. Boy, am I wrong; it's not nearly as fast I thought it would be. Something that is so simple and makes complete sense to me is very confusing to her. After about ten frustrating minutes of trying to tell her how to do it, I make a connection to her. I tell her that she should think of the problems as if the variable represented an object that can hold a certain amount. It is a simple way for her to picture what the problem means. After that she's able to do the work on her own. I give her some extra practice problems to make sure she understands what to do. When she understands all she needs to know about basic algebra for today, I go back upstairs to begin my homework.

I look up at the clock and see that it is seven o'clock and I haven't even started to do homework. I'm able to do the physics problems pretty easily except for two questions around the end. The calculus problems are hard at first then eventually the concept becomes much easier to grasp. The readings take about an hour and a half altogether including the notes I take.

When all that is done it is around midnight and I am relieved to finally be going back to bed. I brush my teeth as well as insert my Invisalign and then I tuck myself into bed. I play music as I fall asleep. I realize this

174

will be the last few minutes I am going to be conscious in Frank's body. As I close my eyes, I think about how much I hate being bullied. My mind drifts and I think about whose body am I about to go into next. I try and think about who's left in my fifth period class and whether or not I'd rather be a girl or a guy. I feel myself drifting as I struggle to try and remember what it was like to be Jake.

CHAPTER 25

Back To The Pool, Considering My Options

This time I wake up alone in a dark room. I feel pretty comfortable. This kid has a bunch of pillows and has made a dent in his bed with his body. I kind of don't want to leave. I like his bed better than Frank's. Couldn't stop thinking about being bullied. I lay there thinking about what might happen today. Then I hear someone open the door and turn the lights on in the room. My mother, no doubt, is telling me to get out of bed and get dressed.

"Hurry up and get dressed," she said. "We're already late."

"For what?"

"You have morning practice. You told me last night I had to wake you at 5:30."

"Whatever you say." After that, I get out of bed and go to the kitchen. I have some Frosted Flakes that were in the cabinet. I go into the bathroom and brush my teeth and do my hair. This is the first time I get a look at my face for today. I have an above average face. I'm more handsome than ugly, but not by too much. I've got straight teeth and a decent smile. My hair is short and I have medium to dark brown hair that is going in every direction right now. After combing it, I leave the bathroom. I pick up two backpacks after I look inside of them. One is a school backpack and the other has workout stuff.

"Let's go!" I hear my "mom" yell. "Your dad is already in the garage."

I walk out the door following her. As I'm walking out, I see some girl still sleeping. I guess I have a sister.

"Ya nos vamos?" I heard my "dad" say when I got into the car.

"Yeah," I shrugged. We leave the garage and I put on some headphones I found in the room. I start some music and look at the clock. It says 6 AM. I'm guessing this kid doesn't live too close to the school. After that, I sleep on the way to school since it's still dark out. When I wake up we are already there. I look at the clock and it says 6:40, so I'm late to this practice. When I walk inside, I hear someone yell something to me. I see him running from the other side of the hallway.

"Hurry up, Ramon! We're late. Coach is gonna be pissed." He says.

"Okay, okay." I respond.

We walk in to the locker room together and change into our workout clothes. We run outside on to the pool deck. I see that the others have already started. I start running.

"Hurry the hell up! You're supposed to be on deck at 6:30! Wake up ten goddamn minutes earlier!" I hear Coach Parnell yell.

We start running around the pool and up the stairs. It looks kind of like a figure-8 when I think about it. After ten minutes of that, we start running up and down the stairs in the bleachers. This part is a little harder since some kids who look like freshman look like they are going to fall down the steps. I just run right pass them; really hoping they don't crash into me. It's a tough workout but I push through it. I think maybe having been Augie and Matt for a day has made me a bit better at this. After that, the coach has us do some drills on the side of the deck.

"First, you're gonna do high knees to the other end. Then run around the back and do high knees on the other side." He says.

We do it in two's and my partner can't really keep up with me. When I see, I slow down a little. We finish one side and run around to do the other. Then, we finish and head back to the coach.

"Now, you're gonna do grape vines. Do them there and back and do them correctly," he says when we are all back.

I start and go at the pace of my partner for the whole time. After that, the coach tells us to do lunges and high jumps. We do three laps of lunges around the pool, which is incredibly hard after that run. After we finish, we go down to the weight room. We get down there and the coach tells us to gather round.

"Okay. It's more of the usual today. It's mainly squats, bench pressing and lat' pull downs. We also have stuff with the medicine balls and the rubber weights. Do the warm up and then get started."

We group together and do the warm up. It's mostly stretching with light weights to make sure we don't pull something during the workout. Then, we disperse and I follow the person I saw earlier in the hallway. We get started with the weights. We go to the squats first.

"Damn," he says. "You're going hard today. You sure that's not too much weight for you?"

"I can handle it. I feel pretty good today," I say.

It's not too bad lifting this weight, but it still gives me a challenge. My partner seems thrown off by what I'm doing. I guess I'm a little stronger than he is, but not by too much.

After a while, the coach says "Okay guys, it's time to head upstairs."

All of us go upstairs and head into the showers. I change into a swimsuit like everyone else and shower. When I get out and finish changing, it's already 7:55. I hurry up and head to my locker. I check my ID to see what class I have first. I see that I have Honors Anatomy and Physiology with Mrs. Smithson. I go to the class and just hang out. We get the same worksheet I had the other day and I work through it kind of quickly. After I'm done, I help the person next to me since he is having trouble. I try not to give him the answers so he can learn, and I'm trying not to confuse him.

"Wow. Are you sure you two want to hand it in that early?" Mrs. Smithson asks.

"Yeah. It wasn't that hard to finish. We worked through them together," I tell her before sitting back down.

I see that everyone takes a little while longer to finish his or her sheets. More than one person asks me for help. I read my book when I'm done helping with any questions.

After that, I head to Honors Law with Mrs. Holzhauser. We get settled down after a couple of minutes and delve into a debate about the legislative intent of laws.

"So, class," she says, "who can tell me what the legislative intent of the law is?"

No one answers, so I help the conversation along.

"It's the debate about what the law actually meant versus the wording of the law. It deals with exceptions and things like that."

"Very good. Now why is this a debate?" She asks the class.

After that, I sit back and just listen to the conversation. I want to see what everyone else thinks about this. When the conversation slows, Mrs. Holzhauser asks another question and the sound of crickets enters the room. I wait a few minutes and then jump in with an answer. It feels good. The bell rings and I head to Division. I wait ten minutes, not really talking to anyone since I have my headphones on. After Division, I head to Art with Ms. Yanny-Tillar. We get to work on our sketches. I really like what the other people are drawing. I flip through my book and see that "I" have been getting better over the year. When the bell rings, I head to Ms. Glass's class. We're still talking Magic Realism. I enjoy the class, but something keeps nagging me while I'm listening. Up next is Honors Accounting. I walk into the classroom and sit down in my seat.

Ms. Meyers says, "Today, we are going to balance more T-accounts. Remember about debit and credit. Always remember that debits equal credits."

Then, she hands out a sheet with a list of accounts. I fill in the titles for all of them and I grab my book.

"The transactions are on page 78." Ms. Meyers begins. "Okay, get started."

I pour through it just like in Anatomy. It was kind of easy since everything is just straightforward. When I'm done, I walk to the front of the class and turn it in, dropping it in the work basket.

"That was quick," I hear Ms. Meyers say.

"Well, it was kind of easy. It's just making sure everything is in the right spot. And you taught us well." I'm not sure where that came from.

I sit down and read my book for the rest of the period. My last class for that day is Honors Probability and Statistics. I look in my notebook and see Ramon has already done the work for today. I guess he works ahead in this class. When the bell rings, I go to my locker. I put my books in and take out what I need for homework, which is nothing. Some people call me over.

"So, where do you guys want to go for lunch?" one of the guys asks.

"How about Billy Goat's?" someone who I've seen in the halls suggests.

"Why not?" I agreed.

We start walking there. I put my headphones on and just walk, staying out of the conversation of the others. When we arrive, we order and start to eat. After finishing quickly, I sit there and just watch the TV while everyone else eats. Around 2:20, we start to walk back. When we get inside, I go to my Seminar, which is watching *The Simpsons*. We watch an episode where

Homer goes back to the pre-historic times. After it ends, I go upstairs to pick up the last of my things. I'm caught by another group of friends and I end up riding the bus and train with them. We just talk on the way back. It's mostly about shows on Netflix and what we should watch. I get off at Kedzie on the Orange Line. I start heading home, which is a ten-minute walk. I'm the only one there when I arrive. I look at the clock as I walk in and it reads 4:51.

I head to my room and turn on the TV. I see that there's an Xbox, so I turn it on. I played Modern Warfare 3 for two hours. Although back in the day I was terrible at it, I impress myself now. After that, I go to the kitchen and heat up some chicken that is in the fridge. I keep playing MW3 until my parents get home. I look at a clock in the room and it says 8:30. They are a little surprised I'm not doing homework.

"Do you want to eat?" they ask.

"Nah. I ate some chicken earlier. Thanks for asking."

After that, they leave my room. I watch TV until 10:30, at which time I turn it off and get ready for bed. I lay there thinking about my day. It wasn't that bad. Ramon doesn't seem to have a bad life. I kind of like his habits. He has settled into a nice little rut, and I although I don't completely like that, I do like the stability of his life. After a couple of minutes, I snuggle into my covers and ask myself, "If I had to stay as any of the people I've been so far, who would it be?"

181

CHAPTER 26
Perfect Chinese

I woke up and looked straight at the clock. It was 6:28, and my alarm hadn't gone off. I don't hesitate to go back to sleep. *Beep! Beep! Beep!*

"Ugh, 6:45 already," I moaned. "Wait, is that the fire alarm?" I smelled smoke.

"*Ahh!!!*" I screamed.

"The house is on fire, everyone get out!" I yelled.

As I ran outside in my boxers, it was cold and snowy. I should've grabbed some clothes. I thought to myself, "Where are my parents?" I started to worry but then I saw them coming down the stairs from outside. All of a sudden … the roof collapsed! I fell to the ground in tears. My eyelids were watery and I could feel the droplets freezing on my face. I couldn't feel anything, and I was probably getting frost bite. The firefighters pulled me back and the paramedics put me in the ambulance for warmth. I cried and cried. I heard a firefighter tell the cops my parents didn't survive. If I had gotten up at 6:28 instead of 6:45, I might have seen the fire, and I could have saved them. The scene of the house collapsing played over and over in my head, my parents lost right before my eyes.

"Screw the world, screw this country, and screw my life." I yelled.

I searched the ambulance, rummaging through their supplies and found a scalpel.

I announced, "I'm coming home, guys," and stabbed myself right in the heart.

RING! RING! RING! I woke up again and shut off my alarm. I thought, "Am I alive? Where am I? Is this a second life?" I had no idea where I was, but I did know I didn't have the Xbox anymore and I was in a new home.

"The fire was just a dream. Thank God." I thought, hitting the snooze button on the alarm, not feeling ready to get up.

It was 6:45, so I went to the bathroom, and showered. I got ready and walked out of my house to go to school. Right as I got out the house, my stomach started growling. I looked around and saw hundreds of Asians on the street. They were talking to each other in all their different dialects. They were all crowded in a circle. I walked over and saw they were all trying to get free food. I tried pushing my way through. I was starving and nothing could stop me. When I got to the middle, all the food was gone. The Asians around me were talking to each other, and looking at me in a weird way. Either I had a booger on my face or maybe they had never seen a white boy before. I went up to one of them pointing at me and asked, "Yow mo see goone?" (Is there a problem?)

I knew how to speak Chinese from school. I was in AP Chinese this year and have been taking it since freshman year. Not only was I in this AP class, but I was in four total AP classes.

The man replied, "Ney yow mo som!" (You have no clothes on!)

I looked at myself, and realized I had nothing on but my boxers. I ran back in the house and put on some sweats on. How embarrassing, I thought. How could I have possibly left the house without wearing….RING! RING! RING!

I looked at the clock it was now 7:00. I got up for real this time and hustled out of the house as quickly as possible.

I found a corner bakery and got a pork bun to eat. I devoured the sandwich. I checked the time; it was 7:36.

"Crap!" I said.

I ran straight to the train. The train takes about 40 minutes to get to school and I start at 8:20. I got to the

183

train at 7:39. I felt I was going to make it on time. The train took six minutes to get to Jackson, where I transferred to the Blue Line. The Blue Line train took ten minutes to come, so I knew I would be late. When it finally arrived, the conductor announced that he was going to go on express to the Racine stop.

"My stop!" I screamed.

I got off the train and it was only 8:00. I walked the rest of the way to school. When I entered school, I had to show my ID to the security guards to get in. I went to my second period Seminar, where I just put my head down and slept. I had no interest in participating in group discussions. The bell rang and I went to my third period class, AP Calculus.

I sat down in my desk, and listened to Mr. Tzu teach. He never looked at us. He taught to the windows and we occasionally heard him. Coming to class seemed stupid, but it always seemed to challenge the other kids in the class. Calculus really wasn't hard for me to understand. All you need is a few rules and formulas, and you're set. I was tired so I put my head down, and slept the remaining 48 minutes in the class. The bell rang, and it was time to go to AP Psychology.

I got to psychology and just slept. The class was just reading, so I never listened in class. The teacher always saw me sleep, but never tried waking me up. He always saw that I got A's on all my tests, so I'm sure he thought, "Why bother him?" The bell rang and I went to my next class.

It was 5th period, and it was time for Ms. Glass's class. Still looking for clues. I remembered Jason as the guy in the back who sat and disrupted her class every day. As I took my seat the guys sitting next to me started cracking on how Ms. Glass looked. "Jason, isn't it amazing that she always has the same ugly dress on. She can change that, even if she can't change her flat face." I laughed a communal laugh with my boys, but I hadn't really ever noticed before. Maybe they were right, but I just wasn't into jumping in on that. Ms. Glass gave me a look. She'd heard us. It would have been hard not to. I decided to stare at the clock; I didn't want to make any eye contact with her, because I knew it wouldn't be pretty. When the bell rang I considered apologizing to her. I went up to her, hesitated, and then left without speaking.

AP Economics was another one of those really easy classes. The class was more like logic. The topics we talked about in class were easy to understand. My view is this: *"Economists can make up stuff and put it in books as long as they dig up statistics to back it up. So if they can research things and make conclusions, so can anyone."*

When the bell rang, I went straight to the lunch room and got something to eat. I had a chicken sandwich from the school cafeteria and, shockingly, I lived. 7th period started, so I went to my AP Chinese class.

I walked in and was somewhat awake now. My teacher started by asking if anything had happened. I replied, "Gnaw ga oek kai hy tong yun giy." (My house is in Chinatown now.)

"Bean do ney ga oek kai tow seen?" she replied. (Where was your house before?)

"Gnaw em gey duk." (I don't remember now.)

"Ney hai ho cheesy." (You're one crazy kid.)

I put my head down on the desk, and just listened to her lecture the rest of the period. She was teaching us how to make a story in Chinese. I was listening and watching all the students, trying to copy all the notes on the board. I thought to myself, "Why do Asian kids in this class have to take notes? Shouldn't they already know how to write Chinese?"

I got up when the bell rang and went to 8th period, Physical Education. It felt good to move. Jason was quite the athlete so it was fun to be asked by people to be on their team. I was sad when the final bell of my day rang. I got up and packed my stuff and went home. I walked to the train and passed by, like, ten street people. Every single one said, "Some change?"

Something inside of Jason almost came out of me. I almost replied, "Don't mind if I do," and imagined sticking my hand in their cups and taking a handful of quarters. But I didn't. I felt a sudden rush of compassion for these struggling folks, and I gave them the little Jason had. I hoped he wouldn't mind.

I got home and opened my book bag. I started doing my homework and got it done in half an hour. My head started aching, so I went to my fridge and got a bite to eat. I found a bowl of fried rice and warmed it up in the microwave. This bowl of rice could not have tasted any better, except for the fact that I had to add a bit of salt. At 4:30, I went on my computer and played Modern Warfare 3. I'm not sure if it was Jason's or Ramon's skills, or maybe a combination of both, but I was tremendous at it. I was really enjoying myself until my parents got home from work and screamed, "Get off that darn computer and start helping around the house! It's a mess around here!"

I thought about screaming "No!" and locking myself in Jason's room until morning. I mean, what could his parents do? Bust down the door? But then I thought about Jason and what it would mean for him tomorrow, and so I went down and cleaned up for a while.

Afterwards, I went to my room, locked the door, and plopped straight on my bed. I thought, "I don't know who I am any more. Inconsiderate, considerate, angry, frustrated, relaxed. Know every damn thing, don't know anything. I've got to get this under control. Otherwise I'm not going to make it."

CHAPTER 27
Party Time

My eyes opened to a small white room. All right, I was a guy again. At least there were no nightmares about fires this time... with luck, I'd get to be a goofball for a day... still, dammit, how long could this continue?

I raised my head and looked at the plain wooden shelf nailed to the wall; there was an alarm clock on it. There were some clothes hanging from the shelf as well. I looked to the right at a T.V. that was bigger than the room in the corner. I bet it was amazing for video games. The television sat on top of a dresser. There was a nightstand right next to me in bed. On the stand were a cell phone and an iPod. I picked up the phone and saw that there were missed calls and texts, but I couldn't figure out the pattern to unlock the phone. I'd have to unlock later. I looked through the iPod to see that there was only rap music. I look in the nightstand and saw an ID. I was Kleave. I knew that kid. It was great, I was a goofball! I walked out of the small room through the sliding door to a small living room.

A small, hyper white dog with black spots ran up to me and ran in circles, breathing rapidly. There was also a person in front of me, I assumed it was Kleave's mom. This is Kleave's mom's place.

She said, "Good morning!"

"Good morning."

"You hungry?" Yes, I thought. This mother gets it. I need food to succeed; I hoped she was a good cook. "Yes I am."

"Okay. Eggs, bacon and hash browns okay? And what do you want to drink?"

"Yes, that sounds delicious, and I'll take chocolate milk."

"Okay, it will be ready soon, can you walk the dog?"

I finished the conversation with "Alright."

I walked back into my room, and looked for a towel. I found one hanging up on the shelf at the head of the bed. I went to the washroom and took a shower. Afterwards, I walked back to my room and looked through the dresser. All of his clothes were too big for him. I picked a black t-shirt and wore some blue denim. I walked out past the living room to a small kitchen slash dining room. My mother had the breakfast ready. I sat down and just began to devour the food. I was starving. After I chugged my glass of chocolate milk, I walked back to my room. I finally just reset the phone and unlocked it. I got 12 missed calls and nine texts. The first few calls were from "Iain." I called him back.

"Hey what's up?" How you doin'?" he said.

"Alright, how are you?" I responded.

"Good, come over!"

"Umm, okay... Where do you live again?"

"Are you serious?"

"Yeah, I'm really disoriented right now."

"Come to Bosworth and Altgeld."

"Alright, coming over."

I grabbed a hoodie and told my mom that I was leaving. I walked over to Iain's. I called him and told him that I was there. A small curly haired blonde boy walked out and said: "What's up?" We exchanged greetings and went inside. Inside there were many other people. I was a little shocked at the number of people in this basement. I recognized a couple people from my school like Logan and Casey, but the rest were unknown. We all shook up and exchanged greetings as well. Then they all start to ask "What are we doing tonight?" We sat in a circle fashion on the couch and everyone exchanged comments and suggestions for the night's plans.

We made sure we had everything we needed for the night then headed out to get food. Deciding on food is always a big fight, it seems, no matter who you are. "I wanna get McDonalds!" said the older looking kid with brown hair.

"Let's get Mexican food, how about Taco Burrito King?" I said.

"Yeah, that sounds good." Iain agreed.

So the big group walked a couple blocks to Taco Burrito King and we entered to sit at the biggest table. I had never gone out to eat with people who were so loud. They just loved shouting and doing whatever they felt like. I can see where Kleave gets his hyper-ness from, but why like this all the time?

I kept silent because I still didn't know everyone at the table and didn't want to embarrass myself. I kept watching and thinking. They were all having so much fun, just joking and playing. It was actually nice to sit there and not take things seriously for once and just have fun. I can see why people do nothing but this with their lives; if you can balance it, this is nice.

So after some delicious tacos I headed outside with the group. Some of the kids started smoking cigarettes. They say it's so satisfying to have a cigarette after a meal.

The older looking brown haired kid came up to me, "You want a drag?" putting the cigarette in my face.

"A drag? Of the cigarette?"

"Yeah…."

"Okay." I took it from his hands and put it in my mouth and inhaled deeply. Whoa! It felt so relaxing and calming to my body. It didn't taste the great and made me cough, but it made me buzz and I could see why it's so good after a meal. It relaxes your stomach as well.

Apparently this girl was having a party on the North Side so after we finished, we all hopped into taxis and headed to the party for the night. During the cab ride, the rowdy kids just couldn't help but shout things out the window and be social with the cab driver. It was a nice environment. It was doubly pleasant because nothing was ever considered too negative, if anything, just sarcastic. Eventually, we pulled up to this big white house and all got out.

It was time to party! We walked up the stairs to the porch and there were some people having a cigarette and a beer outside, talking. They greeted us and we continued inside.

Once in, we ran into a bunch of people hanging out in a combination kitchen and living room. There were people all over, walking around, sitting on the couches or standing in the kitchen. There were even more people on the deck out back. We began to walk through with everyone greeting each other and all these people coming up to me. They all seemed happy and energetic. People were yelling across the house, jumping around and just socializing.

We moved on up some stairs, going on to find a few more rooms full of people doing seemingly nothing but having a good time. We entered one of them, and as soon as I got into the doorway, a lanky kid throws a can of beer at me from his place on a beanbag on the floor.

"Welcome, Kleave."

"Thanks."

Wow that was nice. The kid then said that we had to "shotgun" it. We chugged beers together and I was feeling it. Then, we all sat on the bed for a while and listened to music while we talked about a bunch of different things, half of which I didn't understand. I just sat there sipping on another beer.

After that we left the room and headed downstairs, but this time, all the way to the basement. In the basement was a big meeting room with a few other rooms. In the meeting room was where most of the people were. They were all sitting around on a big couch.

190

There was a giant hookah in the middle, and people were taking turns with the hoses. The different kinds of people running around this house were amazing. It's like my school, with every type of person. It was almost overwhelming.

After I finished some conversations in the basement, I headed to the back porch. On the back porch was this kid who was just kind of hanging out, not really talking to anybody and enjoying the night. He was smoking a thick, rich smelling cigar. He noticed me, then turned and said, "Hey, Kleave, my man. Take a few drags of this, it's freakin' delicious." I accepted the cigar and enjoyed the rich flavor of the smoke...it made me feel like a real boss.

We continued to sit outside and talk. I had a lot of interesting conversations with people, and even though some of those conversations were slurred, they were still quite fun. Everyone outside then headed inside and we turned up the music some more. Everyone started dancing and jamming out. As I moved through the crowd, people just smiled at me and kept on dancing. I danced a little bit, and then sat down again. I finished my beer with some people and we kept talking. Time passed and people left, and I just ended up crashing on the couch, anxious to see who I'd be tomorrow. It was a relaxing day...nice to have been a guy who let loose for a change.

CHAPTER 28
Literally Flying

"Hey, get up!" I awoke not sure what was happening. "Get out of bed; you have a race in an hour and a half!" I rolled over and looked up and saw a collage of race numbers. Not sure who I was, I focused my eyes to read the name on some of the race numbers. I finally found one I could make out the name of and realized that I was Xavier, another person in my class with Ms. Glass. I thought I was close to running out of people in there. I was scared to think of what would happen after that.

I thought about the fact that I had some race and realized this was only Sunday, so no school. Thinking back to the day before: that was one crazy day partying. Still, thanks to the body switching, no hangover! I could take my time after whatever this race was and sleep and then have an easy day for once. I could maybe have one easy day, lying back on the couch and watching some TV. I could sense that was all Xavier really wanted to do, too.

Sadly, right then, out of the hallway I heard a woman, who I assumed was Xavier's mother and the one that woke me up yelling, "And don't forget you and your dad are going to the club later today!" Darn, I almost got away with one nice lazy day, but a club didn't sound that bad either. I looked around and found a clock; it read four o'clock. No wonder I was still half asleep. I continued to survey the room, finally finding a set of clothes lying out and a set stuffed into a bag labeled 'After Race.' That solved any problem getting dressed for the day.

I started putting on my clothes and realized that they weren't something I would be comfortable wearing on myself. I was practically wearing a speedo with short legs! Oh well, not my body I was parading around, just Xavier's. I put the rest of the outfit on, used the bathroom and brushed my teeth, and headed downstairs, only to find that Xavier's mom had already made him breakfast and was shooing him out the door. Right as I got out the door I noticed a text on my phone from a contact labeled 'Charlie <3' which I went on to assume was Xavier's girlfriend since I'd seen both them holding hands in the hallways before.

I looked at the text and it said, "Goodmorning! I'm heading out to work the race so I'll see you there and say hey kay? Good luck! :)" Muscle memory must have taken effect for that one as I quickly responded, "Thanks! I'll see you there! :)." We then drove off to the race. It wasn't long before we were in downtown Chicago and I was being dropped off and told to meet my dad back at that point at 11 to go to the club.

Then I was alone, but muscle memory walked me through it as I went from check-in to the start line, dropping off my bag and clothes at gear check, and in a quick amount of time, I could feel adrenaline pumping through Xavier's body. I had no clue how long the race was until I heard the announcement on the intercom, "We will start the 5k race in 10 minutes! Get loose and have fun! And any roughhousing is an immediate disqualification." Not bad, considering I'd had to run in a couple other kids bodies before and for a lot longer. I looked around and realized that the people looked really fast and I thought, "Do I even have a chance in this at all?" The race was packed wall to wall and it looked like more than 10,000 people total. This being the only race I had been in, it was also the most packed race I'd ever seen.

Before I could measure the size of the crowd, the starter was already at *five* on the countdown. I quickly adjusted my body, thinking to myself, 'Hopefully Xavier is fast or else I'm screwed' and before I knew it the bullhorn sounded. Adrenaline was pumping me up now, as it flowed through me and got me moving faster than I had ever run before. I thought I was flying past everyone, and then I started getting passed by a few people, one by one. I looked around and realized I was still towards the front, sprinting on the side to get away from the crowd of people; Xavier was actually a pretty good runner.

I kept going, saw a 6:25 first mile; pretty good for someone who runs in his free time. Then, all of a sudden, I started feeling pain, and lots of it. I kept going. I wanted to stop, but Xavier just wouldn't stop running, even though his body hurt a lot. His feet felt like they weren't attached to his legs anymore; his legs felt like they were so sprained that he couldn't pick them up; his chest felt like his lungs were giving out, and even his arms were screaming in pain, trying to fall off of his pained body. He kept going though. No amount of pain seemed to stop him, and before I knew it, the mile 3 sign was right in front of me, and the broken down body started to sprint, knowing the finish line was a couple seconds away. His body moved faster and faster until, "With a time 21:08, Xavier Fallstitch, and right behind him…" The announcer kept going as 20 people went through the finish line in a second, listing as many names as possible with their times, and trying to say every kid's name who passed.

I looked around, the finish line was a 6-lane city street wide, 2 blocks long, and filled with after race goods. I immediately went over to the line for chocolate when all of a sudden I heard a girl scream, "Xavier!" By the time I turned around it was too late. I felt the girl jump on my back. I looked back and saw Xavier's girlfriend, Charlie, and then a couple other kids from school walking over to say "hey." Charlie gave me a kiss and said a quick congratulations and I gave her a hug back and said a quick thanks back and said "hey" to all of Xavier's friends. It felt good but I felt a little guilty. They walked me back behind the food station, since she was working there with Key Club. I looked around trying to see if I could find myself there, but evidently this was an event I deemed unworthy to attend. I found my arrogance increasingly annoying.

Charlie came up and let me sit in a seat they had since my legs were about to give out from the run. She went and got some food for me and sat with me for a bit. I looked around in exhaustion, just thinking that my day was over and I was home free and I could sit there listening to Charlie and a couple others talk about school. But then I looked at my watch and saw it was 10:30. It took me another couple minutes to realize I was supposed to meet Xavier's dad at 11 and had to go.

I tapped Charlie on the shoulder quickly said, "Sorry, I need to meet my dad in 25 minutes; I'll see you Monday, all right?" She smiled and responded, "All right, I'll see you tomorrow!" She gave me a kiss and I hugged her and walked over and grabbed my stuff and I got to the place I was supposed to meet my dad with not a second to spare. I got in the car and said, "Hey!"

Xavier's dad responded, "How did you do?"

Not knowing how this time was compared to my other races, I responded with a simple, "Fine."

By then I was about to pass out, but the last thing I remember hearing before I fell asleep for a bit was, "Good. Well, you're signed up for a flight time at 1 with Bob." What kind of club was I going to?

I awoke, startled, looked around and saw open grass fields, my dad yelling "Come on! You gotta be in the sky in ten minutes! Grab a water bottle!" What was happening? Then all of a sudden I heard a roar. Fear hit me when I saw a single engine plane, shooting out from behind a little house. What scared me worse was I realized I was not going to be in that plane, but the engineless glider being dragged from a rope 100 feet behind it.

I looked back in the car and saw a water bottle and glasses and my bag with other clothes, so I quickly

195

ran inside the little house and changed. I ran outside and my dad was signaling me to get over there. There was a golf cart right beside me so I hopped in that and drove over since I knew I had no chance at running away. I got to the little engineless plane when my dad said, "Hop in and we will launch you in a minute." What was happening? Is Xavier insane? Why would I ever?

Yet still, I hopped in, not because I wanted to, but because reflex made me. I heard someone in the backseat go, "Hey, Xavier! How's it going?"

I thought back and remembered that my dad said I was flying with "Bob." "Good, how are you, Bob?"

"Good. Now be careful this week. We are close to getting you your student license and you are gonna need to learn boxing and stalling today."

Well, I don't think you can box in a plane but I was open to the idea of stalling until it was too late in the day to fly, but it was too late; the plane was shut tight and I thought I was about to die when I looked straight forward and saw the plane with the engine speeding up and pulling us straight ahead. Almost immediately, we were off the ground; it took the other plane an extra 15 seconds but it got up and pulled us up higher and higher, then I heard, "I'll take you through the first box, second one is all you. Just feel how I do it for now."

All of a sudden, a stick in front of me started jostling around, throwing the little plane everywhere. I grabbed it and noticed that the other pilot was sliding the plane first to the left. 'Doesn't look too bad yet,' I thought, but then, not even a second of solitude before we started going down. I kept thinking, we have to go back up now; we are getting too far down; but we kept going down and down and down, still attached to the plane above. We were almost directly under it when he started going right. It felt like we were just about to die down there, but then finally he headed back up. As soon as we got right behind the plane again, my body clenched.

I didn't fear this nearly as much as Xavier was then and there. Then, my body clenched as I heard the words, "You have the controls."

Uttering back, "I have the controls," he started to go left. The little plane was shaking violently, and I could only let Xavier take the controls, hoping he knew what he was doing. Left to the far edge, he finally started his descent, but still couldn't make it nearly as far down as before. He quickly went back up, where going straight was turning into a problem for him. I heard from the back, "Close enough for now, next time we will fix those up and go over landings and 2G turns. I'll give you a 2G turn as an example later, too. How about letting go now, though? Pull the knob and turn hard right."

What did he mean, "let go?" Well, only one way to find out. I looked left and found a knob and pulled it and turned right immediately, only to find that the other plane turned left and we now were soaring through the air alone, engineless. I was surprised to feel Xavier's body loosen up; I felt free in there, but I knew I wasn't free. I was trapped in Xavier, at least until tomorrow. I heard from the back, "Do a couple stalls now. We don't have much time up here so let's hurry this up."

I felt Xavier turn left and right quickly. Then out of nowhere, we were going almost straight up. I had a feeling I wasn't going to like stalls. All of a sudden, we dropped straight down. I thought I was going to piss my pants. Xavier felt like he was having the best time of his life though. That's when it hit me, this may be horrible and terrifying to me, but this is probably one of his favorite ways to get an adrenaline rush because he has fun doing it. Still facing straight down, I started to let go of the handle and as much as I wanted to pull up, I knew Xavier was too relaxed to screw up. I let him drop it slowly, and all of a sudden, we were facing Chicago. It may have been 20 miles away but it was a sight that you love to see.

197

"That was great! But we lost enough altitude that we don't have much time for anything else. Let me do a quick 2G turn and I'll land us."

What is this 2G turn? I started to think what it was and then I felt everything start going down, and then, I was pressed up against the seat, going straight down while turning slowly. It was so terrifying I didn't think I would survive the 15 second dive, but when I looked up I saw my dad and a lot more planes a little ways from us. Then, a sweeping turn to the right, then back to my left, and another to my left again, and we were headed straight towards a mowed down strip. "Remember," I heard, "We have no engine, and the first chance is your only chance at this."

At that I was terrified; luckily I wasn't landing this week, but next week it was Xavier, and what if he was terrified about it, too? Luckily for my sake now, the landing was nice and simple. We stopped with the brakes and pulled to the side of the road using momentum. A golf cart came over and picked us up and towed us back to the house. I saw Xavier's dad come over to me and ask how it was. I said "fine" again not knowing how it normally goes, and he helped me out of the plane. I looked back and saw the other pilot. He was a little older than I thought, but I went over and shook his hand and said, "Thanks!"

He responded with a simple, "No problem! I'll see you next week."

I grabbed my stuff and followed my dad to the car, him ranting about resting up, which I take it Xavier wasn't normally too happy about, but I was fine with. I got in the car and it was already about seven. Getting up at four in someone else's body drained me; I would have been happy to fall asleep for the night right then and there. One more small task stood in my way though.

I looked at my phone and noticed another text from Charlie saying, "Good job today and I hope you're being safe flying! I know you said you will be asleep for the night by 8 and I got piano now until 8 so sending this now but I'll see you tomorrow morning! Goodnight! Congrats! :) <3"

I looked at Xavier's old text and made sure it would be something he'd be saying and typed out, "Thanks!!! Have fun at piano!!! And yes I was safe flying! lol, see you in the morning!!! Goodnight sweetie!!! :) <3"

All I could think was, "Finally, I can get some sleep. He may love it, but Xavier has a rougher life than I ever expected."

CHAPTER 29
A Mother's Care

I woke up by the irritating sensation of my eardrums ringing. "Great," I thought, "this must be some sort of side effect from riding in an airplane with 2G force yesterday." But wait. As I gained full consciousness of my surroundings, I distinguished the ringing. Someone was shuffling through the dish pantry. Before I could get up to identify who was making all the commotion, I found myself looking at the pink stenciled name on the wall: ALIZA. Of course, she's one of the two girls left before I had officially lived in everyone from 5th period's life.

I looked at the clock; it was five in the morning. I wished I could go back to sleep. I was tempted to pull the covers over my head, but I continued to hear clanging pans in the distance. I reluctantly got up. As soon as I stepped out of the room, I found a woman smiling and greeting me with a "good morning." The way this woman smiled at me, the way her glare looked into my soul, let me know that this woman was my mother. I smiled back and greeted her, and then I began my morning routine.

I stepped into the bathroom, and I just stood there, in the dark, looking at the mirror for about five minutes. I was prepping myself for the day, telling myself that I had to get through another day. I turned on the radio and the lights, and I began to do all those nasty girl things, which I am embarrassed to say I had gotten used to.

I went into the kitchen and my mother handed me two bagels, assuming that I would help her toast them. I did and before I knew it, I was cooking lunch with her. As she packed it up, I sat down on the chair and listened to her rambling along about her afternoon the previous day. It was hard to know what she was saying; she spoke Spanish but in a slow manner, and I found myself in a frenzy. I understood her, but I was still distracted. Thoughts of what needed to be done for the day were crossing my mind like lightning. Soon, an alarm buzzed and it was now six thirty. My mother was ready to leave for work, and before she left, she reminded me to take the next door neighbors to school and kissed me goodbye. It made me feel awkward. I'm not used to it.

As soon as she left, I began to text the CTA bus tracker for the next half an hour. I got the arrival times, but I lost track of time in the process of getting ready and taking the kids to school. I avoided talking to them, and I used that five-minute walk as a relaxing time. What a bummer. I was now ready for school, but had to wait ten minutes until the bus arrived. I sat on a kitchen chair and a dog approached me. She was cute, but she started barking at me. I wondered if she knew that on the inside, I was not who everyone thought I was . Nah. She was just a dog. I left her alone and started to walk to the bus stop.

I had no idea how perverted these men were! I was walking down the street, minding my own business, when out of the blue, I heard whistling and disrespectful slurs. What the hell is their problem?

I was at the bus stop, and I was listening to some music on Aliza's phone. I sat down on the bench and waited, aware of my surroundings. You never know, someone could just come and attempt to snatch the phone. I remembered that a few weeks ago, Aliza was telling her friends how a girl got her phone snatched by some trouble-makers. I needed to be cautious.

After five minutes, the bus arrived. I got on, used the card that was in her wallet, and began to walk down the aisle. Ugh! I hate when people stare for no reason. I felt like we were at a circus and I was the main attraction. I sat next to a lady near the back of the bus. She was putting on her make-up, which reminded me, I didn't put any on. I looked into Aliza's purse and found all her make-up. I'd seen Aliza plenty of times with make-up on, so I knew her style, but I must admit, it was very helpful to discretely follow the woman's way of applying it. I finished right on time. The bus arrived at the train station, and I got off to board the next inbound train. I waited for a bit, just standing there, and then the train arrived. Once again, men stared at me. I ignored them and sat down, looking out through the window. I couldn't deny it; the scene was beautiful. I got off at the Ashland Orange Line stop, and had to wait for another bus. This was very irritating. Once again, I did the exact same routine. I waited. I got on. I paid. I felt ogled. I sat. I waited. Got off.

I was now a block away from school. I walked past a retirement home, and a woman was waving at me. She was an elderly lady, and I didn't know who she was. Maybe she knew Aliza? I waved back.

I entered the building and ran to Work Study class, but I was late. The teacher looked at me with disapproval, but I couldn't help it. I sat down embarrassed in my seat and waited until the bell rang. I got some work done and saw Denise, but other than that, I was waiting for the bell. It rang.

I got out of class and went to Art. The teacher was really funny. I enjoyed this class very much. I saw a couple of people that I recognized, and before I went say hi, I remembered that I was not in my body...again. As the teacher spoke about famous artists, I began to think about my life: this might be a permanent thing. I conversed with a couple of people at my table, and before I knew it, it was time for Division.

I went into the Division room, and I sat down. Students were all over the place, and I felt awkward. I then heard a voice behind me that said, "Aliza, aren't you going to Best Buddies?" Ah, socializing with the special services kids. Of course. Aliza would be into that.

I turned around. I knew this girl. It was Dania, I'd

seen her with Aliza before. I said, "Ummmm, do I usually go during Division?"

She responded in a funny tone, thinking I was just pulling her leg. She said, "Quit playing girl, you go there every day!"

I tried to hide my distress, and I said, "I'm kidding girl, I know I have to go. But ah! I am so stressed; I don't even remember where they meet."

She giggled and said, "It's alright, all these college applications have me going crazy as well. You meet in room 206."

I said "Thanks," excused myself with the teacher, and left.

I went into the classroom and all these kids were smiling at me. They rushed over to me and I began to feel nervous. I didn't know any of these students, and I had no idea how to react. I smiled and said hi. Some hugged me, which caught me off guard. They began to ask me about my day, and slowly I began to let down my guard. I actually felt happy, which was weird. I didn't know any of these kids, yet they made me feel comfortable and special. The bell rang. I said goodbye and I walked to the third floor for AP Psychology.

I got into the class and the teacher had some groovy music on. I felt hyped and I sat down, dancing a little on my chair. I didn't know what's getting into me, but I was enjoying myself. I felt different. Lunch breezed by and it was time to be with my close friends in 5th Period Interdisciplinary Writing. I couldn't wait. I knew Nia talked to me, and that would be fun. Maybe I'd ask her what she thought of that arrogant boy, Jake Holomann.

I went into the class and sat down. I was nervous. I looked at the class, and I was starting to feel a little like myself. Unfortunately, Nia didn't show up and all we talked about was final exams. Final exams. Hard to believe but one more day and then finals, and that was all

I had left to do to finish my days at Sojourner Truth. Unless I was still body jumping, in which case I might have to stay an extra semester. Maybe that was it. Maybe the lesson I had to learn was going to require me to stay until the end of the school year. Maybe then I'd get released. On the one hand, I was scared to think about it; on the other, I felt a little less in a hurry to leave. I looked over at myself and saw from my body language that I was still itching to call it done. I was still staring at myself when Ashanti nudged me. Evidently, Ms. Glass had called on me. I looked at her and indicated to her that I had no idea what she was talking about and that I hadn't been listening. She seemed to understand. She asked for volunteers and when no one raised a hand to bail me out, I saw myself coming to the rescue.

"It's important in all tragic novels for the main character to come to some deeper understanding of the role he or she has played in his or her downfall. The flaw in the character that led to the downfall is what the Greeks call "hamartia." I said.

I watch as I seemed to go back to reading a book. I quickly raised my hand.

"Yes, Aliza?" Ms. Glass said, suddenly excited that there appears to be a discussion occurring in her class.

"Often the tragic flaw, the hamartia of the character, is arrogance. Don't you think, Jake?"

I watched as being called out stunned me. Ms. Glass jumped in.

"Care to respond, Mr. Holomann?"

"Agreed." I heard myself say, and then I watched as I went back to reading my book, seemingly unruffled by my attempt to get him to wake up.

The bell rang. It was 11:50 and my school day was over. I wanted to go over and talk to myself, but I knew Aliza had work study with Denise, which meant Aliza had to leave right after this class.

I tracked the Jackson bus, as I was now on my way to work. I had seven minutes until the next one arrived, which gave me time to run to the bathroom. I fixed my hair, made sure my attire was clean and unwrinkled, and I stepped out the bathroom. Five minutes later, I was at the bus stop. The bus arrived on time, and I got on. I got off on Franklin, and I walked a block to work. I put on the employee badge that I found in Aliza's purse, and I entered the building. I got on the elevator and went to the 14th floor. I hoped that was right; I was following what the badge said. I used the badge to gain access to the office, and I went sit at a desk that had Aliza's name on it. One of my co- workers looked at me strangely. She said, "Are you sick? Your eyes look a little irritated." It hit me. I accidentally irritated her eye when I tried to clean the smudged make-up before I left the school bathroom.

Oh well, I simply replied with a yes. I sat down, took out the laptop, and began to read all the e-mails of things that needed to get done for the day. I worked and just chatted with some co-workers. They were pretty cool, very hip if you ask me. At five in the afternoon, it was time to go home.

I was so frustrated. Once again, I had to track the train, track the bus, and like in the morning, it took like an hour to get home. I arrived at home around 6:30. I was ready to go to bed, when all of a sudden, Aliza's mother came into the room where I was resting. What the heck was her problem? "¿ Lista para irnos, mija?" I nodded my head. "!Ay niña, vente!" She made a hand gesture to go towards her, and like a dog, I followed her to the garage. She got on the truck and turned it on, so I automatically just jumped in. She was rambling again, and I just smiled. She looked at me again, but she was looking at me with mother's eyes. I wondered if she knew the truth. I was intimidated.

205

We drove into the parking lot, and we were now at a hospital center. I completely forgot. Aliza had been out for weeks when her mother had a stroke.... Her mother had a stroke. Everything made sense now, and I began to feel ignorant. Once the therapy began, I found myself helping the nurse with the therapy for "bonding purposes," as the nurse said. It worked. I felt very connected to her mother even though I didn't know her.

We drove home and I listened to her speak gentle words to me. I am moved. When we got home, I helped her get to bed and then I, too, lay down and closed my eyes for a minute to consider...

CHAPTER 30
Medicated

Unsurprisingly, I woke up to the sound of an alarm clock buzzing in my ear. Instinctively I reached my arm out for the source of the noise, grabbing at nothing. Grudgingly I got out of my bed, reluctant to leave its warm comfort. I turned off the alarm and stumbled out of my room for the day, making my way to the bathroom across the hallway. After a brief cold-water shower, I was alert and able to assess my situation.

Still glad to have both feet on the ground, but thinking about the struggle of Aliza's mother, I looked in the mirror. I saw a somewhat familiar face look back. I had medium length black hair stuck up in unnatural patterns, and acne scattered around my cheeks. I noticed a bottle of prescription medication with the name "Carroll, Avery" taped on the front of it. Was this my medicine? I remembered hearing the name a couple times in class. I was conflicted about taking the drug, as I never had to take any prescribed medication before. What would happen if I did take those pills without having a medical condition? I looked at the label again, "Adderall?" I read aloud "What am I supposed to do with this?" Wincing, I swallowed one of the pills bracing myself for the worst...and...nothing. I felt a bit silly making such a big deal over so little, and after completing my standard hygiene routine, I returned to my room.

After browsing through Avery's wardrobe, I picked out a sweater and a pair of jeans and got ready for the day. I saw a train card in my wallet; so I had to use public transportation. Once I had directions to the nearest train station, I set out on the mile-long bike ride. While riding, I realized that I managed to get through the entire morning without encountering anybody. I guess it was a nice change of pace from waking up to people's parents yelling at you. I was beginning to feel a bit optimistic about the day, but I wiped that hope from my mind. Every day since I started this entire body-jumping thing hadn't been nearly as enjoyable as a day in my own body. I could liken the experience to having a random animal at the dinner table every day and I'm the only one who seems to notice. There may be times when it doesn't cause too much of a disturbance, and occasionally it's enjoyable, but I would still rather not have to deal with it. It was still dark out, and by the time I arrived at the station, my bare hands were red and numb. The map on the train platform said I had an hour-long train ride to school, meaning that I had to find something to entertain me for an hour. I took a seat at the back of the train, and waited.

When I finally reached my stop, the other students and I shuffled out of the train station like cattle. I checked the time; it was thirty minutes before class started, and with nothing to do, I headed to the tech lab. The first bell rang, and I made my way to my first class of the day.

A short Asian man was already at the front of the classroom, and he greeted every student in Chinese as they walked through the door. The second passing period ended, and the lesson began at a rapid pace. Even with Avery's understanding of the language, I could only pick out bits and pieces from what the teacher was saying. With my head spinning, I suddenly felt as if the edges of my vision were under pressure. "This must be the Adderall kicking in." I muttered to myself. Everything that the teacher said came out crystal clear, and my mind began translating everything into English. Class ended with the medication sending me into a state of incredible focus. I don't know if Avery feels like this all day long, but it felt incredibly odd. I felt like my brain was on hyper-drive, and I could take on anything! Then I stopped, stepped back, and took a candid look at myself. Adderall was meant to cure mental problems, but if I didn't have Avery's mind then his medication would affect me like it would any normal person. So I was going through the school day high on ADHD meds. I had no idea how this was going to affect how I thought, but I hoped I wouldn't do something incredibly stupid.

This thought weighed heavily on my mind all the way to Avery's piano class. I sat down at my designated keyboard, uncertain of how well I would be able to play piano. This was a beginner's piano class, anyways. The pieces that were assigned didn't look complicated, until I noticed the extra pages of paper that peeked out of the book. Apparently Avery had printed out another song that he practiced in his free time, one that was much more difficult. However, once I placed my hands on the keys, my entire body seemed to relax. It didn't feel like I was thinking, my fingers moved up and down the keyboard as if they had minds of their own. By the time the period had ended, I was regretting turning down the piano lessons that my parents had offered to sign me up for back in grade school. So far I was pretty happy that nobody bothered me during my first two classes, but I knew that I'd have to talk to Avery's friends for the duration of Division at least.

Being "Ackies," Avery and his friends had gotten to know each other for two years more than everyone else. One of his friends cordially greeted me, but a disagreement between another two kids distracted him. With any luck, I could manage to get through the entire ten-minute period without drawing any attention to myself. Though I was trying my best to stay out of the situation, I was beginning to become more and more interested with what was happening between Avery's friends. They were at each other's throats, but they didn't seem to be genuinely angry at each other. It was like watching a brother and sister harmlessly arguing with each other. Considering how long they knew each other, they practically were siblings. I began to wonder where I would be if I actually took the time to become good friends with somebody during my stay in high school. Certainly I'd seen the benefits of such an endeavor; having a companion, confidant, and someone to help in times of need seemed like a win-win scenario. But at the same time it meant relying on somebody else and trusting them, two things that I don't particularly like doing. Why would I rely on anyone's abilities other than my own, especially when I know I could do a better job? How did I know that I could really trust them? Though I tried to convince myself that how I had been going through high school was right all along, I still felt jealous of people who had a close knit group of friends.

I don't know whether or not it was the medication, but I was beginning to feel a bit fuzzy. Fourth period was a blur. I understood everything the teacher said, and I even answered a few questions despite not knowing the material. Even with the side effects, this drug definitely made studying lessons easier. Speaking of side effects, I never really noticed that my heart was practically pounding through my chest, that I was breathing like I had just run a marathon, or that the room seemed to be spinning when I focused too hard on something. There was no reason why I shouldn't be perfectly content with how the day was progressing, but for some reason I felt unsettled. It must be the pills. I headed to Ms. Glass' class reluctantly. Something about taking control of a person for the day left you feeling a bit dirty. Now I had to sit in a class filled with people whose lives I had lived or will live for a day while high on prescription meds. I contemplated cutting class, too scared that I would lose my grip on sanity and blurt out what has been going on with me. On one side I might save Avery from being shipped off to a mental institution, but on the other hand, I would be sentencing him to disciplinary action sometime in the future. I decide to head to the nurses office; it might provide a solid enough alibi to get me out of fifth period at least.

The nurse looked at me a bit skeptically as I walked in. I guess she expects people to be on death's doorstep when they walk in. Despite this, she didn't send me straight back to class and I managed to escape 5th period for the day. I went through the next two classes without incident, chatting with a couple of Avery's friends that sat near him. Well, maybe chatting isn't the right term, more like listening. I looked back at why I didn't talk to many people before this. Did I feel that I was above talking to others, or did I fear it? I didn't want to answer the question, but it kept gnawing at me until lunch. Or maybe that was hunger. Apparently Avery was one of the unlucky students to have been assigned the last lunch slot of the day, meaning that he had to wait until almost the end of the school day to eat. I wasn't too hungry though. Not only that, but I couldn't bring myself to eat. Anything that I had to eat didn't seem appealing, and it felt like I had to force feed myself.

I normally took these lunch periods to have some precious alone time, which was normally uncommon in another person's body. But now I didn't want to be left to my own devices; I didn't want to face all of those questions that I had been asking myself all day. I walked awkwardly around the lunchrooms hoping that someone would recognize me, until one kid around my height with curly blonde hair greeted me. I followed him into a room next to the dean's office, reserved only for members of the school's academic decathlon team. There were two girls in the room; we exchanged pleasantries with before sitting down. I sat and listened, as the blonde who led me there ran the discussion. He was smart, social, and entertaining, but he lacked humility. The more he talked, the less I began to like him. Maybe it was because he was mouthing off, but I never had a problem with people like that before. I mean it's not bragging if you can do it, right? Then why was I so bothered by this? Then I knew. This kid verbalized every bit of my suppressed superiority complex, like I was having my innermost thoughts being read aloud to me. The less I liked him, the less I liked myself. Fortunately my thoughts were cut short by the shrill ring of the bell, and I followed everyone else from the room to Avery's last class. The entire class was a presentation by a student on one of the topics that needed to be studied for upcoming competition, but I couldn't bring myself to focus. The medication had begun to wear off, and I felt completely drained.

School ended and I headed back to the train station, trying to retrace how I got there in the morning. The second I got back to Avery's home, I dropped my backpack and collapsed on the bed. After a short nap, I felt somewhat functional again. Nobody was home and I was alone. Walking past the refrigerator, I saw a note intended for Avery.

"Your dad's at the firehouse today and I have to work the night shift at the ER today. I left some spaghetti in the fridge for you for dinner."

I was alone with nothing to bother me. This was what I wanted right? This was practically a quintessential day for me, even with the Adderall. I couldn't shake that feeling of regret, like I've been doing something wrong the entire time. I climbed into bed longing to go to sleep, to drift away from my problems.

CHAPTER 31
Panic Attack

BEEP. BEEP. BEEP. I wake up way too early for any human being. 5:30. Don't tell me; I'm another athlete. I look around the room I have just woken up in and notice a desk and clothes everywhere. Not in the mood to explore at this hour of the morning, I head to the shower.

As I walk into the bathroom, I look in the mirror to confirm who I am for the day. I have dark, wild, curly hair, hazel eyes, and pale skin. My suspicions are correct; I am Samantha, an energetic girl who sits in the front of the class. She is the only person I have not been. I've never really spoken to this girl before, and I have to admit I'm kind of excited to get to know her a little better.

In the shower, I think about yesterday's events; I was struggling with the medication for most of the day; I did not like the way it made me feel. On the other hand, I felt I did sort a few things out.

After my shower I go to my room to get dressed. My "mom" brings me breakfast and my lunch. I love when parents do this. I can't believe that some parents take time out of their morning routines to make their kids breakfast and lunch. As I'm brushing my teeth, my mom yells at me that it is 6:30 and I have to leave or I'm going to miss the bus. I run outside and my legs instinctively take me to the bus stop around the corner. As I wait for the bus, I think about my new arrangements: average sized house, no siblings, sweet and caring mother, and no father. Interesting. As I am about to ponder this further, the bus arrives, and my mind carries on thinking about other things.

After seventy-five minutes, I'm finally at school. I walk up to my locker and take out what I need for the beginning of my day. As I'm finishing up, an overly energetic girl comes over to me to remind me about a Yearbook meeting after 9th period. I've gotten used to the idea of after school activities, so it does not bother me as much as it used to when I have to attend them.

I'm in easy senior classes. While I do not approve of taking the easy way out senior year, I notice that Samantha was an Ackie by her Division number, so I guess she kind of deserves the break. The first two classes, Division, and fourth period are a breeze, and they leave me time to think of what the rest of the day will bring. Yearbook sounds interesting; I never get a Yearbook and I hadn't planned on getting one, but I surprise myself by thinking I should get one.

The one strange thing about today is that a lot of people have said hi to me in the hallways while I'm on my way to class. I'm definitely not used to that. I generally keep to myself at school, but at this point I have had a few days where I have had to talk to a bunch of people in between classes. A month ago, I would have thought that talking to people in the hallways only holds me up on my way to class, but now I don't mind it as much. I still hate being late though. While I'm walking to fifth period, a teacher stops me in the hallway. She tells me that there will be a meeting next week for Habitat for Humanity and that since I am on the executive board I need to spread the word about it. Executive board? I'm impressed that Samantha is in charge of so many things.

I sit down in Ms. Glass' class and start to write in my journal when I see myself walk in and slump into my seat. All of the sudden, I start to feel my heart race. I shudder, and my body tenses. All of the blood rushes to my head, and my ears and face are burning. My mind starts to race and my body starts to shake. I don't know what's going on. This has never happened to me before. I can feel adrenaline coursing through my veins, almost as if I have taken a shot of it. My heart feels like it's about to beat right out of my chest and my hands are shaking as if I've had too much caffeine. For a split second, my eyesight is blurry. I can't see anything in front of me, only the images racing through my mind. Luckily I am sitting down, or my shaky legs might have given out and I would have fallen down for sure. Once I calm down, I continue to journal and try to shake it off.

The rest of my day continues on as boring and as easy as the beginning. I get handed papers with above average, but not excellent, grades and I make small talk with those around me. At lunch I ate what my mother had packed for me; it was clearly made by someone who has great care for whom she was making it. I try to field as many people in the hallway as I can; however, many people seem to know me and constantly say hi to me. I can't imagine knowing that many people, let alone be willing to talk to that many people in a day. Maybe it's the Samantha in me, but I like it. A couple of my teachers pull me aside after class and ask me if I was feeling okay because I didn't seem as cheerful as usual and I didn't participate as much. While my initial reaction is to roll my eyes at them and walk away, I tell them that I'm just tired and should be better tomorrow.

Finally the last bell rings and I am excited to start heading home. As I am about to walk out of school, I hear my name being called. It's the same girl from this morning.

"Are you on your way to the Yearbook meeting?" she asks, albeit a little to perkily.

"Yes," I reply, and with that I reluctantly follow her to the meeting in hopes that it will be over quickly.

During the meeting I find out that this girl is an editor on the yearbook as well. I'm even more impressed. As I start to get a feel of all of the responsibilities she has, I begin to sympathize with her. Or something.

Finally I begin the long trek home. Because I am traveling alone, I take out my iPod and look for some music to listen to. A majority of the music is oldies, rap, relaxing music, and alternative. Lucky for me, I am a huge Lynyrd Skynyrd fan, and I listen to them the whole way home. After about an hour and a half, I walk through the door to find my mother for a day sitting on the computer.

"How was your day, sweetie?" she asks.

"Fine," I mutter, with the hopes of being able to get to my room as quickly as possible.

Unfortunately, she continues to ask me about my day and all of the things that happened. I give her one or two word answers, and she seems hurt. I don't really know why; she was practically interrogating me about my day. After about two or three minutes of this, she finally gives up. I feel kind of badly, but I was kind of out talked for the day. As I head to my room, she tells me that dinner will be ready in an hour and a half. I shout an acknowledgment through the walls and say thank you, hoping to ease her hurt about our short conversation. I enter my room and close the door tightly behind me.

As I'm sitting on my bed thinking about all of the things I need to do tonight, I find myself staring at the pictures all over the walls. Collages like this seem to be a trend among girls. They really tell a story. They start off with a very little girl, and progress on throughout all of the stages of her life thus far. There are pictures with various friends and family members in many locations. One location that continues to pop up appears to be in the forest. It must be some sort of camp. Deciding that I want to get to know this girl further, I decide to look around her room to see what I can find.

I examine the room more closely than I did this morning. It isn't that big; it's about eleven feet in either direction. The main features are a full-sized bed, a desk, three sets of shelves, a dresser, and a radiator. The shelves are covered with personal items, ranging from small knickknacks to old art projects to journals. I pick up one of the journals and being to read. It starts in the fall of

2009 and goes into the beginning of 2010. Reading someone else's thoughts is definitely a weird experience. Some of her thoughts seem so vapid while others are deep and emotional. One in particular describes the relationship of her parents; her dad moved out when she was young, and while she still sees him a lot, their relationship has not been the same since. That explains the living situation. While sad, she seems well adjusted.

After becoming bored with searching the room, I decide to work on some homework until my mom calls me and tells me my dinner is ready. I engage in conversation with my mother, and it seems to brighten her mood. After loading the dishwasher and taking out the garbage as I was told, something I never do at home, I head back to my room to finish my homework. Unfortunately, by this point it is only eight o'clock. I'm dying for the day to end. My world either comes back together tomorrow or I don't know what.

Two hours pass and the only thing I have left to do is review Existentialism and Magic Realism for Ms. Glass' Final. I review my notes on Sartre's *No Exit* and consider whether or not I believe "Hell is other people" as the play suggests. After the month I've just had, I think "living the lives of other people can be hell" but I'm not sure such a thesis would be easy to defend. I take a look at my notes on *Like Water for Chocolate* and try and formulate an opinion about Magic Realism. A month ago I'd have said it was all bull shit, but that was thirty lifetimes ago.

All of the sudden, I am hit with the same feelings as before; my heart starts to race, my body starts to shake, adrenaline courses through my body, blood rushes to my head, and I can only see my thoughts and nothing else for a few seconds. When my body starts to calm down, I grab my phone and research these symptoms. After a few minutes on Google, I discover that I had an anxiety attack. Wow. That's what she's been going through. I had two of

217

them in one day; I can't imagine how many this girl has had in her lifetime. It's strange though; the one at school made me feel awful, but this one just made me more aware of what was going on. I don't feel great, but I don't feel that bad either. Not that anxiety attacks are good things, but it seems that this body is used to them.

As eleven o'clock draws closer, I decide to try and get to bed. I pack Samantha's bag for her for the next day and turn off the light. Unfortunately, the adrenaline that flooded my veins only minutes earlier has left me wide-awake, and I can't stop thinking about the past month and everything that has happened to me. I go over every one of the different days I have experienced and all the things I've done. It's definitely been a wild ride, but all I can think is, "Please make it end." Nothing. I lay there for hours. At five in the morning I get scared that I'll never fall asleep. At six I'm sure I'm losing it. At 6:30 my heart started to race, my body started to shake, adrenaline coursed through my body, blood rushed to my head, and I could only see my thoughts and nothing else.

CHAPTER 32
How It Happened

I wake up one eye at a time, afraid of where I might be. I've done the math and there's no one else left in the class for me to be unless I am Ms. Glass; as cool as that might be at another time, I'm hoping my journey has ended; I had spent one day as each of my classmates. Who else could I be, if not me when I woke up? Then it hit me: What if I'm not me but another person from another of my classes, say someone from 6th period, what then? I start to panic when I look around. I don't recognize where I am.

After a month of bouncing around the City in the minds and bodies of my classmates, I suppose I have a right to be a bit disoriented, but when I look to my right and see the handwritten calendar I'd made, I'm simultaneously stunned and then relieved as I read "One day left of mindless drivel ---- you made it." I had forgotten that I had written that congratulatory addendum to the otherwise straightforward calendar.

How odd to feel strangely out of place in one's own bed. But here I am. I feel like Dorothy in the Wizard of Oz. How had I traveled so long and far only to find myself back in the bed where I had started? It doesn't matter at the moment. I'm home. Finally, home. I'm not hung over, I'm not in jail, and I'm not worried about my mother or my rent. I'm home and I'm me. I grab the calendar as if it's Zuzu's petals. I start to tear up as I gather myself up to run to the mirror and look at myself, when I hear a harsh, familiar voice.

"Where are you going?"

"I'm going to the bathroom to check and see if I'm me." I say mechanically, as if my answer were a perfectly logical statement.

219

" Check and see if you're you? What does that even mean?" the voice retorts coldly, as if I'm insane.

"You know what I'm talking about. I'm talking about not being in anyone else's body except my own. Not Sophie's not Tessa's not Zach's not anyone else's."

"Are you nuts? What are you talking about? People in your class? What do they have to do with anything?" The voice is mine, cynical, arrogant *old* Jake.

"You know what I'm talking about. I spent a month in each of their shoes. Today I'm me. I'm back. I'm Jake Holomann, and I've got to quit talking to myself and hurry up and get to school. I've got three finals to take."

"Relax, you're going to ace them. After all, just take a look at your competition."

"Look, I don't have time for you. Get away from me." I mumble just as my mother knocks on my door.

"Are you okay in there?" she says, with a tone of concern.

Shocked that I had been heard, but astonishingly happy that it's my real mother's voice, I casually reply. "I'm fine."

"Sounded like you were talking to someone in there. You sure you're all right?

"Yeah, just reviewing some English terms," I say in a way no one listening would have believed.

"All right, well, breakfast is ready and your lunch is on the counter."

I head for the bathroom and get a jolt when I look into the mirror. I have a tough time recognizing myself. It's me, and yet, I look different.

"What's wrong?" That voice again.

"Look, I don't want to talk about it." I say too emphatically.

"Honey, are you sure you're okay?" my mother's voice wafts through the door.

220

"I'm fine!" I yell back, then, whispering to myself, I add, "Leave me alone." How my mother hears this, I don't know, but somehow she does, even though I'm sure I had said it under my breath.

"Honey, is there someone in there with you?"

"No, mom, I'm just talking to myself. Trying to pump myself up for finals."

"Okay. Let me know if you need anything."

"I'm good, thanks."

But I'm not good. The inner voice, my old me, won't leave me alone. It keeps rambling on about how great it's going to be to be finished with school. How I've finally, finally finished high school and I'm less than nine hours from being home free.

I try to ignore the inner voice as I grab my Honda keys and head down Ashland Avenue towards school. It feels good to drive a familiar road in a familiar seat. I listen to WBEZ, the local Public Radio station, and I'm not surprised to hear them begging for money. My old self would be aggravated, but the new me considers pledging.

When I arrive at school, I want to head straight to English class, but the English final is the last period of the day. I have to get through my first two finals.

I head to my AP Calculus final, which is more difficult than I had assumed. I begin the test pre-occupied, looking for anyone from my 5th period class whom I could recognize and lock eyes with. I don't exactly know what I'm looking for from any one of them, except maybe an encouraging smile, a sense of communal uncertainty. No such luck. Everyone in the class looks like they know what to do and they all seem to be doing it.

It occurs to me that my bizarre month of masquerading as my classmates has impacted my thinking and my confidence. I can't remember a single function. Although I know now is not the time, my mind keeps drifting off to the days and nights of my classmates. With less than half an hour to go through the ninety-minute test, I have yet to answer a single question.

I keep looking around, lost, uncertain, and I start to panic. I close my eyes and think about giving up. I recalculate my Calc grade, assuming an F on the final, and realize it would bring my final grade down below a C, as Mr. Mack had insisted the final was worth 60% of our grade. Not good, and a severe blow to my Ivy League chances. It momentarily alarms me until I hears my inner voice say, "Stop thinking about the human muck that surrounds you and ace the test. What you can do in half an hour, none of these people can do in an hour and a half."

I'm no longer so sure. What's happened? In the thirty days since I've truly been myself, have I forgotten everything I know? Hard to imagine. I sense the problems in front of me weren't that difficult, and yet I have a sense of paralysis, a deep inertia somehow brought on by... by what I can't at first understand. "You're thinking about others too much. Stop it." I hear myself say.

"Maybe, but I can't help it. I wonder how they're all doing?" I reply.

"They're all taking their math finals, not thinking about you!" my inner voice snaps.

"Well, I can't do this." I say, impulsively about to raise my hand and ask to go to the bathroom for no particular reason except to get out of the class.

"Oh, no you don't." a voice says, although this time it's not my inner voice. This time it has a different tone, one I recognize as not my own, but that of someone else. Someone vaguely familiar. I can't quite place it. "Sit yourself down and ace this test. Don't you be coming home with no D, girl." Girl? What? And then it hits me. It's NeNe's mother.

222

I don't have time to answer her, nor would I know what to say. I realize four-fifths through my last answer that NeNe's mother isn't looking for any answer from me at all. She doesn't have time for any back talk and she realizes that in the precarious position I'm in, that I don't have any time for it either. I just need to act and act right. And so I do. I do the best I can with the time remaining and when the bell rings I look up and realize I probably aced the test. Partly because of what I know but, more importantly, because the woman who had urged me on recognized that self-absorption is a luxury not everyone can have.

I walk out of the class thankful for a mother's voice I barely know. I want to say something to her like "See, ma, I did it, " but as I create the scene in my mind's eye, I realize no words are appropriate. When I get into the hallway, I see Zach in the middle of half a dozen friends. I smile at him briefly, and he seems to look my way and nod his head. It feels great to be acknowledged.

AP French is next and this time I'm better prepared for the paralysis I assume will come. When I put on my headset in the lab to translate and respond to what is being said to me, I imagine myself talking to classmates and I find the test to be *"tres, tres facile."* The ninety minutes still seem twice as long as it is, as I cannot stop thinking about 5th Period English and my chance to talk to Ms. Glass. I know she is the only person in the world whom I can talk to about the past month who won't think me insane. *"Pourtant, il était arrivé, j'étais sûr de lui." Je me suis dit.* Oh, no, no, no. That's French, I tell myself, and then translate, "Yet, I know it happened."

It did happen. I'm about to find out how. When the bell rings I jump out of my seat and head in the direction of Room 129. On the way, I decide to take one very quick detour. I go to the school bookstore and order a yearbook. When I reach the bottom of the stairs, just before I reach the bookstore, I see George, the guy who had bullied me when I was Frank. He's lying on the floor, holding his arm, wincing in pain. Evidently he has either fallen down the stairs or been pushed. In either case, it looks like he has broken his arm. For some reason, my arm starts hurting, too.

I keep moving because I want to be the first to arrive for my Interdisciplinary Writing final. When I reach 129, even Ms. Glass has yet to get there. I take my familiar seat and wait for others to trickle in. When each of my classmates enters the room, I look at each one in the eyes and say a quick "hello" and even try to call them by name. Most of them are stunned, a few look at me as if I'm a foreign exchange student unfamiliar with the American custom of not uttering any comments to classmates who aren't your friends. I defy the cultural expectations and greet every one of them as if I am once again Jimmy Stewart, happy to be back in Bedford Falls. No one objects, some even return my greeting. I am feeling sort of nostalgic as I think of Mel in the silo and Kleave at the party, and Ashanti's poems. My mind is all over the place. Adderall?

I wait for Nia. When she comes in I didn't hesitate. I go straight up to her and take my chance.

"Listen, after finals are over, you want to go out with me and celebrate?"

She looks at me as if to say, "It's about time." Then she smiles and says, "It's about time."

When Ms. Glass arrives I resist the urge to lunge at her and scream, "How did you do that to me?" I realize that to do so would be problematic, as the rest of the class will definitely want to know what I'm talking about, and then the final will be delayed, and eventually the class will break down into a hot mess. As difficult as it is, I decide to take the final first, and then approach Ms. Glass after it's over.

The final includes a multiple choice section followed by a single essay. The ninety question multiple-choice test is easy enough. I may have missed two or three answers, but I race through most of them with confidence. When everyone completes that section, Ms. Glass hands out the essay portion of the final. It's the last test I'll ever take in high school.

When she passes out the writing prompt, I quickly see that the verbiage was familiar. The prompt reads, "In a well written formal essay, choose a novel, short story or event from this semester which details a character's journey from self-deception to self-awareness. Remember that both form and content are important."

I look up at Ms. Glass as soon as I finish reading the prompt. Our eyes meet briefly as she scans the room looking at her students. I think I see a glint in her eye, but I may be imagining it. I'm looking for an acknowledgement that she knows what I know. If she gives me such acknowledgement, I've missed it, because she seems to treat me no differently than anyone else in the class. I decide I'll focus on the essay first and solve the mystery later.

I start to write about Garcin from Sartre's *No Exit*, a character in hell as a consequence of his own actions. Half way through the essay I tear it up, realizing it's not what I want to write about. I consider a number of options from novels and plays we've read, but nothing seems to fit and, in any case, I don't feel like writing about the struggle of a fictional character.

Almost hypnotically, I start writing what happened to me in the previous month. My paper has no thesis whatsoever nor is there any explanation of what I write. I don't care. I have barely finished writing the intro to my fantastical tale, when the bell rings and time is called. I never hear the bell ring and keep writing until Ms. Glass comes over to my desk, puts her hand on my pen, and tells me time is up.

I look around and notice everyone has left the room. Out of kindness, I suppose, Ms. Glass has let me

225

continue writing for a few extra minutes. Slightly embarrassed, I hand her my test and explain I haven't had enough time to finish.

"You seemed very intent on whatever you were writing."

"I was trying to explain something that had happened to me this past month, something I think you know."

"Well, the question I asked wasn't really about you, Jake, it was meant to be used as a prompt to write about something we had read this past semester."

"I know, Ms. Glass. But after what I've been through this month, I needed to write it down."

"Well, if it was that important."

And then it just pours out of me. "I spent each day of this month living as every one of the students in this class. I know it's not possible, but that's what happened. I've been all over town, in all kinds of circumstances." I keep rambling on, waiting for her to interrupt me, but she just listens. I babble on with the hope that she'll acknowledge her role in my mysterious transformation, but she just let me talk. I tell her everything that's happened as I remember it. Every once in a while, she nods, as if to indicate she's still listening and that what I'm saying is rational.

When I finish, I wait for her to offer a response. She says nothing.

"Tell me I'm not crazy," I say.

"You're not crazy," she says.

"How did you make it happen?" I ask, convinced she has somehow bewitched me into a month long set of experiences. "Don't act like you don't know. We had a conversation a month ago about 'empathy,' don't you remember?"

"Yes, I remember."

"It all started happening the day after you and I talked. The day after you told me to go to bed thinking

226

about what it meant to be empathic. You called it my homework assignment. You tricked me or hypnotized me or cast a spell on me or some sort of weird thing because what happened to me this past month can't happen. Not in real life."

"It does sound like the stuff of fiction. Still...."

I get a bit heated; it feels like she's playing with me. "Come on. No one can actually spend a day living someone else's life. That's impossible and you know it." She looks at me and almost seems to smile. "Come on, Ms. Glass. Let's not go around and around about this. You know what happened to me was more like magic realism than reality."

"Nice allusion."

I ignore her pedantic response. "How'd you do it?"

She shrugged her shoulders.

"You must be some kind of a mystic or a guru or an Albus Dumbledore or something."

" Look, Jake, I think you may be overthinking this. Plenty of people can do what I do and they do it every day. It's about connecting with students. Good teachers do it on a regular basis. Great teachers do it all the time. So do good students. They connect."

"Yeah, yeah, yeah. But you, you've got some kind of special magic power."

"I'm telling you, whatever I've got, other people have. Trust me, there are a lot better out there."

"What, mystics?"

"No, teachers."

"Well, I've never met anyone like you, and I'm about ready to graduate."

"Then I'm glad I was your teacher before you did. At least it happened to you once. Maybe if you're open to it in college, it'll happen to you again."

"No, no. It's too weird. It's never happened to anyone and it'll never happen again."

"You're too pessimistic. Tell you what. Why don't you go home and text all of your classmates and ask them if it's ever happened to them. You might be surprised by what they say. Will you do that for me?"

At that moment I would have done anything she told me. "Whatever you say," I said.

"Great." She said as if it was the end of the conversation, and she started packing up her papers.

"Then what do I do? I mean, what if what you did to me, you've done to them? What then?"

She looked at me as if I knew the answer all along. "Tell them to tell their stories. Have them write them down. Share them with others."

So I did.

About the Authors:

Taylor Berghoff
Taylor Berghoff is currently a senior at Whitney M. Young Magnet High School. Sports (primarily softball and volleyball) have played a strong role in her life since grade school. Once she entered high school she found a deep love for music, which is what she currently spends most of her time working on. Her favorite classes have always been art and writing, so it is no secret that *30 Days to Empathy* was very enjoyable for her to take part in.

Sydney Burdin
Sydney Burdin is a senior who lives in Rogers Park with her family, dog, and turtle. She spends her time in school, swimming, and volunteering. She also enjoys time with her family and hopes to become a Pharmacist.

Joli Chandler
Joli Chandler is a senior attending Whitney M. Young Magnet High School in Chicago, Illinois. She is one of the many authors of this class-sourced book, and took pride in adding her work to this novel. She is an only child and lives with her mother and father in Chicago's South Shore neighborhood. In addition to being an occasional fiction writer, she is a hard working student, avid skier, and sailor.

Mateusz Chorazy
Mateusz Chorazy was born on January 16th, 1996 in Chicago, Illinois. He is currently a junior in high school. Matt enjoys sports and is a member of the school's swim team and the water polo team. He is also a member of other clubs and organizations and often volunteers in his free time. Although the plans for his future aren't definite and set in stone, he is steering towards a career in the medical field as an anesthesiologist.

Zachary Deitz

Zach Deitz is a junior, and an honors student. He is on the Varsity baseball team and also plays on a Club team that travels around the country in the summer. He is currently being recruited to play in college. In his free time he enjoys drawing, hanging out with friends, and doing other athletic activities besides playing baseball. He lives in Chicago's Lakeview neighborhood and loves to explore the city.

Marc Deming

Marc Deming is a senior at Whitney M. Young Magnet High School and has been in the school band for three years as a percussionist. Marc is an artist and enjoys drawing, which translates into a sketching aptitude for his other passion, mechanical engineering. Cars and engineering are a passion of Marc's, and he plans to study engineering in college. Marc Deming is an interesting guy, and has been known to engage in some sordid activities. He has grand dreams and sharp wits; hopefully they will keep him alive.

Adeyanira Escuadra

Adeyanira Escuadra was born on August 9, 1995, and still resides in the south- side of Chicago. She is an aspiring accountant, pursuing a career through her internship with PricewaterhouseCoopers. She currently works on the Marketing & Sales team, but she hopes to one day work as an associate for the firm. Adeyanira also enjoys giving her time to volunteer around her community. One of her biggest passions is working with special needs children. She is president of the Best Buddies club this year, a program that works with special needs children in her school: one of her biggest achievements thus far.

Justin Galowich

Justin Galowich is a student at Whitney Young High School, a competitive racer, and a student pilot. He has raced in mostly 5k runs and triathlons; competing often and in the family name. His coach/mentor is his uncle, who lives in Florida, who sends him weekly workouts so that he can keep up with his uncle. He also pilots multiple types of aircraft (normally twin-engine aircraft and gliders) with his father, and comes from a long line of aviators.

Jasmine Grayson

Jasmine B. Grayson, born on January 12th, is the youngest daughter of Theresa Manney. Jasmine attended KIPP Ascend Charter School for middle school and went on to attend and graduate from Whitney Young High School, in Chicago, IL. While in high school Jasmine was in charge of the Activities Committee for Best Buddies, a club where regular education students get paired with a student with a disability. After being accepted to Tuskegee University, she decided that's where she would study Occupational Therapy and began her career in the military by doing ROTC.

Jacob Haase

Jacob Daniel Haase was born June 24th, 1995 in Chicago, IL. Among familiar company, he goes by the nickname "Jake." Jake is a senior at Whitney M. Young high school. He does a lot of volunteer work and has in fact accrued over 270 hours over the course of his high school career. Jake is exploring the world of digital media with the intent of pursuing a major and career in the field. Jake will be attending college at one of the top 20 video game design schools in the nation.

Susan Jiang

Susan Jiang is a high school entrepreneur who owns her own eBay business. She was born in Chicago, Illinois and has one younger sister. Susan attends Whitney M. Young Magnet High School as a senior and will graduate in 2013. During her free time, she enjoys crocheting and running her online business. She is vice president of Chinese club and treasurer of Ping Pong club. Susan plans on majoring in business in college next fall.

Alyssa Komish

Alyssa Komish grew up on the North Side of Chicago in West Rogers Park. She is currently enjoying her senior year and keeping busy with the yearbook and volunteering with Habitat for Humanity. In her free time, Alyssa enjoys babysitting, volunteering, and hanging out with her friends. This summer, she will be a camp counselor at an overnight camp for 4 weeks.

Victoria Lei

Victoria Lei was born on May 12th, 1995 in Streator, Illinois. She is currently a senior at Whitney M. Young High School. She has one older brother and one younger sister. Victoria enjoys playing instruments, reading books, and spending time with friends and family in her free time. She is planning on majoring in Biomedical Sciences and becoming an orthodontist.

Marlene Lenthang

Marlene Lenthang is a Chicago native and culturally unique individual. Coming from a half Indian and half Ecuadorian household fostered her love for culture and diversity. She is an aspiring writer and journalist and currently is Editor-in-Chief of her school newspaper, the Beacon. Marlene is a lover of music, sports, and literature. She enjoys travelling to different countries, spending time with her family and friends, and dancing.

Patryk Lipski

Patryk Lipski is a pirate astronaut firefighter. In his spare time he writes best-selling children's novels, like *The Friendly Lesion* and *How To Charm Hostile Cyborgs*. His future plans are to become a neuroscientist and freelance mathematician. He enjoys grilled octopus, chats with his neighborhood cats, and if he could tell you one quote to take heed to, it'd be "We must be careful about what we pretend to be" from Kurt Vonnegut. He'd bet ten dollars you can figure out which chapter's his.

Ashanti Marshall

Ashanti Renee Rose Marshall was born in Chicago, Illinois on December 11, 1994. She is a senior in high school. Marshall enjoys sunshine and happiness. She loves writing poetry and taking care of small children. Her goal is life is to open free-standing birth centers in every state. This young lady loves R&B music, art, and freedom. Currently, Ms. Marshall is obtaining her doula certification.

Logan McClure

Logan McClure. was born in Des Moines, Iowa, and at age six moved away. He currently lives on the North Side of Chicago with his mom, dad, brother, and two sisters. Logan values things such as family, success, and education. A senior at Whitney Young Magnet High School, he enjoys activities such as lacrosse, swimming, and socializing with friends. He plans to attend college next year and major in Mechanical Engineering.

Somyiah Nance

Somyiah L. Nance lives in the Bronzeville area of Chicago with her supportive mother, Kimberland. She attended Whitney Young's seventh and eighth grade program then went on to their high school where she will be graduating in June of 2013. Somyiah is a passionate dancer and

current captain of Pom-Pon team. She enjoys
volunteering with children and people with disabilities.
She is a new participant in the Best Buddies program at
her school and was accepted into the honored Chicago
Scholars program her junior year. Somyiah plans to study
medicine at a university in the Midwest and pursue a
career in pediatrics.

Kevin Ngo
Kevin Ngo was born in Evanston, Illinois in 1996. Raised
in Chicago, he is a high school junior who went to John
B. Murphy Elementary School and now attends Whitney
M. Young. He has an older brother and a younger sister.
Activities he enjoys are playing video games, learning
about sciences, playing sports, listening to music, and just
hanging out with his friends. He is currently considering
pursuing becoming an Environmental Engineer.

Aidan O'Carroll
Aidan O'Carroll is currently a junior at Whitney Young
Magnet High School. He hopes to attend college at the
University of Chicago, and plans to study economics. In
his free times he likes to run cross-country and play video
games.

Sarah Quinn
Sarah Quinn is a senior at Whitney M. Young high school
in Chicago. She likes to read in the winter. More often
than not, you can find her at home cuddling with her two
cats, Pickles and Bacon. Sarah writes autobiographies in
her free time, and loves watching obscure films on
Netflix. Her goal for the next ten years is to stay alive.

Jay C. Rehak
Jay C. Rehak is a teacher, author, lecturer and
videographer who has collaborated with thousands of
students over the years to create literature. A proponent

of student creation and collaboration, Jay is a National Board Certified instructor who has taught English for the past 25 years. Jay's 27 plays and 2 screenplays are available at www.jaycrehak.com; his ACT Test Tip videos can be found on YouTube and through the Chicago Public School Safari website. Jay lives in Chicago with his wife, award winning children's singer Susan Salidor. He has three children, Hope, Hannah and Ali.

Antonio Romo
Antonio Romo was born in Chicago in 1996. He was raised there and is a student attending Whitney M. Young Magnet High at the time this is being written. He is a student athlete who is on the swim team and the water polo team. Antonio was diagnosed with diabetes in 2006, which he is able to handle with help from family and friends. He aspires to become a pediatric endocrinologist so he can help other children who have diabetes.

Brian Scheff
Brian Scheff was born in Chicago, Illinois in March 1996. He grew up with his mother, father and older sister. Throughout his childhood he enjoyed playing sports, playing video games, and hanging out with friends. Brian is currently a junior at Whitney M Young Magnet High School, and has been attending there since seventh grade. He hopes to one day become an engineer or some sort of game designer.

Matthew Scott
Matthew Scott was born in Chicago on December 23, 1994. He is a senior at Whitney Young High School. He has lived in the same Lakeview apartment for his entire life. Matthew is currently interested in business and engineering. A football player for six years, he aspires to be a coach. Matthew is currently interested in business

and engineering. His dream is to remain involved with the game of football for the rest of his life.

Veronica Skital

Veronica Skital is a senior at Whitney M. Young High School. She plans on attending a prestigious university and studying biomedical engineering. She recently completed the Bank of America Marathon and enjoys running long distances. She also loves dogs and owns an Australian Shepherd. In her spare time, Veronica likes to sew.

Da'Manise Smith

Da'Manise Juanita Smith grew up on the South Side of Chicago facing many adversities. This led to her passion for writing and expressing her creativity. She attends Whitney Young High School and currently works at Kirkland & Ellis LLP. Da'Manise also enjoys singing, dancing, and modeling. She intends to attend a university and major in psychology to become a therapist. This is Da'Manise first published piece of writing.

Jonathan Villasenor

Jonathan Villasenor is a current junior at Whitney M. Young Magnet High School. Jonathan is an outstanding track athlete, who with his team, qualified for state in the 4x800. Jonathan also runs cross-country, and hopes to do so in the future. Jonathan is involved with choral & solo singing, as well as an avid player of the guitar and piano. Jonathan is also a part time model.

Rielle Walker

Rielle Walker has always appreciated literature. At a young age, she became fascinated with the art and magic of language, which sparked her love for reading and, not long after, her desire to write pieces as beautiful as those that she read. Currently, she is a senior at Whitney Young

High School (c/o 2013) and is undecided about where she will be attending college in the fall.

Cory Y. Wong
Cory Y. Wong was born on April 26th, 1996 in Chicago, Illinois. He is a junior. He grew fond of sports at a very young age. He excelled through school giving him time to play on the volleyball and baseball team for school. As of now Cory is undecided on exactly what his future has in store, but he plans on studying business or engineering. He sees life as a gift and a blessing, which shouldn't be taken for granted.

Hannah Wong
Hannah Wong is a senior in high school. She loves to bake, chase fashion trends, study at local coffee shops, and explore thrift stores. She plays the piano and knows a little here and there about the ukulele. She loves God and dedicates a lot of time to planning games and organizing events for her Friday night youth group. She hopes to go to college and eventually medical school to study to become a pediatrician.